Day and Night, Forever

ISBN-13:
978-0615531052 (Pompano Press)

ISBN-10:
0615531059

Third edition

Library of Congress Control Number: 2006903418

Pompano Press
936 Intracoastal Drive 4F
Fort Lauderdale, FL 33304

For my son KARL, wherever you are

Day and Night, Forever

Jack Nease

Fort Lauderdale, Florida

*The terrible, cold, cruel part [of New York] is Wall Street....
There, as nowhere else, you feel a total absence of the spirit:
herds of men who cannot count past three, herds more who cannot
get past six, scorn for pure science and demoniacal respect for the
present. And the terrible thing is that the crowd that fills the street
believes that the world will always be the same and that it is their
duty to keep that huge machine running, day and night, forever.*

Federico García Lorca, Spanish playwright

*The day is not far off when the economic problem will take
the back seat where it belongs, and the arena of the heart and the
head will be occupied or reoccupied, by our real problems—the
problems of life and of human relations, of creation and
behaviour and religion.*

John Maynard Keynes, British economist

Chapter One

Go was there waiting, on-time as Maureen knew he'd be, standing just beyond the security gates at the Lauderdale airport, thinner and tanned but otherwise exactly the same as before, his black hair mussed in front, arms and chest almost too big for his legs, a little gold ring in his ear. Thirty-five but didn't look it, not to Maureen, anyway. And until he moved, neither she nor anyone else could see one leg was shorter than the other.

He limped toward her, and Maureen walked faster. Finally she was past the last guard. They hugged, touching only above the waist, the way distant relatives greet at weddings and funerals. She resisted an impulse to kiss him on the cheek, and a real kiss was out of the question.

"You look great," Go said, and Maureen smiled. So much better to hear him say it than someone at work. There'd been no time to change so she wore the same black suit skirt and light green blouse as at the office, but on the plane she'd added her favorite necklace, gold with a platinum angel, and matching earrings.

He said, "I've rented a car."

"Why not use yours?"

"They won't let me have one down here. Rules of the rehab program."

"How's it going?"

"Six months next week. Then I can get a real job."

"Where?"

"That's what I want to talk to you about. Come on."

Go—she always thought of Gregory by his nickname—took her carry-on, and they walked toward the parking garage. Calls of jungle birds screamed from loudspeakers in the terminal ceilings. Flat video panels flashed rotating photos of beaches, boats and homes on canals, even stunt planes. Palms and tropical plants grew everywhere. Already she felt she'd entered another world. The misgivings of the morning began to fade.

Maureen's job being what it was—partner in a mid-sized Wall Street brokerage house—she always kept a small suitcase in her office, packed and ready to go. She believed in keeping things simple. She dyed her hair herself, a reddish-brown shade of Clairol called Burgundy Borga, and never spent more than twenty-five dollars for a cut. A woman's worth, she was convinced, is inversely proportional to the amount of time and money spent at a beauty salon.

Thirty-nine now and proud of it. If people wanted to think she was younger, that was their problem. She didn't tell them how far she jogged almost every morning before work. Just as she hadn't told anybody about this rush trip to Florida. Most of her friends and the people she worked with would think it was foolish. She'd know soon enough.

They drove along A1A in a yellow Mustang convertible, one Maureen called gaudy but which Go said was regulation outfitting for tourists and visitors. The Atlantic Ocean passed by on their right, the beach separated from the road only by a low wall curving along the sidewalk, a strip of neon lighting making a continuous wave of pink, blue, and green in the barrier. On the other side, new condominiums and buildings full of restaurants rose into the sky, not at all like the tawdry bars and T-shirt shops she remembered from twenty years before. Spring Break. Seemed like a million years ago.

Some things had stayed the same. The smell of salt water still filled the air. Out in the ocean, cruise ships and freighters floated in place, their bright lights forming little cities at sea. The street lights were new—electric but made to look like gas lamps—and shielded so light didn't go out to sea. Something about turtles, she'd read.

Maureen said, "Now will you tell me what this is all about?"

"You ever hear of Providence Place?"

"Read about it." In some sort of trouble once, she remembered.

"There's one here on the beach, one in Orlando and a few up North. They take care of homeless kids."

She nodded, not caring that with his eyes on the road Go couldn't see her. He seemed to know her thoughts, no matter what.

"Without them, the kids would be out on the streets begging and prostituting themselves. Boys and girls alike."

"So?" Maureen said.

"The nuns who run it want me to go to work for them when I finish rehab. As a counselor."

"You'd be good at it." Gregory had excelled at all three of his professions—a nurse practitioner, a hospital administrator, then a youth counselor. All interests, she was convinced, he'd absorbed when she helped nurse him back to health when they were kids. It's good to help people. That was the message he'd picked up. But it's possible to do too much for others, too. Had he learned that yet?

She said, "The woman, tell me about the woman."

"There's no woman."

"When you phoned, you said there was."

"Oh, Bridget," he said. "She's a girl, really."

"You're involved with girls now?"

Gregory didn't say a word. Maureen knew what he was doing. Breathing deeply, starting over, so the interruption wouldn't bother him. She liked that about him. She'd never seen him get angry or shout or scream, but he always insisted on explaining things his way.

Finally he said, "I'd work with the boys. Someone else would counsel the girls."

"So what's the problem?"

"There's a philanthropist who wants to give fifty million dollars to Providence Place so they can build a larger building."

"Doesn't seem like a problem to me," Maureen said, but she felt something tickle the back of her neck, much like what happened at the office that morning. She lifted her hand to push aside whatever had touched her, but there was nothing there.

"The nuns who run Providence Place want to accept the money. But the kids somehow got word of it, and they're in revolt."

"Why?"

Gregory turned left onto a wider road. "They say he's evil.".

"What's his name?"

"You'll see. He'll be at the party."

"Why do you care what the kids think?"

"They've got the nuns worried. They say kids sometimes sense things adults don't."

"And Bridget?" Maureen said.

"She's their ringleader."

Gregory turned left one more time, drove to the end of the street where it dead-ended at a tall rock wall, and pulled through an open gate. A two-story house, vaguely plantation in style, old and substantial, a mansion by anyone's standards, stood before them, the structure and surrounding grounds brightly lit by floodlights.

Maureen said, "Is this Providence Place?"

"This is headquarters of a trust fund. They call it Trust House."

Again Maureen felt something in her neck, but this time the warning didn't puzzle her. She was beginning to form an idea, still fuzzy but getting clearer, about what was going to happen. The man had been on her mind all day.

Gregory surrendered the car keys to a guy with a pink Mohawk, valet parking their only option. Maureen took his arm, and they walked down a flower-lined path at the side of the house, Gregory body's swaying as his short and long leg alternated on the paving stones. She was exactly his height but knew she appeared taller. Five nine, tall for a woman but an advantage in what until recently was strictly a man's business.

Sounds of a jazz band and a babble of voices floated in the air. They entered into a large garden at the rear of the house. Men and women, stood in clusters, drinks in hand, most wearing their work clothes—suits and ties for men, jackets and skirts for women. Then Maureen saw the whole set-up, and despite herself something inside said, Wow!

Stunning cascades of purple, red, and pink bougainvillea vines grew up sides of the house and spilled over walls. Small electric lights twinkled overhead. Gas torches illuminated trees and bamboo stalks in the shadows. A scene from a fairy tale.

Before the dragon arrived. The thought came out of nowhere.

"There he is," Go said. "The man I want you to tell the nuns is OK."

Roland Pettigrew walked toward them, glasses of something bubbly in each hand, his arms held high and away from his body, as if in greeting. Midas Man. The last man on earth Maureen wanted to see. Or talk with. Even be close to. She'd flown a thousand miles to meet him?

Chapter Two

Pettigrew looked older and smaller than his photographs. Early to mid-fifties, thin gray hair combed back at the sides, a cream silk blazer over a lavender shirt open at the neck. Physically frail. Even so, there was an aura of power about him. Maureen thought of Aristotle Onassis.

Why here of all places? Pettigrew's corporate holdings were scattered across the country. Then, from somewhere deep in her mind where not-yet-useful information was stored, Maureen remembered his holding company was headquartered in South Florida. No wonder her neck tingled. She'd been talking about him back in New York.

Go said, "He must have been waiting for us."

"Looks like it." Damned obvious, in fact.

"Have you met him before?"

"Never. But I've heard a lot about him."

Oh yes, Maureen knew all about Roland Pettigrew. A shark, a manipulator, a Wall Street operator who skated on the edges of the law. Probably shot right over them, but nobody had caught him yet. Magazines and television shows usually referred to him as a brilliant billionaire philanthropist. They had it backwards. He'd started with a charitable trust fund of a few hundred million, and built it into a billion-dollar powerhouse. Along the way he'd made himself a fortune.

Ruthless. Everybody on Wall Street said that about him. He bought and sold corporations like Monopoly pieces, gutted them, and forced once-profitable companies into bankruptcy. Or sent their assets and jobs overseas. Populations of whole towns were left unemployed, their divorce and suicide rates climbing, the pain and suffering reaching into every home. All completely legal, and no one could stop him. Not that anyone on The Street wanted to interfere. Just give them a share of the millions to be made, Maureen's firm included.

Already the party seemed less glamorous. Those drinks in the flat, wide stemware in Pettigrew's hands, for example. Champagne, probably, but being served in the wrong glasses. Punch glasses, for God's sake. Somebody had no taste. Pettigrew, probably. Or someone he'd hired.

A big woman in a modern nun's habit—gray and white, the skirt at mid-calf and a sheer black veil on the back of her head—crossed Pettigrew's path. He stopped abruptly, and liquid spilled from the glasses. Pettigrew smiled, let the nun pass, then did a little dance step that ended with a foot stopping just short of her rump. People around them laughed, but by the time the woman turned to see what the laughter was about, Pettigrew had resumed his journey.

"They say he likes to kid around," Gregory said.

This could be a very long party, Maureen thought, Go already making excuses for the man, me biting my tongue.

Pettigrew reached them, handed her one of the glasses, and said he'd always wanted to meet her. The same thing all company officials said when Maureen showed up to question them. "When the nuns told me you were coming, I said, 'Wonderful.'"

Maureen looked toward Gregory, knowing only he could have tipped them off, but Go was looking away, holding up his palm toward Pettigrew, rejecting the other glass of champagne in Midas Man's hand. Pettigrew knew, she thought. His gesture was so half-hearted he knew Gregory would refuse the drink. How?

"And I've heard about you." Maureen's standard answer.

His smile. Good God! Practiced, calculated to charm, but a hundred percent phony. Then she noticed his thin white mustache. Another strike against him.

Maureen had theories about facial hair. Men with beards have something to hide. Men with mustaches are invariably vain.

Also: The more of his face a bearded man concealed, the more secrets he had. And the vanity of mustached men? You could take it to the bank. She'd seen her father looking in the bathroom mirror, admiring himself as he trimmed the tiny bit of hair on his lip.

"You're quite a TV star," Pettigrew said. "CNBC, CNN, Lou Rukeyser's show. And now that I see how attractive you are—"

"It's part of the job." Maureen always cut them off when they sucked up with phony compliments. She felt the same way about make-up as she did hair styling. A little pink blush on her cheeks in the morning, a minimum of eye shadow and brow pencil, and that was that. Let other women try to make it on looks. She'd stick with brains and hard work. When people called her gorgeous, as they did from time to time, she pretended she hadn't heard them.

"And now you've come to check me out." Pettigrew let the words ease from his mouth. Again, the no-caret smile.

"Gregory wanted me to meet you."

"I've known Mo since we were children," Gregory said. "She helped nurse me through polio when I was a kid."

Pettigrew studied him. "I didn't know anybody in this country got polio anymore."

"A fluke. There was a weird set of circumstances, and I didn't get the vaccine."

"Pity." Pettigrew turned back to Maureen. "Anything I can do to help your research, please let me know."

Gregory said, "Maybe Luther and Kennedy could help her."

Pettigrew frowned. "Somebody who works for the holding company would be better."

His words came out so quickly that Maureen knew if she ever wanted to learn Pettigrew's secrets, her first step would be to talk to Luther and Kennedy. Whoever they were.

Gregory said he wanted to talk with the nuns, and Maureen motioned him to go ahead. Pretty obvious he wants to leave the two of us alone, Maureen thought, but who cares? Sooner or later she'd have met Midas Man somewhere.

Now there were only the two of them, a billionaire and a Wall Street skeptic standing in the middle of a party, no one else near. Maureen could see it as a movie, the camera somewhere overhead, the crowd around them out of focus. How this came out depended on what sort of film this was. A western duel, a thriller, an adventure in the jungle? She decided to let Pettigrew pick the plot, at least the way the story began. *You can learn a lot by listening.* Who had told her that first? Her mother? Her father? Or had she discovered it herself?

Pettigrew touched his throat, put a hand to his mouth, then lowered it as he sipped champagne. Why so nervous? Maureen wondered. Surely the powerful Midas Man couldn't be worried about a lone analyst coming to town. Former analyst, actually.

"Do you plan to stay here long?" he asked.

"As long as necessary."

"I imagine you'll stay longer than you think. This is when spring arrives down here."

So they talked about the weather and the market, Maureen knowing considerably more was going on between them. Pettigrew was studying her, not even trying to hide his appraisal, a human calculator at work behind steel-blue eyes. Was she friend or foe? Could she be bought? Could she be scared away?

She knew what was coming next. She'd heard it before.

"Years as an investigative reporter, then straight into stock analysis." Pettigrew said. "You can't possibly understand finance."

"I've learned how to find out the truth. I do a lot more on-the-scene investigation than most analysts, and if I run into problems on financial sheets, I know a dozen people who'll help me," she said. "And remember it wasn't an MBA analyst who first caught on to Enron. It was a writer from *Fortune*."

Without warning, Pettigrew leaned closer and lowered his voice. "Fuck with me, and you'll regret it."

"Better men than you have told me that," Maureen said, barely missing a beat. "They couldn't frighten me off."

"None had the clout I have. I could destroy you."

"Or maybe you'd be the one—" Maureen searched for a different word. "Demolished."

"Don't sell me short."

Maureen heard his words, but something didn't compute. Pettigrew's voice came out too gruffly, like a boy covering up fear. Why?

"Or you me," she said, intending to leave it at that. But remnants of the conversation she'd had earlier in the day were lodged in her head, and she abandoned professionalism.

"Do you ever think about the results of your actions? The jobs lost. The towns destroyed."

Midas Man looked at her as if he'd never been asked the question. "Our job is to make profits. We do a good job of that."

A textbook answer, Maureen thought. One she couldn't argue with under most circumstances. "But you and your Trust are supposed to be helping people."

Pettigrew stared at her in silence for almost a minute, then shook his head, straightened up, and stepped back. "Duty calls."

"Don't let me keep you," Maureen said.

"Don't forget." He looked toward the nuns and then back at Maureen. "Mess with me, and you'll be sorry you ever came down here."

With that Pettigrew walked away, too quickly, Maureen thought looking at his back and concluding mustached men must have a lot to hide, too. Especially ones who're so nervous. Why? Why is such a powerful man so insecure he must make childish threats? What was Midas Man afraid of?

Should she tell Go about Pettigrew's threat? Probably not. She wasn't worried, so why bother him? Too bad the nuns hadn't heard the exchange, though. It'd have shown them what their potential benefactor was really like.

Chapter Three

They'd been at the party only an hour, maybe a little more, but Maureen was ready to leave. She'd had enough. She'd seen some things neither she nor Gregory could have expected, and she wasn't going to get involved This hadn't been a party; it was a circus. Or one of those zoos with the animals roaming wild. But none of it was any of her business. All she wanted now was to find a hotel, take a long, hot shower, and sleep ten hours. When she'd told Gregory she wanted to leave, he didn't object. Now they walked toward the same path they'd used to enter the garden.

The flashing lights of police cars someone had called flickered through the mansion, entering front windows and leaving through the tall glass doors that opened into the garden. All the more reason to get out of there. They reached a lagoon she had walked around earlier.

Gregory pointed. "Look."

But Maureen had already seen it. Something pink lay among the hyacinths ten to fifteen feet from shore. A pink beach towel simmering below the surface, she thought at first. No, not as substantial as that. A piece of light cloth. Like a frilly dress. That was it. A woman floating on her stomach, face down, almost still.

And then she remembered. She'd seen the dress and met the woman at the party. Grace Pettigrew, Midas Man's former wife. His second ex, someone had said. The woman who'd heckled Pettigrew in front of the television cameras. The woman who'd been invited to the party only because of her lifetime appointment as a trustee of Providence Place. Dead. Maureen was sure of it.

Gregory jumped into the shallow water of the lagoon, his feet sinking into the slime, his body seeming to shrink. He sloshed toward Grace, every step an obvious effort, the floating hyacinths grabbing around his waist. He bent down and tried to spread the plants apart with his hands, but they sprang back into his path. He leaned forward and plunged ahead.

Maureen thought of getting into the water, too, but stopped herself. She knew Go could drag Grace's body to the shore by himself, then attempt to revive her with one of the respiration techniques he'd learned in nursing. Her job was to stand back and stay dry until he asked for help. No use calling 9-1-1. The cops were already at the front of the house and would be at the lagoon in minutes. They could call medics quicker than she could.

Finally Gregory got to Grace, reached out, and put his hands on her shoulders. Her body slipped deeper below the surface. Try again, try again, Maureen's thoughts yelled but she knew Gregory would anyway. He stuck an arm deep into the water, worked it under Grace's back, put his other arm over her chest, and pulled upward. Grace rolled over on her back but fell deeper into the hyacinths.

Maureen became vaguely aware that other people had reached the edge of the lagoon and stood on either side of her now. Someone jumped into the pond and splashed toward Gregory, shouting "Hold her up." Kennedy. Yes, that was his name. He'd said he was Midas Man's chauffeur but acted as if he were much more important. Well spoken. Knowledgeable. Likeable. But something mysterious about him, too.

Now Maureen saw Gregory point in her direction, and the other man seemed to understand. They began pulling Grace toward shore, but her body insisted on sinking. The voices on either side of Maureen grew louder. She looked along the edge of the lagoon, and saw the television crews, the ones that had been there for Pettigrew's speech, every camera lens pointed toward Gregory and Kennedy and Grace now, their microphones on booms reaching over water. How long had they been there?

Suddenly the water filled with brown uniforms, police splashing toward Grace's body, Gregory and Kennedy in their way, one cop yelling, "Leave her alone." The two men held Grace above the water until the police reached them, then waded toward shore. Maureen put her hand out, braced herself, and helped Gregory up.

He said, "Let's get out of here."

"I doubt they'll let us leave."

A man in civilian clothes, suit and tie, but something about him saying cop, pushed his way through the cameras. "What happened?"

"We found her floating there," Maureen said. Stupid thing to say maybe, but that's what came to her mind.

"Suppose you come along, and tell me all about it." He looked at Gregory's wet clothes. "Both of you."

"OK. But then we leave." Set some limits, Maureen was thinking.

"You'll leave when I say you can."

Maureen saw the cameras focus on the cop, on Gregory, and on her, then swing back to the uniformed men around Grace's floating body. She could see the future. She and Gregory and the police and poor Grace's body were going to be on the eleven o'clock news all over South Florida. Pettigrew's little speech and all the rest would be eclipsed by the discovery of his ex-wife's body and the arrival of the cops.

Then it hit her. Not just in South Florida. New York and the rest of the nation, too. How could the networks resist? A billionaire, a Wall Street figure of some repute, and a drowning, maybe a murder. The networks would love it. On the other hand, her partners in New York....

They'd hate it. Absolutely hate it. To hell with them. She hadn't done anything wrong.

Chapter Four

The cop—he'd said his name was Carlos Fourquet and that he was a lieutenant detective with the Fort Lauderdale Police Department—questioned Gregory first, Maureen sitting twenty to twenty five feet away, two uniformed cops standing nearby but not so close as to be intimidating. A few television crews pointed cameras at them from the other side of a yellow crime scene tape, but others, nearer the house, were already broadcasting

Gregory had taken off his shoes and socks, but there was nothing he could do about his wet trousers. The air had turned colder and occasionally Maureen saw him tremble involuntarily. He sat with his hands on his lap, sometimes putting one in front of his mouth, the way shrinks do, not wanting the detective to see his expression, smiling or whatever. Suddenly he spread his arms as if startled, and Maureen thought she heard the word "ridiculous." He looked her way. She smiled, trying to be as encouraging as possible under the circumstances. Ridiculous was the right word for it, Maureen was sure, whatever it was.

Finally it was her turn. Fourquet sat on a gray metal chair not more than four feet in front of her, the two cops standing closer now. The detective was about Gregory's age and height but with a smaller frame. Vain, of course. With that little black mustache he couldn't be anything else.

Fourquet started asking his questions, and Maureen told him about Gregory meeting her at the airport, their arrival at the party, and Pettigrew's limp little threat. The detective fingered his mustache. "Take your time now and tell me everything you remember after that."

"You don't want to hear every detail, do you?"

"Yep."

OK fellow, but you'll be sorry, Maureen thought. She had a fantastically good memory, one trained in her newspaper days and honed by stock analysis, so she started giving him every detail she could remember. Why not?

After she'd clashed with Pettigrew early in the party, Maureen told the detective, she stooped down and poured the remainder of her champagne, almost two-thirds of a glass, into the ground at the base of a hibiscus bush. She figured it wouldn't hurt the plant, and she wanted to be as clearheaded as possible for the remainder of the party.

Then, since Gregory was still talking with the nuns, she decided to explore the grounds by herself. She remembered walking around the large lagoon covered with floating hyacinths. Lights from the city lit the sky. A few pleasure boats passed by on the wide strip of water at the garden's edge. Maureen hadn't been to South Florida for years, but she knew this was the Intracoastal Waterway, the liquid highway connecting Miami to Maine.

A floodlit boathouse, weathered and old, sat on the shoreline, the chain-link fence that surrounded most of the grounds pushed down on either side. On its roof, a much newer diving board stuck out over the water. Strange. Must have been put there for looks, she'd thought. Who would ever dive into that dark liquid?

"Not bad if you like this kind of shit." The voice came from behind her. Maureen spun around.

The guy was young, early twenties probably, clean-shaven and dark-skinned but not from the sun, Puerto Rican maybe, his blue blazer and tan slacks fitting perfectly, a white handkerchief barely sticking out of the jacket pocket.

"Mr. Pettigrew asked me to see if there was anything you wanted." He grinned. "And to say he didn't really mean what he said to you. Whatever that was."

Maureen liked the guy immediately. Something about him radiated optimism and hope, something more than his obvious good health.

"Who are you?"

"Name's Kennedy." He didn't extend a hand.

Ding, ding, ding! The Kennedy of Luther and Kennedy, she'd thought. "You have a first name?"

"Kennedy's my middle name. It's what I go by."

"And you are—"

"Pettigrew's chauffeur."

More than that. Mingling with the guests, acting like he was one of them. The clothes he wore. So Maureen said, "And what else?"

"The man's personal trainer."

"What else?"

"Law student."

"What else?"

"That's it."

"Bodyguard?"

Kennedy laughed. "There're enough of them around here without me."

"Where?"

"Anybody wearing a shirt so loud no man of taste would wear it. Anybody wearing a waiter's suit who's not waiting."

Maureen saw two, figured there must be half a dozen more. "Pettigrew live here?"

"Nah, but I do."

Maureen kept silent. Long ago she'd learned the effectiveness of saying nothing and waiting for the other person to speak first. Nine times out of ten, people will explain themselves.

"I live here over the garage. The man lives in a penthouse on top of a hotel down on the beach."

Maureen was on auto pilot now, the questions coming quickly. "Anybody else live here?"

"Nope. Luther and the staff work here, but they all go home at night."

Ding, ding! The other half of the Kennedy-Luther pair. "Who's Luther?"

"He's the accountant who runs the Trust. Wouldn't be surprised if he's up in his office looking down on the party now." Kennedy pointed upward, toward the house. Maureen turned her head. Light glowed from windows on the second floor. A dark silhouette filled one. Or was she imagining that?

"He'd be down here now if tomorrow wasn't the deadline for some report. For my money, he's the smartest man around here."

A strange thing to say. Wouldn't he assume his billionaire boss was smarter?

"Now," Kennedy said, "I've got a question for you. Are you and Mr. Overman an item?"

The question startled Maureen, coming out of the blue like that. She stalled for time. "You've been watching us. Why?"

"The man told me to. He's done his research and knows quite a bit about you two. Like you drink a little, but Mr. Overman doesn't drink at all."

"I could tell he knew that."

"Well are you? An item?"

"What does his research tell him?"

"Everybody's got a different opinion," Kennedy said. "They say it's a puzzling relationship."

Maureen wanted to say something, but how much should she tell him? That when she helped nurse Gregory, he'd been five years old and she was nine? That when you're in high school a four-year difference is an eternity and that no self respecting sixteen-year-old girl would be caught dead even holding hands with an twelve-year-old boy? That even now that she'd almost reached forty and he was thirty-five, the thought of an intimate relationship seemed absurd? No. She wouldn't say any of those things. It was much, much too late to even think about becoming what Kennedy called an item.

"We're just friends," she said finally, not liking the way it sounded but at a loss to come up with something better. "Now you tell me what this party is all about."

"See that bamboo hedge over there?"

Maureen turned away from the house.

"Providence Place is on the other side. That's where Catholic nuns take care of homeless kids."

The bamboo stalks and Australian pines that Kennedy pointed toward grew together so densely that Maureen couldn't see anything behind them except pieces of chain-link fence, but she'd take Kennedy's word for it.

"Who's here besides the nuns?"

"You sure ask a lot of questions," Kennedy said.

"I get paid for asking questions."

"Who you working for?"

"Nobody right now." At this instant, she meant, at this party.

"Well, chill out."

Maureen looked into Kennedy's face until their eyes locked. "Pettigrew told you to ask if there was anything I wanted. I want you to answer my questions."

Kennedy thought for a couple of seconds, shrugged, and pointed toward a man in the crowd. "There's the mayor."

"Young for a mayor."

"This is the new Lauderdale." He pointed again. "Over there are some un-indicted county commissioners. The people kissing up to them work for agencies that need money. The nuns are networking for the same reason, but not so obvious about it. The corporate suits are here because Pettigrew's here. The kids will serve the food. "

Maureen had wondered about them. They stood behind linen-covered tables at the rear of the garden, fifteen or more young people, most in their teens, a few in their early twenties. Each wore shorts or jeans and a dark blue T-shirt with a large white letter "P" on the front. At first Maureen thought the big Ps stood for Pettigrew. Then Providence Place registered.

One of the young women waved. Slim, a little taller and older than the others, her long blond hair tied into a ponytail, legs browned from the sun, purple polish on her nails. Her age? Somewhere between fifteen and twenty-five. Maureen couldn't call it any closer in the flickering light of the torches.

Kennedy waved back. "That's Bridget."

The girl Gregory had mentioned. "You like her."

"She's a troublemaker."

"But one who attracts men."

Kennedy laughed. "Look but don't touch. That's my motto."

Indeed. Kennedy called her a troublemaker, Gregory used the word ringleader. No matter what her age, she was old enough to draw the attention of these two men, probably others.

Bridget, she'd thought. Someone to watch.

A woman in her late thirties, maybe forty, her frilly pink dress a size too tight and her complexion ruddy, wobbled toward them on the high heels of her pink shoes. Probably very attractive before she got into booze, Maureen thought.

"Who's that?"

"Grace Pettigrew," Kennedy said. "The second Mrs. Pettigrew."

"I didn't think he was married."

"She's an ex. Ex-wife Number Two. The first one's out in Santa Fe."

"What's this one doing here?"

"She's a trustee for Providence Place. It's a lifetime appointment."

The second Mrs. Pettigrew reached a spot five or six feet in front of them and stopped. When she spoke, her words came out indistinctly, slow and slurred, the intense concentration going into forming the words barely succeeding.

"You Maureen O'Neal?"

"Yes."

"I heard 'bout— I heard 'bout you."

Maureen waited.

"You don't know what you're getting into," Grace said, her voice stronger and clearer.

Kennedy said, "Now Grace."

Maureen said, "Getting into what?"

Grace said, "You should stay away from it."

Here less than two hours and already two people have warned me away, Maureen thought. Some sort of record.

"Stay away from what?"

"Some other time would be better." Kennedy put an arm around the woman. "Right now Grace needs to get over to the stage."

He guided her away with a gentleness that made Maureen realize he'd done it before. Grace, she remembered thinking: Another woman to keep an eye on.

Maureen watched Kennedy and Grace until they turned a corner of the mansion and vanished, then followed at a distance until she reached the far side of the house and saw the set-up. A makeshift stage stood near the Intracoastal, rows of gray metal chairs in front, a platform of metal scaffolding behind, a half-dozen television cameras peering down from the top of the platform, their lenses pointed toward a microphone at center stage.

No wonder they'd taken down the fence near the boathouse. This part of the garden is going to be in pictures, she thought, someone at the microphone in front of the water, floodlights illuminating boats passing by, the old boathouse giving the scene an historic look. The images should be spectacular. And phony. Phony as the backdrops used in presidential campaigns. Phony like Pettigrew.

"Mo."

Maureen turned at the sound of Gregory's voice.

"They're about to start the show. We can sit together."

She had a better idea. "Remember when we were kids? We said two could see better than one only if they have different sight lines."

"Yes."

"Let's do it now. One of us sit in a chair, the other stand somewhere else."

Why? Maureen could see him start to say, but he didn't.

"OK. I'll find a tree to lean against."

"Watch Grace."

Gregory nodded, and Maureen walked away. The band stopped playing. The saxophonist unhooked his horn, propped it against a tree, walked toward the microphone, and told people to take their seats "for the announcement we've all been waiting for."

Maureen listened to people talk as they passed.

A woman said, "I hear he gives a million a year to charity."

"I heard it was a million a month."

"Such a nice man."

"I heard it's drug money."

"Shush. He's Providence Place's biggest contributor."

"From the Trust or from himself?"

"It's all the same."

"No, it's not."

Not at all the same, Maureen thought. Spending someone else's money is so much easier than spending your own. She followed the crowd and found a seat near the front. Gregory stood under a palm tree. Grace sat in the middle of the second row, Kennedy a few seats away. The nuns and social agency people took seats around them, corporate and government officials sitting in the rear.

Pettigrew mounted the stage and stood behind the microphone. "Tonight I'm pleased to announce a contribution of fifty million dollars to Providence Place."

"Bull!" Grace Pettigrew stood up, shaking her fist.

Pettigrew ignored her. "It will be used to build a new residence—"

"Millions for buildings and not one penny for operations," Grace shouted.

Two men who fit Kennedy's description of bodyguards, one in a white waiter's outfit, the other in sports clothes, moved toward her from either side of the stage. Pettigrew kept going. "Bigger, farther west, away from tourist activity."

"Bull!" The voice, younger than Grace's, came from the Providence Place kids.

Pettigrew fought on, irritation showing on his face. "A much larger facility, the most modern—"

"Bull." No doubt about it this time. It was Bridget's voice.

"Four stories tall, more than a hundred thousand square feet, every amenity—"

"Bull, bull, bull," the youngsters from Providence Place chanted.

The bodyguards, almost to Grace, reversed direction and ran toward the teenagers. Two nuns stood and followed. Bridget saw them, grabbed the shiniest thing on the table, a big silver platter full of little sandwiches, and bolted toward the boathouse. The other kids ran after her.

"Get her!" Pettigrew's amplified voice rang through the garden, Midas Man's patience and self-control giving way to fury.

Another loud-shirted bodyguard, this one younger and bigger than the others, emerged from the darkness and chased after Bridget, the distance between them narrowing quickly. Gregory abandoned his post by the palm tree and ran toward the guy. Maureen wanted to shout he shouldn't risk his leg but didn't. She'd quit playing big sister.

The bodyguard got within a few feet of Bridget before Gregory hit him, Go's shoulder thrusting into the man's side, striking where he was most vulnerable. They tumbled to the ground, the guy with a surprised look on his face, Gregory in obvious pain. Now they'll pound each other, and Go will get hurt, Maureen thought. But the security guy lay on the ground, stunned. Or maybe they didn't pay him enough to really fight.

Bridget stopped, blew a kiss to Gregory, then turned and climbed the wooden ladder on the side of the boathouse. The other kids from Providence Place ran toward her, television crews in pursuit. Maureen wanted to stay near the stage to see how Pettigrew was reacting, but it was more important to get to Gregory. She followed the crowd.

Now Bridget stood on the diving board holding the silver platter above her head as if performing some ancient rite, her eyes closed, her face expressionless. She began rolling her hips slowly, the effect more mystical than seductive.

Police sirens wailed in the distance, the muted sounds coming from somewhere across the Intracoastal. Bridget heard the sirens, opened her eyes, and lowered the platter, fingers of her right hand around one edge. Her arm moved smoothly to her left, then quickly to the right. The platter flew into the air and sailed over the Intracoastal like a Frisbee, sandwiches flying into the darkness. Then it lost altitude, hit the surface, skipped once, twice, three times, and sank into the black water.

The sirens grew louder. Bridget bounced on the board twice, her slim body brightly lit by floodlights. The kids chanted, "Go, Bridg, go." On the third bounce the girl sprang into the air, grabbed her legs, coiled into a ball, somersaulted, unwound, and cut into the water, barely making a splash.

The kids cheered. A few adults applauded. The television cameras swung away from Bridget to pan the crowd. Every eleven o'clock news program in South Florida would use the footage, Maureen figured, Pettigrew's big announcement overshadowed by the antics of Bridget and her friends.

Police cruisers, lights flashing and sirens screeching, raced over the bridge from the mainland. Maureen searched the dark waters of the Intracoastal, looking for Bridget. The girl had disappeared.

"Bridget," Go said. "She'll catch something in that water."

"You shouldn't have," she told him. Shouldn't have gone after the security guard, she meant. And you shouldn't nag, Maureen added to herself. "Let's get out of here."

Go started walking. Maureen looked back at the stage. Empty. Pettigrew had vanished, too.

Chapter Five

Maureen looked at the detective now, reviewing in her mind what she'd told him. Yes, she'd related everything of importance that happened in the last hour. She finished it up. "Then we left the others. When we got to the lagoon we saw Grace's body. Gregory jumped in to try to save her."

She watched Fourquet's face for reaction, but it showed nothing. Over his shoulder she saw Gregory tremble again. It was time to get out of there.

She stood up. "And now we'll leave this mess to you."

"I know you'd like to," Fourquet said.

Maureen look down at him.

"But like I told you before, you leave when I say you can."

What would happen, Maureen wondered, if I just walked away? The answer came back in an instant: She and the cops who stopped her would be on television again. She sat down.

Fourquet said, "You understand, Miss O'Neal, that Mr. Pettigrew is this town's most prominent citizen."

"If you say so."

"So when your friend tells us he invited you to come down here and vouch for Mr. Pettigrew, I have some difficulty seeing why."

"I doubt if that's exactly what he said."

"Close enough."

"Doesn't matter. This is a simple drowning case," Maureen said. "Grace Pettigrew was drunk. She fell into the lagoon and drowned. Simple as that."

"She had a few drinks, no dispute about that." Fourquet nodded. "Whether she drowned is something only the medical examiner can say."

"Most people who are found dead in water drowned."

"Yeah. But there are questions." Fourquet paused, and Maureen realized he was enjoying this, the situation, the questioning, him being the star of the show. "The questions are…." He held up one finger. "One, was she so inebriated she couldn't stand up once she fell into three feet of water?"

"And your answer is?" Maureen said.

"Maybe so, maybe not."

"And the other question?"

"Could someone have held her head beneath the water long enough to drown her?"

"And your answer?"

"Probably, considering the state people say she was in." Fourquet looked around the garden. "More than a hundred people here when her body was found. A hundred of the most influential people in South Florida."

"So?"

"Notice the way they're being treated? All we're asking is to see some ID. Show us a driver's license and they can go home."

"Except for Gregory and me."

"You two say you saw Grace Pettigrew's body in the water as you were walking by," the detective said. "But when a third party, Kennedy, arrived, Mr. Overman was already in the lagoon next to her body, pushing her down."

"He was trying to save her." Maureen felt the adrenaline start to rise, her body preparing to focus, fight, or flee.

"You were the only person who saw your friend jump into the lagoon."

"Most of the others were down at the boathouse, milling around after watching the girl from Providence Place."

Again Fourquet nodded. "Except for you two and Mr. Pettigrew, who we've already determined had walked to his car.

Then Kennedy saw his boss had left the party and ran after him. He stopped when he saw your friend and Grace in the lagoon."

Maureen said nothing.

"The point is," he said, looking directly at her, "you're the only one who knows what your friend did when he jumped into the pool. And the only alibi either of you has is each other."

Maureen stayed silent. Fourquet hadn't asked a question.

"Your friend Gregory lifts weights."

Another statement, one Maureen knew was true. He'd been working out at a gym ever since he recovered from polio.

"He says he can bench press a couple of hundred pounds," Fourquet said.

"I didn't hear him say that," she said.

"He did." For the first time since they started talking, Fourquet sounded annoyed. "So Mr. Overman—no, make that a man like Mr. Overman—is strong enough to hold a drunken woman under water no matter how much she struggles."

"Ridiculous," Maureen said, realizing only after the word was out that she was echoing Gregory. She looked toward Gregory and saw him smiling, giving her a thumbs up. Dated, maybe, but she didn't mind.

"And you," Fourquet said, "If you knew of his plans, you'd be an accomplice. Same as a murderer."

"Absurd."

"Or even if you didn't know of his plans and didn't yell out when you saw what he was doing, you'd be considered an accomplice."

Maureen didn't know anything about criminal law and didn't want to, but she wondered if Fourquet wasn't stretching things a bit. "But why? What would be his motive?"

"Don't know."

"And mine?" Maureen said. "Why in the world would I be suspected of anything?"

"Easy." A big grin crossed Fourquet's face, his white teeth flashing under the mustache. "You're a stranger in town."

Absurd, ridiculous, irrational, preposterous, all those words and more crossed Maureen's mind but she kept them inside.

"To be more precise," the cop said, "we don't know anything about you or your friend. Twenty-four hours from now we'll know almost everything about both of you."

"Neither of us has any reason to hurt Grace Pettigrew."

"Maybe. But until we learn more, don't leave town."

"Don't tell me that. You didn't read me my Miranda rights."

"Don't have to. You're not in custody."

"You got it," Maureen said, the adrenaline finally getting to her. "So I'm free to go anywhere I want. Gregory, too."

Fourquet smiled, straining. "Technically, I suppose."

"So charge us or let us go."

Again the teeth flashed. "Let me rephrase my statement. The Fort Lauderdale Police Department requests that you not leave town for a few days. That suit you?"

"I wasn't planning on going anywhere."

"Let us know where you're staying." Fourquet turned and walked away, not waiting for an answer.

Maureen stood up. Midas Man had predicted she'd stay in Florida longer than she planned. Score one for him.

Chapter Six

They rode from Trust House with the convertible top up, the air cooler now, Maureen thinking, Who said Florida doesn't get cold in February? "I'll need to rent a room."

"It's late. You can stay with me until tomorrow." Gregory looked over at her. "I'll sleep on the sofa. You get the bed."

"The girl. Bridget. You think she was in on it?"

"In on what?"

"Grace Pettigrew's murder," she said. "If she was murdered."

"What could Bridget have to do with it?"

"Her show—throwing the silver platter and diving off the board—she distracted everyone's attention from the rest of the garden while someone killed Grace."

"That seems far-fetched. Who would she do it for?"

"Pettigrew maybe. Kennedy maybe."

"Too wild to even think about," Gregory said.

"Don't you find it strange that Pettigrew, supposedly one of the most powerful men in the country, let his big announcement get out of hand so easily?"

"He was at his car when Grace drowned."

"How do we know that?" Maureen asked.

"The police— That lieutenant who questioned us said they'd established he was at his car."

"I'll bet they asked him, Pettigrew told them he was there, and they took his word for it," she said. "Fourquet didn't seem keen on challenging the town's most prominent citizen."

"I picked that up, too. In fact, he didn't come across as a real professional."

"Something was off-key about him, all right." No good cop would act like Fourquet had, Maureen figured, but what did she know? When she'd worked for newspapers she left the cop beat as quickly as possible, preferring City Hall, Courthouse, and legislative assignments. Early on she'd discovered that the best stories are found where money and politics meet.

A1A split, one-way north near the ocean, one-way south nearer the Intracoastal, and Gregory had no choice but to turn away from the Atlantic. Now the street felt different, nobody walking on the sidewalks, the lighting dimmer.

Gregory said, "When Bridget returns, I can talk to her."

"No. This whole thing is none of our business."

"But we're suspects."

"Surely you don't take that clown seriously."

"I don't know what to think," he said. "But I notice you have some fancy theories."

"Just speculating. It's not something for us to get involved in." Change the subject, Maureen thought. "Did you tell the police you were in rehab?"

"They wouldn't understand."

"Sometimes I don't understand."

"I burned out. That's all there was to it."

"And started drinking again."

"Yes."

"Drugs?" Maureen thought she knew the answer, but she wanted to be sure.

"No."

"What happened?"

"A boy I was counseling killed himself."

"Surely not your fault," Maureen said. But she knew Gregory would blame himself forever. She decided to spend the night in his apartment, then move to a hotel tomorrow.

Gregory turned the Mustang to the right. "This is Las Olas. It means 'the waves.'"

They crossed a bridge over the Intracoastal, and the road became a divided boulevard, tall royal palms in the median strip, the sidewalks lined with more coconut palms and fake gas streetlights. Big yachts filled the canals on either side, and occasionally Maureen spotted a sailboat mast sticking up over a house, something she hadn't seen since they were in Lauderdale before.

"They hide the wires and cables underground and put the cell phone base stations on the roofs of condominiums," Gregory said. "Makes everything look tidy."

No, Maureen thought, he can't bury this in small talk. She had to say something now, get it out in the open early during her stay. "Gregory, you've let yourself be influenced much too much by the little help I gave you years ago. Your whole life, your professions, determined by those two years."

"You were wonderful. Without you I'd—"

"Stop it. I helped nurse you because I was the girl next door and you were a little kid. I did what I did for my own motives."

"You did more. You taught me to read and do some pretty fancy math."

She'd say it as clearly as she could. "You don't owe me anything. Stop treating me like you do." There. He should understand that. Stop treating me like a sister. Stop treating me like your nurse. Wake up. I'm a woman.

Go turned right again. "This is where I live. The Isle of Venice."

He didn't get it, didn't understand at all what she was talking about. So she said, "That the name of the apartment house?"

"The street."

"Silly name for a street." But not as silly as being told you were suspected of being an accomplice in a murder only a few hours after you arrived in a city. Maureen had fun here twenty years ago, but she didn't particularly like the new Lauderdale. Maybe this whole trip was a bad mistake. Maybe she should have listened to her intuition. It had warned her.

Chapter Seven

That morning Maureen had been in New York, standing in the middle of her firm's trading room floor, knowing something was wrong but unable to locate the source of the trouble. Was it in the market or somewhere else? She closed her eyes. All around her dozens of men and women stared into flat computer monitors, tapped commands on keyboards, and talked into phones. They bought and sold stocks, bonds, and fancier things, betting millions.

It was a Friday and she was in charge. Stock prices had moved steadily upward since early morning, and the traders were riding the wave. But there was a feeling in the air, an undercurrent, not just the low trading volume. Something....

"Mo," the guy at the central desk yelled over the din. "Phone."

"I'm busy," she shouted back.

"He says his name is Go, and you'll talk to him."

Her eyes opened. "I'll take it in my office."

She started across the room, one almost as large as a basketball court, the clicks and clatter growing louder. Big money at stake. Seconds counted and minutes mattered, but she was never too busy to talk to Go. She'd given him the nickname when they were kids, just as he had dubbed her Mo. Simple as pie. Take the initials from their full names—Gregory Overman and Maureen O'Neal—and they had it. Mo and Go. Go and Mo.

They'd been close then. Long time since she saw him. Months? A couple of years, actually.

"Mo, stop a minute and look at this." Rebecca, a trader she'd mentored, mid-twenties with an Ivy League muted attractiveness about her, smart, ambitious. She wanted to short 100,000 shares of Qualflex, a bet the high-flyer would crash and burn soon. Up a point and a half, trading at 36, but Rebecca thought the gain was temporary. Maureen nodded approval. She'd researched the company earlier in the week and concluded its stock would be trading in the teens within a month.

Across the floor a trader yelled, "Damn, damn, damn." One of the new men, a curly-headed youngster barely out of business school, his MBA still damp. He held the keyboard in his hands as if to smash the monitor.

Maureen rushed over and looked at his screen. "Get out of it."

He pushed some buttons. "Lost half million in five minutes."

She put a hand on his shoulder. "You'll make it back Monday." He would, too, but she made a mental note to watch him more carefully. "Take the rest of the day off."

The smile that brightened his face was somewhere between boyish and manly. Maureen replied with a stern look so he wouldn't think the loss was a minor matter. Or that her attitude conveyed forgiveness. With only two hours left in the trading day she hadn't given him much of a gift.

Now to get to her office before there was another emergency. Maureen liked the excitement of the job, the adrenaline rush that wiped out the doubts and anxiety that came at her at times. She was good at managing the floor but felt she'd been even better as an analyst. Give her a couple of days to wade through a company's financials, talk to suppliers and competitors, maybe find a disgruntled executive or former lover of one, and she could discover the secrets and Achilles' heel of any corporation in the country. What separated her from others of the breed was that two-thirds of her reports recommended against purchase of stock in the company she'd researched. No other analyst could say that. Too many became carnival barkers for the companies they were supposed to cover.

But now the partners had made her a managing director, and she no longer wrote reports on individual companies. Instead, she spent most of her time talking with major clients—insurance companies, pension funds and other institutional investors—or, alas, supervising trading. This was the third time this week she'd been assigned to manage the floor. Three times last week, too. One of the partners had suffered a heart attack, another had a new child he wanted to spend time with, and another wanted to leave town early for the weekend. She'd heard someone joke she was so busy managing the floor she couldn't screw up any underwriting deals. Who said that? Neither a name nor face would come to mind. Maybe she'd imagined it.

Finally in her office, she'd pick up her phone. "What's up, Go?"

"I need help."

"Anything." She felt good, just hearing her voice.

When he'd asked her to fly to Lauderdale, Maureen agreed without hesitation. Why not? Later she'd wondered if she'd been too eager. Maybe she should have asked more questions. Maybe she should have pinned him down about the man he wanted her to meet. Maybe Gregory's reference to another woman had thrown her off balance. What had he said exactly?

"Why, Go? Why do you want me there?" she asked.

"To attend a party with me. To meet someone."

"A woman?"

"No." he said. "Or maybe so."

Oh Lord, not again, she'd thought. Go had been involved with the biggest collection of losers she could imagine. Control freaks and whiners, alcoholics and addicts, users and bimbos—not a keeper in the bunch. Sometimes Maureen wondered if she was the problem. Their background. So close, but never a couple. Never would be.

Not that she had done any better. Most men she'd met wouldn't adjust to her work schedule, traveling out of town so much, often not knowing when she'd get back. A workaholic, some called her. But how do you do your best without working long and hard? Others said she was too smart for her own good. How could that be true of anyone?

"It's not what you think," Gregory had said. "It's the man I want you to meet. You can see him and everybody else at the party."

"What party?"

"I'll meet you at the plane and take you straight there."

Maureen rubbed the back of her neck. It always hurt when something was wrong. Ordinarily she stopped and listened to whatever part of her brain was trying to talk to her, but this time she couldn't. Rebecca stuck her head though the door. "The market's turned, everything's falling."

Into the phone, Maureen said, "Meet the first flight that leaves LaGuardia an hour and a half after the market closes," hung up without saying goodbye, and rushed past Rebecca into the trading room.

Decisive. Everybody said that about her. What they didn't know was she was absolutely wrong about investment decisions almost half the time. She always admitted errors quickly, though, getting out of a bad stock position with minimum losses. The other half, the right calls, she let ride. Those were the ones that made her clients rich.

Crossing the trading room, she wished she'd acted on her hunch about trouble in the market. Alerting the traders might have helped. Or had a premonition about Go's phone call set off her alarms?

Thirty minutes later, after she'd checked to see how well the traders had adjusted to the market's new direction, Rebecca wanted her to look at another special situation. Red, green, and gold lines on her monitor tracked trading in a dog of a stock, one that had scraped along the bottom of the market for years. In the last few days it had showed surprising strength, rising thirteen percent on high volume.

Maureen pushed buttons on Rebecca's keyboard. A new graph popped onto the screen showing volume adjusted moving price averages, an old tool to flatten bumps in trading. Then she created more graphs, each more sophisticated than the last.

"It's Pettigrew," she said.

"You think so?"

"It's his pattern. Buy in front of him and make him pay dearly for this one."

Rebecca nodded and started pushing keys. Those keystrokes and the phone calls that would follow committed the firm to wagering millions that someone—probably Roland Pettigrew—was trying to gain control of the company, gut it, and move on. They were going along for the ride.

"Ever met Pettigrew?" Rebecca said, her eyes still on the screen.

"No. And I don't want to."

"They say you have to count your fingers after you shake hands with him. If you have three left, you're lucky."

Maureen had heard the joke a hundred times but laughed anyway.

"Ever think about what he does?" Rebecca asked.

"I try not to."

"Do we help him by buying stock in his companies?"

"We don't whip the horses," Maureen said. "We just bet on them."

True enough. But sometimes she'd wondered how everyone on The Street could disassociate themselves from the effects of Pettigrew's actions. Was it like buying stock in tobacco companies? People rationalized those decisions. They think: Tobacco companies are profitable, their shares go up, and there's no reason I shouldn't make money on them like everyone else. I don't own enough shares to influence what they do, therefore I'm not responsible for it. Besides, almost half their profits come from food products.

Bull! Maureen always thought when someone on Wall Street made those arguments. She couldn't own stock in a company whose main product killed people. But other companies? Where do you draw the line? So far, she hadn't been above owning stocks in Pettigrew's companies as short term speculations. But only that.

Rebecca looked up. "Who's the man? Who's Go?"

"A friend."

"One you're not going to talk about."

Maureen nodded, turned, and walked away. Her relationship with Go was special, and she'd be damned if she'd let the two of them become a subject of office gossip.

"Thanks for the assist," Rebecca shouted after her. Not something she needed to say. The girl had been kissing up a lot lately.

Later in the afternoon, after most of the others left, her door closed but still able to see stragglers through the glass window in her office, Maureen reviewed events of the day. Thanks to the afternoon action, all the traders had made millions. The market turned and bounced up twenty minutes before the close. The traders got out of their short positions at a profit. Except for one. Rebecca's Qualflex short was in the money, and Maureen had felt so confident about the position she decided to leave it open for the weekend. At the same time stock in Pettigrew's presumed target company had continued climbing, and Rebecca bought more and more right up to the close. The computers would sort things out overnight, but she was sure they'd find an eight-digit gain for the session. Not a bad day.

All was well. Except for the man in the round glasses staring down from the wall. Maureen looked up at the framed poster Go had given her years ago, a burnt-orange line drawing of Mohandas Gandhi printed on stark brown paper and overlaid with a quotation in bold black type. You have to do the right thing, the bald one admonished.

Rebecca's question about Pettigrew, silly as it was, stuck in her mind. Do we help a man like Pettigrew by buying stock in his companies? Of course not. Stock and bond prices rise and fall for the same reasons as anything else, supply and demand. Markets don't know who moves them.

Her only part in it was to do her job well. And that, as a partner and a managing director of a mid-size New York-based broker-dealer, was to study and deal in stocks, bonds, and their exotic offspring—options and indexes, some with nicknames like Tigers, Spiders, Leaps, and Diamonds. Strip away the bells and whistles, though, and like everyone else on The Street she was motivated by the same maxim that inspired desert traders more than two thousand years ago. Buy low, sell high. What was wrong with that?

Rebecca came in again, this time having changed from heels to Nikes. "You do a great job," she said.

"With a little bit of luck."

"I can't understand why you're leaving."

"What?"

"That's the rumor."

"I plan to stay here a long time." Maureen made her words sound as firm and confident as she could. She wouldn't ask where Rebecca heard the rumor. Treating such tales seriously only fanned them.

Rebecca beamed. "I'm glad. You're so good at what you do."

There she goes again, laying on flattery like peanut butter. Why?

"The market," Rebecca said. "You think the worst is over?"

Two years after The Bubble burst and everyone Maureen knew was still asking that. She was glad she'd gotten her clients out in January and February 2000, just before the market fell apart.

"People are coming back," Maureen said. "Stocks are way up."

"But almost every day, there's a new scandal. Companies, accountants, stock analysts, brokers, mutual funds—all being accused of crimes. Dirty linen everywhere."

Yes, and things could get worse. But Maureen wouldn't tell Rebecca that. How old was she—mid-twenties, maybe younger? Too soon to encourage cynicism.

"You don't have to worry about that. Just keep your skirt clean."

Rebecca looked up at Gandhi. "And do the right thing."

Maureen shook her head. "Watch your back. Look out for yourself. First. Foremost. Always."

A strange expression crossed Rebecca's face. Puzzlement? Surprise? Fear? Maureen was tired, and it was too late in the day to figure it out. She waved Rebecca away. "Get out and have a good weekend."

A good weekend. Fat chance. Outside the sky was gray, the temperature a windy thirty. Par for New York in February. Go was in Florida, soaking up rays. Be good to see him, she'd thought then.

But now, climbing the stairs to his Venice Isles apartment, she wondered if she'd made a mistake. She was going to be away from New York longer than she'd thought. Without her presence, those rumors Rebecca heard would grow.

And Gregory? What did he really want of her? What was this trip all about?

Chapter Eight

They entered Gregory's apartment through the kitchen door, the one nearest the stairs, and the first thing Maureen saw was the poster hanging on the wall next to the refrigerator. A hurting little boy stood in front of a triumphant unicorn, the caption proclaiming, NEVER PLAY LEAP FROG WITH A UNICORN. She'd given it to Gregory years ago as a continuing reminder to guard against impetuousness. A lot of good it did. He was still at it, crashing into the bodyguard at the party to help a girl he barely knew. And later, jumping into the lagoon, even saying on the way to his apartment they ought to find out more about Grace's death. It was none of their business.

A red light blinked from the answering machine on the counter between Gregory's kitchen and living room, two messages waiting. He pushed a button. The first message was an automated one, telemarketing of some sort. Gregory zapped it. Then the digitally reconstructed voice of a woman filled the kitchen.

"Grace Pettigrew," Maureen said when she recognized it. She'd talked to the woman only briefly, but she wouldn't forget that slurred voice for a long time. Gregory nodded.

You there, Mr. Overman? Grace paused. *Oh fuck.* Silence, then, *I guess I'll leave a message anyway. I hear you're going to work at Providence Place.* Another break. *You don't know what you're getting into.* A short pause. *You should talk to me before you commit yourself.* Another pause, one so long that Gregory reached toward the machine to replay the message. He pulled back when Grace started talking again. *I've really got some important things to tell you about that bastard.*

Then nothing.

"Let's hear it again," Maureen said.

Gregory pushed a button. The dead woman's words sounded more urgent, shriller, this time, but when she finished they had more questions than answers.

"Is she warning you about Providence Place or Pettigrew?" Maureen asked.

"You can interpret it either way."

"The reference to 'that bastard' is unmistakable. But why is she calling you? Why did she warn me away at the party?"

"First question, first," Gregory said. "I've been to Providence Place two or three times for interviews and orientation. Grace saw me there, introduced herself and we talked briefly. The answer to the second question is, I don't know."

Maureen looked toward the poster with the unicorn and hurting little boy, then back at Gregory. "Did you tell anyone at Providence Place I was coming here?"

"I told them I would invite you."

"Who?"

"A couple of the nuns. We were talking about Pettigrew's donation." Gregory opened the refrigerator. "Some of them had the same doubts about Pettigrew as the kids."

Well, that explained a few things. The nuns must have told Pettigrew she was coming. That gave him time to find out more about her. And Gregory. And maybe make plans for the evening. He certainly had a motive to kill Grace. She was a trustee for life at Providence Place. Her death ended that, along with her opposition to Pettigrew's donation. Was it a coincidence that Pettigrew's chauffeur, Kennedy, showed up so soon after they found Grace's body in the lagoon? And Bridget's diversion—was it so far-fetched to think she'd do something to help Grace? Or someone else?

All and all, a fascinating puzzle, Maureen thought, a problem susceptible to methodical analysis, like researching a company for a stock market report. She could.... No. Stop it, stop it, stop it. Don't let yourself get dragged into this.

"Grace's death is none of our business," she said.

Maureen's words came out so forcefully that Gregory swung around. "Except that Lt. Fourquet suspects us of killing her."

"He'll change his mind quickly. We don't have any motive."

"Still—" Gregory turned back and reached into the freezer.

Maureen knew what he was doing. "I don't want any."

"A little bit won't hurt." Gregory laid the carton of Chunky Monkey on the counter next to the sink. "I've been Jonesing for some all evening."

"OK," she said. "Just one scoop."

They ate the ice cream in the living room, the Mohandas Gandhi poster on the wall, a duplicate of the one in Maureen's office. Gregory had bought two of them years ago, one for her, one for himself. Gandhi looked down, his owl-like glasses giving Maureen the feeling that he could read their minds. His words didn't change.

It's the action, not the fruit of the action, that is important.

You have to do the right thing.

It may not be in your power, may not be in your time, that there will be any fruit.

But that doesn't mean you stop doing the right thing.

You may never know what results come from your action,

But if you do nothing, there will be no result.

It's not so simple, fellow, Maureen thought, not at all. What the heck was the right thing? What about leaving well enough alone? What about minding your own business?

"People who see that tell me Gandhi's first name is misspelled." Gregory said. "It's not."

Maureen nodded. "Mohandas was his first name. Mahatma was a title." But she knew Go was just warming up.

"If you believe Gandhi, we have to do something," he said.

"We aren't cops."

"Grace's death could jeopardize Pettigrew's gift to Providence Place."

"Why?"

"He expected praise. Now all he'll get is bad publicity."

"If he backs off the gift, people will realize he's a schmuck," Maureen said. "Those that don't know already."

"Mo, you've had nothing but bad things to say about him ever since you arrived."

She spooned the last of the ice cream from the bowl. "I haven't said all that much about the bastard."

"So tell me, what's he done that's so bad?"

"It would take some time."

"I've got little else." Gregory settled into his chair, a leather one shaped like a shell.

Maureen sat on the leather sofa and told him everything she could remember about Pettigrew—the shady deals, the buy-outs and sell-outs, the unnecessary cost cutting to give the bottom line a quick boost, the thousands of jobs lost in the process, the double crosses, the inflated price of initial public offerings, the times he bailed out of a company's stock not long before it tanked.

When she finished, Go said, "What's he done that's illegal?"

"Nothing he's been caught at. But there's a stench about him. Rumors."

"You're judging him by rumors?"

"By the results of his actions."

"That's strange. You used to talk about the wonders of a free economy and the marketplace—'the moving hand' that allocated resources. And how temporary dislocations can cause short-term pain, but in the long run they're good for everybody."

"But Pettigrew knows no limits," Maureen said. "He uses the system to screw the system."

"He gives millions to charity."

"The Trust's money or his?"

"I don't know, and I don't care."

"It makes a difference." Maureen started to elaborate but looked up and saw Gregory's face was flushed. Time to end the argument. "Let's drop this."

But Gregory said, "Haven't they passed a new law that cracked down on bad practices in the stock market?"

"You're talking about the Sarbanes-Oxley Act. Much of what Pettigrew did came before its passage." Maureen paused. "Besides, you can't reform a jungle."

"So my question remains, what's Pettigrew done that's illegal?"

Maureen thought about the question. No answer came. Pettigrew's actions were morally wrong, but.... "Why is it so important to you that he's actually broken a law?"

"I invited you down here. If your trip has messed up Pettigrew's gift to Providence Place, I'll be very disappointed. On the other hand, if he's a crook, I want to warn the nuns."

So now the whole thing was up to her. Unfair, unfair, unfair, Maureen thought. But keeping Gregory's friendship was more important than arguing about fairness. She said, "I'll find out more about Pettigrew, enough to satisfy you, in a couple of days."

"Tomorrow's Saturday, the next day's Sunday."

"Doesn't matter." Maureen stood up.

Gregory began unfolding the sofa bed.

"Want help with that?"

"I can do it myself."

"Go," she said. "Don't be mad at me."

He rested the bed's metal legs on the floor and turned toward her, hands at his side. "You don't like Pettigrew because he reminds you of your father."

Maureen recoiled. "What a terrible thing to say."

"But true."

Maureen stood there, fighting down a scream. No. She wouldn't discuss it tonight. They hadn't talked about the subject for years and this was the worst possible time to start. She turned and walked into the bedroom.

Sometime during the night Gregory came through the bedroom on the way to the bathroom. Mo pretended to be asleep, but she'd been awake for hours. Her thoughts keep going round and round.

Their relationship had started so innocently. She'd been in the third grade when Gregory came down with polio. He was only five and hadn't even begun grammar school. They were next-door neighbors in Sumner, Maryland, a suburb of the District of Columbia, their fathers each foreign service officers.

At first it was curiosity, Maureen going over to see him one afternoon when she heard about his illness, then the next afternoon, then another. There was something about him, or maybe the situation, that kept her going back. It wasn't long before they gave each other the nicknames.

Every day after school she'd climb the stairs, rush into his room and say something like, "Hi Go, guess what happened today?" He'd listen to every word, paying equal attention whether it was about what she learned in class or something that happened in the cafeteria. That must have been when she developed her interest in news reporting. To keep Gregory's interest, she learned to give almost word-for-word accounts of the things that happened in school. Soon she discovered he especially relished the stories kids brought to school from their homes, spilling secrets in class that their parents thought nobody would ever learn. Maybe those were the roots of his interest in counseling young people and families.

Maureen had read about the iron lungs people with polio had to use in the old days, before the new medications, but Go didn't have to lie in one. Instead, the regimen for him was to take a bunch of pills, stay in bed, and keep the oxygen mask on a lot. After a while, Maureen started bringing books to read to him, then went on and taught him how to read and work simple math problems. She wasn't any good at telling jokes, then or now, but she made him laugh anyway.

The next year, when Go could get up and walk with crutches, she got tougher. She'd climb the three flights of stairs and say, "OK, time to get your ass out of bed and get to work!" He lapped it up, willing to be taught anything. When Gregory started school, he was able to skip two grades.

They remained close until Maureen started dating, and even then saw each other from time to time. Later, after they'd gone to separate colleges and started different careers, they'd kept in touch by phone and e-mail. She knew everything important, professional and romantic, that happened to him.

That was all there was to it. Except for two ugly scenes: The one at high school and the one in her parent's bedroom. She didn't want to think about either of them now.

Chapter Nine

The next morning neither Maureen nor Gregory said anything about Maureen's father, Roland Pettigrew or even poor Grace Pettigrew while in Gregory's apartment or as they walked down Las Olas to the Floridian, a restaurant Go said she'd like.

"A twenty-four-hour diner on the low-rent end of the ritziest street in town," he said. "They have a secret formula for success."

Maureen waited.

"Good service, plain food, and reasonable prices."

"It'll never work." She smiled.

"No credit cards, no checks, no tablecloths."

"Maybe it will."

Flocks of wild parrots, green and noisy, flew overhead. Rays of the sun, still low in the sky, struck palms, yachts, and big houses. Enormous wealth here, Maureen thought, people making it somewhere else, then bringing it to Florida to play with. They've got half-million-dollar sport fishing boats, multi-million-dollar houses and tons of cash, while most people in the country live paycheck to paycheck, credit cards maxed out, bill drawers full. It's the way the system works. She'd quit fighting it, but still....

"This is it," Gregory said when they reached the restaurant. "We're lucky to beat the Saturday rush."

They walked through the main dining area to a side room, philodendron vines and television sets hanging from the ceiling, each turned to a different channel, the sound off, the walls covered by mirrors and campy cartoons from the sixties, photos of Marilyn Monroe and the Beatles. Maureen wore jeans, a pink blouse and beat-up running shoes, some of the emergency clothes she kept at the office, nothing special, but as they passed half the guys in the restaurant turned and stared.

When the waitress came Maureen ordered a poached egg, orange juice and whole wheat toast, dry. Gregory went for two eggs over light, Canadian bacon, raisin bread toast, and tomato juice. Then the silence between them returned, just as Maureen knew it would. Eventually they'd have to talk about what happened between them last night, about her father and all. But not now. So she said, "After a night's sleep, what do you make of Grace's message?"

"When she tried to talk to me at Providence Place. I told her I didn't want to get involved in her personal affairs."

Maureen stopped her coffee cup halfway to her mouth.

"Looking back," Gregory added, "that may have been a mistake."

"Any idea what Grace wanted to tell you?"

"No clue."

"You heard what she said about Pettigrew. Millions for buildings, not one cent for operations. True or false?"

"Don't know."

"Ever talk to Pettigrew before last night?"

"No."

"You ever hear anyone threaten Grace?"

"No."

The waitress put plates on the table. They ate, again in silence, and were about finished when a guy at a corner table pointed upward. Someone else stood on a chair and turned up sound on the television set. On the screen, a young woman no older than Rebecca, blond hair perfectly coiffured, sat at a desk reading, some of her words lost in the noise around them, a banner screaming BREAKING NEWS running across the bottom of the screen.

There's been a new development in the mysterious death of Grace Pettigrew, wife of famed Fort Lauderdale billionaire.... The clatter of dishes broke into her words. *...medical examiner...and now to the crime scene.*

The picture switched to the rock wall in front of Pettigrew Trust House, another young woman standing in front of it with a microphone, her appearance much the same as the other but with black hair. Someone in the restaurant turned the sound higher.

Yes, Greta, there has been an important development in the case. The Broward County Medical Examiner has just released a preliminary report, and it looks like foul play may have been involved in the drowning of Grace Pettigrew at a fancy party given by her former husband.

The images on the screen changed, first to a picture of Pettigrew at a podium, then to Bridget running toward the boathouse, throwing the silver platter, and diving into the Intracoastal.

The Medical Examiner said Grace Pettigrew's death was caused by drowning and that marks on her body 'are not necessarily consistent' with accidental drowning.

Now the screen filled with a shot of Gregory with Grace's body in the lagoon, his hands on the woman and her body sinking below the water's surface. Then a cop waded into the pool and arrested him. Or so it seemed.

In other words, she could have been murdered. Police said they have an active investigation underway.

Images of Gregory sitting across from Fourquet, the lieutenant wagging a finger at him, came then, Maureen and cops in the background.

Sue, did you see the images we just showed?

Yes, I did Greta.

Sort of looks like he was drowning her, doesn't it?

Well, yes, that's the way it looked. But we have to remember this is just a preliminary report.

So it is. When can we get that final report?

Well, it could be days or it could take weeks. The examiner is very careful in cases like this.

And all of his cases, I'm sure. Thank you, Sue, we'll be getting back to you....

Gregory said, "I was trying to save her."

"Those damn women were almost giggling." Maureen wanted to reach across the table and hold Go's hand, but didn't. *"Sort of looks like he was drowning her, doesn't it?* Stupid."

"Let's get out of here."

There was a line at the cash register so it took a while to pay the check. People at nearby tables nudged each other and pointed at Gregory.

"First time I've had breakfast with a celebrity," Maureen said, thinking maybe that would cheer him up.

Gregory didn't smile. "You know how we could put an end to all this?"

"How?"

"We could solve the crime, turn the murderer over to the police, and walk away heroes."

"This is reality, Greg." One of Mo's favorite lines, right out of E.T. The Extra-Terrestrial. Elliott and his brother were helping E.T. escape. *He's a man from outer space and we're taking him to his space ship,* Elliott told a boy on a bicycle. *Well, can't he just beam up?* the kid said. *This is reality, Greg!* Elliott scoffed.

The line got a laugh from every movie audience that heard it, and now Maureen saw Gregory smiling almost in spite of himself.

"And besides," she said. "The murder is none of our business. It doesn't affect us and I don't want to get involved."

When they walked back to Gregory's apartment, he asked Maureen to take a ride with him. "I want to see if Bridget got home last night."

"You're showing a lot of interest in her."

Gregory pursed his lips. "Want to drive?"

"Later."

The sun had warmed the morning air so they took the Mustang's top down. Gregory drove east on Las Olas and turned left on A1A. A two-story pink and aqua bar stood on the corner.

"Recognize the place?"

"The Elbo Room." Maureen remembered it from twenty years before. "But where's The Button?"

"They tore it down and put a parking lot there."

"No loss." She thought back a couple of decades. Things that were so marvelously exciting then seemed absurd and obnoxious now. Almost every bar had a wet T-shirt contest, but only The Button had Wet Willie competitions, too. Guys would stand on the stage wearing nothing but T-shirts, and girls would throw buckets of water on them.

"The World Famous Button" it called itself, and the worst acts on the beach took place there. The banana-eating contest, for example. Guys would put bananas between their legs and girls would eat them. Later the bar started an Absurd Acts Contest that got completely out of control. Guys masturbated on stage while the crowd yelled encouragement. Then things got even worse.

Now all that had vanished, eliminated—Maureen had read—by stringent enforcement of "open-bottle," jaywalking and other laws. But the surf and sand were the same. The ocean, azure blue close to shore, green farther out, lay completely flat, sailboats passing leisurely beside anchored freighters. Hundreds of bodies—thin, fat, grotesque and beautiful—lay on the beach, more naked flesh than Maureen had seen in years, the bikinis getting smaller and smaller, even some men wearing thongs that were little more than G-strings. Made their bellies look bigger, she thought. The young men—smarter—wore pants almost as low as those of pro basketball players.

Maureen inhaled salt air, thinking, Be fun to put on a swim suit and get out there, lie in the sun. Couldn't do it, though, because of the stupid investigation they'd stumbled into.

Gregory turned left. "Providence Place is two blocks down."

"Oh, goodie," Maureen said.

Maureen sat in the Providence Place parking lot waiting for Go to finish inside. The residence looked like two motels cobbled together and painted tan. Nice enough, and only two blocks from the beach. No wonder Bridget and the others didn't want to move. Their feelings may have nothing to do with Pettigrew as a person. And he probably didn't care about them. Maybe he had another motive.

Last night Kennedy told her Trust House and its garden lay adjacent to Providence Place, only a bamboo hedge and chain-link fence separating the two properties. Pettigrew might want to buy the residence and annex it to the Trust House gardens. Or get it free, part of the deal for his contribution. What was wrong with that? Providence Place would get a new, much larger home. Pettigrew could expand his showplace. He'd be using trust fund money to enhance his prestige, but most billionaires did such things. Didn't they? Maureen shook her head to banish the sympathy. She was getting soft.

A young black woman, seventeen or eighteen, maybe nineteen, came out of the residence carrying a baby. Then a guy and a girl covered with tattoos went in. Not kids, not by a long shot. About the age she and Go were when the made their trip to Lauderdale long ago.

Go was taking forever. There must be something she could do. Providence Place backed up to Trust House, but could a person walk from one place to another? Maureen got out of the car, went to the far side of Providence Place, and walked down a rough path made of concrete blocks sunk into the sand. Soon the bamboo, Australian pines, and chain-link fence stopped her. Crouching down, almost crawling, she made her way along the back of the building, all the while wondering what the heck she was doing. She should turn back. Then she saw a place where links of the fence had been cut and pushed down to form a passageway, a trail worn though it. Cautiously she took a few steps through the bamboo. She could see the Trust House gardens, the lagoon, even portions of the mansion.

A lot of foot traffic down this path, Maureen realized. Why? Find out later, maybe. But it's clear one of the young people, the adults, even one of the nuns who lived at Providence Place could have sneaked through the hole and killed Grace Pettigrew. Surely the police knew about the opening. She'd seen them searching the grounds while Fourquet questioned her, but he'd acted as if it was absolutely certain that someone at the party killed Grace.

CRACK! The sound of a breaking branch came from somewhere behind her, but when Maureen turned no one was there. Maybe it was the wind. Time to return to the car, though. Before someone came.

Gregory walked up to the Mustang and said, "Bridget didn't come back last night."

Maureen, barely back in the car, said, "Did you expect her to?"

"I hoped."

"Why are you so interested in that girl?"

"I'm interested in everyone there, all of the kids." Gregory slid behind the wheel.

"You're fooling yourself."

Gregory started the engine, looked to the rear, and backed the car into the road.

"She's not a kid." Maureen raised her voice so she'd be heard. "She's a young woman. And she's got a great little body."

Gregory didn't say anything until they were at the parking lot off Cordova, almost back to Las Olas. He pulled off the street, cut the engine and turned to her. "Mo, I'm a counselor. You know that. I'm interested in all of them."

"Some more than others."

"I keep my distance."

"I know that. But you're giving her special attention."

Gregory looked back, toward Providence Place. When he turned to Maureen, he said, "There's a reason, Mo. Not any reason you could guess. I'll tell you about it later. Not now."

Should she trust him? Why not? He's never lied to her. Not yet.

"OK?" Go asked.

"OK." Maureen smiled. "But you'll have to do something for me. Right now."

"What?"

"Forget about Bridget and give me all your attention. Give me the deluxe tour of Lauderdale. Like you would the biggest VIP you can think of."

"Sure." Gregory started the engine. "I was planning to, anyway."

Chapter Ten

Gregory took her on what he called a Great Circle Route, driving up A1A as far as Deerfield Beach first, then back to downtown Fort Lauderdale via US 1, the road they called Federal Highway here. Every little beach community displayed a different personality. Maureen liked Lauderdale-by-the-Sea best—no buildings over three stories high.

"Like a beach is supposed to be," she said.

In Deerfield Beach, Gregory said, "That's Boca Raton on the other side of the bridge. It's another world."

"More sophisticated, I've heard," Maureen said.

"Prissy. That's the word I'd use."

The sleek new buildings in downtown Lauderdale were pretty much standard issue for medium-sized cities, and Maureen wasn't surprised when Gregory explained that half-million-dollar waterfront residences near town were often torn down to make way for three-and four-million-dollar showplaces. But she wanted to know, "What are those funky little boats?" On both the New River and the Intracoastal she'd seen green and yellow vessels with squared-off bows, not tugboats, not fishing craft, something else.

"Water taxis," Gregory said. "They'll pull up to almost any dock around here to pick up people or drop them off. Seven-fifty one-way, fourteen dollars roundtrip, sixteen bucks all day. Up and down the Intracoastal from Shooters at Oakland Park Boulevard to the Seventeenth Street Causeway, and up the New River to the Performing Arts Center."

"Do a lot of business?"

"Mostly between bars and restaurants, but people use them for anything."

Something else fascinated Maureen.

"Pettigrew's name is all over town." Almost everywhere she looked, signs in front of large buildings announced a Pettigrew Memorial this, a Pettigrew Family Memorial that, and sometimes simply Pettigrew Something. A mixed bunch—a residence for battered women, a shelter for homeless men, a hospital wing, a store that sold recycled clothing, and a university library.

"He gives a lot to charity," Gregory said.

"He's buying naming rights," Maureen said. "Like companies buy naming rights for football stadiums and sports arenas."

"That's cynical."

"Before the donation is made, there's usually a contract. X will donate Y millions if Z will name the building for X. I'll bet Pettigrew won't donate a penny unless he gets to put his name on something."

"You don't know that," Gregory said.

"I said I'd bet on it."

Gregory went into his deep breathing routine, counting to himself Maureen knew, just as she knew he'd change the subject when he spoke next.

He said, "What else do you want to see?"

"I want to see Trust House again."

"It'll be closed."

"We can look through the fence," she said.

In the daylight the mansion seemed ordinary, still big but nothing magical about it now, its white paint fading, a black Lincoln Town Car and a Honda Civic parked behind the spiked metal fence.

Maureen took her cell phone from her purse.

Gregory said, "There won't be anybody inside on a Saturday."

"Two people are. The owners or drivers of those two cars."

"Probably guards."

"How many guards own Lincolns?"

Gregory sighed. "Go ahead if you want."

"Bet?"

"No."

The exchange took less than a minute, but that was long enough to irritate Maureen. She wasn't used to defending what she planned to do. Later. She'd discuss it later. Now she phoned information and discovered the Pettigrew Trust did indeed have a listed number. She dialed it. A man answered.

"I want to talk to Luther." Thinking, I don't even know his last name.

"Who should I say is calling?"

Like this happened every Saturday. She told him her name and the name of her firm.

"I'll put you through."

Just like that. As if someone had been waiting for her call.

Luther's voice, soft and Southern, came through the air. "What time would you like to come by?"

Maureen could almost see him, a white coat, a Colonel Sanders goatee and a black string tie. The feeling that he'd been expecting her grew stronger. "Right now."

"I can accommodate that. Come to the second floor. My office is in back."

We know that already, she thought. You were up there last night, watching everything that happened. You looked down on the party, witnessed the hijinks that disrupted Pettigrew's speech, and watched Bridget's dive. Maybe you saw who murdered Grace Pettigrew. Maybe not. Maybe you killed her.

The thought startled her, coming out of nowhere like that.

The front gate buzzed.

"The elevator's broken," the guard in the lobby said. "Take the stairs."

They climbed the formal, curving staircase, something out of *Gone with the Wind*, Maureen trying to calculate how long it would take Luther to run down the stairs, drag Grace into the lagoon, drown her, come back into the house, and climb the stairs. Too long, she concluded. Getting up the stairs took forever, no time left to do anything else. And why suspect Luther anyway? She was getting just as loony as the people at the party.

Luther stood at the door of his office, not at all like Maureen had pictured him. He didn't have a Colonel Sanders goatee; he was clean-shaven. Neither did he sport a white coat or a string tie; instead, he wore a muted purple brocade vest (must have cost a fortune) over a white shirt open at the neck. And—the big surprise—he was black. So much for picturing people over the telephone.

He shook her hand, then Gregory's, and motioned for them to sit in the brown leather wing chairs in front of his desk, a big chunk of mahogany imposing and solid as a battleship. The words African-American came to Maureen belatedly, the proper language not yet automatic, and she finished her inventory. In his sixties, head almost bald, the little hair that remained gray and clipped close.

Gregory said, "You always work on Saturday?"

Luther ignored him and turned to Maureen. "Mr. Pettigrew told me you may want to talk to me." As if that explained everything.

Maureen's eyes went to the paneled wall behind Luther's desk. On either side of his chair hung a framed Bachelor of Arts degree from Florida Agricultural and Mechanical University and a Certified Public Accountant's license, both awarded to Luther Benjamin Washington. An Honorable Discharge certificate from the U.S. Army and a crucifix were suspended on the right and to the left were two smaller black-and-white photographs that Maureen couldn't see clearly. These are the items this man wants people to know about him, she was thinking, the things he's proudest of. Remember them.

Luther said, "Do either of you have a cell phone?"

Maureen nodded.

"Please turn it off. I don't like them in my office, and I won't allow anyone who works here to bring one on the grounds. We can all get along quite well sticking to phones connected to a wire." Luther leaned back in his chair. "Otherwise, you're always on someone else's string."

Maureen reached in her purse, found her cell, and put it on vibrate. She was willing to humor Luther. He was just being an old man, afraid of progress, not willing to learn about its benefits.

Now Luther said, "What do you want of me?"

"I want to know everything you know about Roland Pettigrew, Mr. Washington." She paused for effect. "That's all."

He laughed. "All I am is a humble bookkeeper."

Humble bookkeeper my foot. Too many things gave him away. He wore a gold pinky ring on his left hand, the diamond bigger than any Maureen owned, and a Rolex on his right arm. Even without the jewelry, he couldn't pass for simple or humble. There was an old-fashioned sense of dignity about him, an aura of power even. Maybe the way he held his body straight, almost rigid, or looked her in the eye without wavering. Appraising her, judging her, just as Pettigrew and Kennedy had last night.

"Call me Luther," he said. "And tell me what you really want."

What Maureen wanted was to know whether Pettigrew had broken the law and how he did it. Just that. If Luther thought Pettigrew killed his ex-wife or knew who did, Maureen would be interested, of course, but she wasn't going to let herself get sidetracked. The police—if they ever assigned someone to the case other than that stupid Fourquet—would discover who murdered Grace.

She started the way she usually worked, opening with a broad question, then adopting an I-don't-know-anything-so-please-explain-it-all-to-me attitude, saving the tough questions for later. "Tell me about the Pettigrew Trust."

"What about it?"

"Start at the beginning." Another of Maureen's favorite lines.

Luther looked toward Gregory, but he turned away. This was Maureen's game, and he wouldn't interfere. Luther turned back. "You know what a testamentary trust is?"

"Vaguely." A small lie.

"A testamentary trust is a financial entity established by a will." Luther put his hands together and made a steeple with his fingers, a professor giving a little lesson. "They're the way rich people try to beat death."

"Beat death?" Play along with this, Maureen said to herself, see where he takes it.

"The pharaohs built pyramids. We establish testamentary trusts. Within limitations, a testamentary trust allows a person—you, me, anybody—to direct how our money is used after we die. We're gone, but our directives—our ego, you might say—live on."

Luther looked between Maureen and Gregory for reaction. Neither moved.

"The money in the Pettigrew Trust comes from the estate of a man named Reginald Pettigrew who died almost forty years ago. We invest the money, and—"

"Wait," Maureen said. "Tell me about Reginald."

Luther spread his hands apart. "Is that important?"

"To me it is."

"I don't usually—" Luther took a pack of Camel Lights from a shirt pocket, pulled out a cigarette and tapped it on the desk. A curious half-smile crossed his face. "Mr. Pettigrew told me to answer your questions, so I will."

His smile. Mischievous or cunning? Either way he's decided to tell me more than he has to, Maureen thought. Why? She was beginning to like this man. There was something about him, his mannerisms maybe, that she'd seen and felt good about not long ago.

"Reginald Pettigrew was a piece of work." Luther held the unlit cigarette in his hand. "He was an accountant, like me, but much more ambitious and with absolutely no scruples. He went to Washington before World War II and became an aide to a member of Congress. When the congressman was defeated, he found jobs at a couple of federal agencies, then moved to the Pentagon."

"Military?"

"He worked there as a civilian. He was 4-F, which meant—Never mind." Luther moved the cigarette to his left hand. "By the time the war ended, Reginald had saved some money and knew almost everybody of importance in the Capital. He quit the government and went into business for himself."

He stopped. "You sure you want to hear all this?"

Maureen nodded. You could never learn too much about anything.

"Harry Truman was president and started the Marshall Plan. Reginald brokered contacts. Then the Korean conflict came along, and he went from brokering contracts to brokering companies. After that he was able to buy companies on his own. He became very, very rich."

Like father like son, Maureen thought. Roland Pettigrew is following in the old man's footsteps, buying and selling companies.

"Soon Reginald was one of the most influential men in Washington. He made big campaign contributions and threw lavish parties. There were rumors he bribed people, but nobody proved anything."

Crookedness nobody could prove. Again, father and son.

Luther picked up a round, black object the size of a tennis ball with his right hand. "Maybe they would have gotten something on him eventually, but when he got to be fifty-five, he announced he was retiring to Palm Beach. Made a big production of it."

Palm Beach. Yes, that was the place Maureen associated with the Pettigrew name. That's the reason she was surprised to see Roland Pettigrew in Lauderdale.

Luther pushed his shoulders forward. "That's about it."

"I don't think so." Maureen knew there was more. She'd read there'd been another scandal.

"You mean you want the dirt?"

"Yep."

Luther shrugged, looked at the cigarette, then back at her. "The man told me to tell you whatever you want to know."

Again the half-smile. I was only following orders, Luther could tell Pettigrew. The man. Sounded just like Kennedy when he called his boss that.

"Reginald Pettigrew was married three times." Luther's voice picked up speed, as if to get it out all at once. "His first marriage lasted more than twenty-five years—until he started making some money. Three children from it, all grown and away from home at the time of the split. The second marriage didn't come until a few years later, but it was over almost as soon as it started. Reginald said she was crazy. She said he was. It was a messy, messy divorce, because by that time everybody knew about Sara."

Luther clicked the black ball. A three-inch flame erupted from the top, bright and big. Startled, Maureen pulled back. Gregory, too. Luther smiled, lit the cigarette with the fire and inhaled deeply. Maybe now, Maureen thought, maybe this is the part Luther wants to tell me for his own purposes.

He exhaled, laid the cigarette on the edge of a black ashtray next to the lighter and looked up. "Sara Fitzgerald must have been the Lolita of her time. When Reginald first met her, she was fifteen or sixteen. He was visiting the Eastern Shore of Maryland on a hunting trip. She lived there with her little brother. Dirt poor, but she must have been something to see."

He took another pull from the cigarette, then snubbed it out. "I'm trying to quit."

Maureen said, "You were telling us about the Lolita of her time."

"We don't really know what went on between them then, of course. But we can guess. He was in his forties, still married to his first wife, but he kept going back to Sara off and on, right through his second marriage." Luther stopped. "Do you really want to hear all this?"

Maureen nodded.

Luther's forehead furrowed, Maureen figuring there might be doubt in his mind now. But he kept going. "After he divorced his second wife he married Sara, sold all his companies, and moved to Palm Beach. He bought her a mansion, one of the biggest on the island. They lived there, just the two of them and their servants, and eventually little Roland."

Eventually little Roland, her thoughts echoed. Their son.

"They threw big parties and invited all of Palm Beach society, but the 'A' list never came. He gave huge gifts to charities. He even got a hospital named after him. But he couldn't buy himself into the inner circle of Palm Beach society. He couldn't buy respect."

Things don't change, Maureen mused, his son trying to buy respect now, getting his name on all those buildings.

"He was a sad case in the end," Luther continued. "Bitter. Cantankerous as hell. Almost deaf, almost blind, refusing to wear hearing aids or have a cataract operation. That was the shape he was in when he had his attorneys draw up the will that established the Pettigrew Trust. A testamentary trust, like we were talking about. He was seventy when he made the will, a year before he died, not terribly old by today's standards, but worn out. You can tell by what he did."

Luther stood and walked to a file cabinet in a corner of the office. He opened the top drawer and took out a thick document. "Here's a copy of Reginald Pettigrew's Will and Trust Agreement. The will set up the Trust, then directed that as long as Sara lived, she should get all of the income it produced. A very common provision. Then when she died...."

He flipped through pages until he found the one he wanted. "When Sara died, income from the Trust was to be used, get this, 'to aid the sightless, the deaf and the hard of hearing, particularly the elderly who cannot secure other assistance, and for the benefit of crippled children similarly situated.'" He looked up. "Strange wording, eh? You can't imagine how much lawyers have argued about it."

Maureen looked at Gregory, no doubt in her mind what a crippled child was. He'd been one.

Luther said, "Medicare and Medicaid came along, and every old person in the country could get medical care. And how many truly 'sightless' people are there in the country who don't qualify for those or other programs? Or deaf people?"

He held out both hands, the will still in one, and at that instant Maureen knew what was so familiar about Luther. His mannerisms—the way he moved his hands and arms, the way he talked, the way he smiled, even the pauses to see how she was reacting—were exactly like Kennedy's. They could be father and son.

"The old man may have thought he was going to help thousands of elderly people, but he didn't," Luther said. "The provisions of his will don't apply to anybody now. It provided money only to the elderly, the blind, the deaf, and crippled children 'who cannot secure other assistance.'"

Maureen said, "The trustees could, if they really wanted to help them."

"There've been a couple of court rulings saying they can't," Luther said. "Except for children. The trustees went to court and got a ruling that said the 'crippled children' clause means the Trust's money can be used to help any child with any disability, physical or mental. Even homelessness. That's why Mr. Pettigrew was able to announce the gift to Providence Place last night."

"*Millions for buildings, not one cent for operations*," said Maureen, repeating Grace's words. "Was what Grace said true?"

"Ever since Sara Pettigrew died, the policy of the Trust has been to donate money only for construction and equipment. Operating funds must come from somewhere else."

"Since Sara died. When was that?"

"A year or so after the old man died."

"Died of grief?" Maureen said.

"Hardly. A merry widow, if anything."

"So Roland Pettigrew inherited the money? Or control of it."

"Not exactly," Luther said. "Reginald Pettigrew's will appointed three trustees—Sara, Roland and a bank."

"Lifetime appointments?"

"For the individuals. The two human trustees could change banks."

"And when one trustee died?"

"A successor was appointed by the survivor and the bank."

And the bank would agree to whoever the survivor wanted to appoint, Maureen thought.

"Sara wasn't interested in the Trust," Luther said. "Only parties and having all the money she could spend. So Fritz and the bank ran things."

"Who's Fritz?"

Luther took his time putting the will back into the file cabinet. When he turned around, there was a frown on his forehead, as if he slipped and said too much. "Oh. Nobody calls him Fritz anymore. I'm talking about Roland Pettigrew. The man you met last night. My boss."

Maureen felt her head jerk back involuntarily, her neck telling her something was wrong. A part of the story didn't fit with the rest. Maureen's intuition was telling her that. Which part? What part of the story was wrong? She'd listened to every word, absorbed every detail, noted every nuance. One fact followed another, just as it should have, every development making sense, and yet—

Something was missing, something had been added, something— She'd figure it out later.

Chapter Eleven

Gregory stood, stretched his arms as if he'd been uncomfortable in the chair and walked to the window on the left side of Luther's desk. He's up to something, Maureen thought. He didn't get up simply to stretch, she was sure of that.

"We're proud of the work we've done," Luther was saying. "The Pettigrew Trust started with a hundred million or so. Now it's worth almost two billion."

Gregory reached the window and looked down. From where she sat, Maureen couldn't see anything but palm fronds, big ones like royal palms. She stood, did the stretching thing like Gregory, walked to a spot next to him, and looked out. Things looked about the same as the night before, the makeshift stage still there, workmen beginning to dismantle the scaffolding the television crews had stood on, only the sound system gone. But where was the lagoon they'd found Grace Pettigrew's body floating in?

"Good view, if you like what you see." Luther's voice, behind them, sounded like Kennedy's. *Not bad, if you like stuff like this.* But Maureen didn't have time to think about it. She understood what Gregory had been looking for. Their view of the lagoon was blocked by branches of two royal palms. Luther couldn't have seen the murder from this window.

"I know what you're looking at." Luther moved closer. "I couldn't see Grace Pettigrew before or after she got into the water. That's what I told the police."

Gregory turned and faced him. "What did you see?"

"Mr. Pettigrew's speech. The disruptive young people from Providence Place. The girl's dive. Then I stopped watching. There was some work to do on my desk."

"You heard the police sirens," Gregory said. "How could you stay away?"

"Oh, eventually I got back up and watched the medics and the police take Mrs. Pettigrew's body away."

"And then?"

"Then I realized the police would want to talk to me. So I went down and talked to that lieutenant, Fourquet. I told him the same things I'm telling you. I don't know anything about Grace Pettigrew's death. I didn't see her killed, and I didn't see anyone following her. I don't know why anybody would want to kill her."

"Did you like her? Did you like Grace?"

Luther thought a minute. "Yes," he said. "She was a lush, but I think she was well-intentioned."

Maureen didn't like where Gregory was going, his line of questioning. She'd agreed to find out more about Pettigrew, but she'd made it clear they shouldn't try to solve the murder. She knew Gregory was innocent, he knew she was, and sooner or later the police would conclude the same thing. They shouldn't get involved.

Maureen turned her back on the two men and found herself staring at the two black-and-white photographs on the wall behind Luther's desk. The one on the left showed an attractive black woman in a graduation gown, high school probably, pride and determination on her face. The other was of the same woman, older, still proud but showing another quality, too, wisdom maybe, or skepticism. She held a baby in her lap.

Who could she be? Maureen wondered. She'd ask Luther. But not now. It was time to leave.

Maureen moved toward the door. Luther handed her a stack of papers from the file cabinet. "These are copies of the Trust's annual reports. They should answer any questions you have."

"Reports to whom?"

"Anyone who shows an interest. We file more detailed reports with the clerk of court. A legal requirement." Luther pulled a pocket watch from his vest. "Now, if you'll excuse me."

Maureen knew they were being dismissed but didn't care. Luther had given her documents to study. If she wanted to know more she could check the court filings, even come back and talk with Luther again. He'd been extraordinarily candid, something she could speculate about later. She took the reports from his hands and said, "These explain why you can't give away all the money you have?"

"I told you the trustees went to court and got permission to expand the scope of our work. We're spending more every year."

"But still not for operations."

"The Pettigrew Foundation helps there. Mr. Pettigrew's personal foundation." Luther looked at his watch again. "I must break this off. I have an important appointment."

On Saturday? Maureen doubted it. But enough for today. Someday she'd asked Luther how he got his job, who the woman in the photograph was, how he and Pettigrew justified using a charitable trust to invest in companies that treated workers like widgets. But this wasn't the time. She decided to give Luther a present, something that would make him feel good about helping her.

"I like you," she told him. "And I like Kennedy. So far, you're the only people I've met down here I can say that about."

Every word true.

Luther stopped. "You met Kennedy?"

"At the party."

"And you liked him?"

"He's a likeable guy."

"A fine young man," Luther said, breaking into a big smile.

Beaming with something like fatherly pride, Maureen realized. What's that about?

Luther shook hands with Gregory, who surprised Maureen and said, "I'd like to walk through the gardens."

"Of course. Spend as much time there as you want."

Then Luther held Maureen's hand longer than necessary for a handshake and looked into her eyes. "Remember. Everything I've told you is true. Every word of it."

I hear you, Maureen thought. I hear you, but I don't believe you.

Maureen and Gregory walked down the curving staircase together, Maureen thinking too late she should have timed their descent to calculate exactly how long it would have taken for Luther to get down the stairs.

In the lobby, Gregory asked the guard, "Is there a back door we can use to get to the garden?"

"They're all locked. You've got to go around the house."

So they went through the front door, turned right, and backtracked along the same flowered pathway they'd walked down the night before. Maureen was even surer now that Luther couldn't have descended the stairs, walked around the house, drowned Grace, and got back up the stairs without being noticed. The doors were locked during the party, too. She remembered trying one.

She asked Gregory, "What are you looking for?"

"I want to be sure." He marched to the side of the lagoon and stood on the spot where he'd jumped into the water the night before, close to where Grace's body floated. He looked up. "Luther's right. You can't see this spot from his window. And vice versa."

Maureen said, "So?"

"Whoever murdered Grace may have deliberately picked a spot where he—or she—knew Luther couldn't see them."

Interesting, Maureen thought, but so what? It wasn't their job to solve the murder and she'd resist every effort Gregory made to get them involved. She'd be subtle but firm. "Do you want to see anything else?"

Gregory shook his head. They walked to the front of the house and turned the corner.

"Look," Maureen said. "There's Kennedy."

Pettigrew's chauffeur, law student and sometime personal trainer sat behind the wheel of a big, black Mercedes, an S-class Maureen knew cost between seventy and ninety thousand dollars. His boss had to be close by. She looked toward the front door. Too late. Pettigrew's back vanished into the house, the door making a solid clunk when it closed.

Gregory opened the Mustang's passenger-side door. "Pettigrew was Luther's big appointment."

Maureen nodded, got into the car, and carefully laid the trust reports on the floor beneath her legs. Now Pettigrew would talk to Luther about their visit, trying to gauge from their questions how much they knew. Have at it, fellow, she thought. We know less than you think.

Chapter Twelve

At Gregory's apartment, Maureen dug her cell phone from her purse and checked for messages. Four from Rebecca saying to call her, the last two using the word "urgent" twice. In the morning, Maureen decided, no business tonight. She sat on a stool at the kitchen counter knowing Gregory would fix ice cream soon.

"Go, I really should find a hotel room. It's unfair for you to sleep on the sofa."

"I don't mind."

Maureen knew he didn't, but it was time to move out. The closeness made her feel uncomfortable. "Any suggestions for a hotel?"

"The Marriott Harbor Beach is the best in town, but my favorite is the old Pier 66. It's called a Hyatt Regency now, but it's still got a bar on top that rotates."

"I thought you were supposed to stay out of bars."

"By myself. But I could go there with you."

Maureen's cell jiggled. She looked at the number. Rebecca again. Might as well find out what she wants, she thought. She'll be calling all night if I don't.

The girl's voice rushed out, shrill and excited. "I've been trying to reach you all day."

"I've been out, away from the phone."

"The partners have been calling me all day, saying I just had to get in touch with you."

"What do they want?"

Rebecca said nothing for a moment, the silence between New York and Lauderdale building until Maureen knew bad news was coming. "I hate to be the one to tell you this but— They've axed you."

"What?" Maureen thought she hadn't heard right.

"The partners have suspended you without pay."

"They couldn't have."

"They told me to tell you. They're writing a letter," Rebecca said. "One of them even leaked word to the papers that you're no longer an active member of the firm."

"Why? What reason did they give?"

"You're a suspect in a murder."

"I'm not."

"They're saying so on television. They say police questioned you about the murder of Pettigrew's wife. They keep putting your picture on the screen."

"It was his ex-wife." Maureen realized she was almost shouting. She lowered her voice. "And questioning is not the same as being accused."

"It sounds the same. Most of all, though, the partners don't like the name of our firm being mentioned every time they show film about the murder."

Maureen began counting. A thousand one, a thousand two, a thousand three.... Maybe the partners had been looking for an excuse to get rid of her.

"They say it puts a cloud over our firm," Rebecca added.

"Why didn't one of them phone me?"

"I asked that, too. They say they don't want to get within a hundred miles of a criminal investigation."

Maureen began counting again, but Rebecca barely paused.

"Another thing. They're saying you took an unnecessary risk on the Qualflex short."

Bull, Maureen thought. She'd done the research. And the stake was well within the limits established for floor managers.

"I'm supposed to cover it first thing Monday morning," Rebecca said.

"Tell them—"

"Keep in touch."

Rebecca clicked off, leaving Maureen to remember that Rebecca was the one who proposed the Qualflex short. She wondered if Rebecca mentioned that to the partners.

Of course not.

Maureen's mind wouldn't focus. She heard herself telling Gregory what Rebecca had said, her voice mechanical and emotionless, but all she could think about was the laminate on the counter. It looked solid green from a distance, but now she saw specs of white, yellow and red that gave it texture. Nor had she really seen the kitchen appliances before—the stove, refrigerator and dishwasher amber instead of white, a fad that had come and gone long ago. How many years? Twenty at least. No wonder they were tearing the building down to build an expensive condo. Gregory had told her that in explaining the reason he could afford the place. No lease. Just month to month. Like all of life.

"It seems so unfair," Gregory said.

"The concepts of fair and unfair don't exist on The Street. Everything just is. "Think of every slimy, underhanded thing you've seen or heard about in corporations—back stabbing, lying, cheating, deceiving and all the rest—and multiply it by ten. That's Wall Street."

Gregory stood close, behind her. He put his hands on her shoulders. "Can they do this to you?"

"They can't and they can. A partnership is a collection of legal contracts. They can't break my contract except for—" She stopped. "There's a vague provision. Moral turpitude or something."

"That's not what this is about."

"But they can claim it is. They'll say I've brought disrepute on the firm."

"By being at a party where a murder took place?" His fingers kneaded her shoulders.

"By being a murder suspect."

"Interpreted as such."

"Same difference." She felt his fingers on her neck.

"Who would decide whether what they've done is justified."

"Courts, I guess. But by that time I wouldn't have a reputation left."

"You could phone one of the partners," Gregory said. "Confront him directly."

"If any of them were willing to talk with me, they wouldn't have left it to Rebecca."

Neither said anything for a while, Gregory continuing to work on Maureen's neck, Maureen thinking, figuring. Now she swiveled the stool around and faced him. His hands dropped away.

"You know what this means?"

He shook his head.

"I have to solve this stupid murder."

Gregory didn't say anything to that, but Maureen knew he'd help. He'd been pushing her to get involved all along. She slid off the stool, her body inches from his. "Hug me."

They pressed into each other, their bodies touching everywhere, eventually even the rhythm of their breathing in sync, the first adult hug of their lives. How long did they stay that way? A minute? Two? Five? Ten? Later Maureen tried to remember that and other details but couldn't.

She pulled back enough to look at Go's face. The brown of his eyes was flecked with hazel. She hadn't noticed that before. They moved together again, their lips almost touching.

Who turned away? Maureen couldn't remember that, either. It happened too quickly. All she remembered clearly was standing at the bedroom door looking back at Gregory as he folded down the sofa, his head down, the look on his face confused, puzzled, and somber, exactly the way she felt.

Chapter Thirteen

Sunday morning they walked to the Floridian again, but there was a long line and Gregory said he wanted to go somewhere else. Maureen saw a newsstand a few doors down the street and bought copies of *Barron's* and Sunday's *Times* before they walked back to his car. She could look at the papers while he drove.

The *Times* hadn't carried a real story, just a brief, and in the eyes of some rewrite person there were only two important points about the events of Friday night. One, Grace Pettigrew, former wife of the billionaire financier and philanthropist Roland Pettigrew, had been found drowned, possibly murdered, at a party in Florida. And, two, Fort Lauderdale police were questioning Maureen O'Neal, a widely known New York stock analyst—they named her firm—and someone named Gregory Overman, otherwise not identified. No mention of her suspension.

Sure they questioned us, Maureen thought. We found the body. But that's all. Putting it in print like that, mentioning our names like we were the only people questioned, makes us look like suspects. She remembered a line from an old movie: It's accurate, but it's not true. Exactly. But maybe Rebecca and her partners weren't the only ones that would draw the wrong conclusions. Her clients. Would their faith vanish as quickly?

Maureen tossed the *Times* in the back seat and flipped through *Barron's*. Nothing about the murder that she could find. Not that she'd expected a story. Barron's was the weekly racing form of the stock and bond business. Facts, figures, and speculation about what was going up or down in the coming week. A tip sheet, with the predictions no more accurate than those they sold at race tracks. Only if the paper had learned of her suspension would it be interested in something as off-the-subject as a murder.

Gregory turned off Federal Highway into the parking lot of a restaurant called the Original Pancake House. A woman at the door said there'd be a thirty-minute wait, and Gregory gave her his name. The food is worth it, he said. Maureen bought a copy of the *Herald* and read it while they sat outside.

Grace's body had been discovered too late for the paper to get much of a story into Saturday's edition, so it went all out Sunday:

Billionaire's Ex-Wife Drowns,
Broker and Counselor Questioned
The subhead read:
Maybe Not Accidental, Coroner Says
All true, but the devilish stuff was in the details. Police said the only reason Maureen and Gregory had not been taken to the police station Friday night was that there had been no finding of foul play at the time. They'd been told not to leave town. If someone drowned Grace, Gregory was a suspect and Maureen might be an accomplice. Police were still investigating and had reached no conclusions.

Maureen read the passage aloud. "But they know enough to smear us," she said to Gregory.

"Don't take it personally. They'd do it to anybody," he said.

Maureen wanted to laugh but couldn't.

Inside the restaurant, Maureen ordered the Cherry Kijafa Crepes, Gregory the chocolate chip pancakes.

"You must be the only person over twelve who's ever ordered those," she said.

"It'd be better with ice cream."

Good. Go was relaxed now. Time to tell him what she had to do. "Greg, I need to work today. I need to do some research."

"This is Sunday."

"Doesn't matter."

"What in the world are you going to do?"

"Find and use a Bloomberg."

"What's a Bloomberg?"

Maureen explained as simply as she could. A Bloomberg is an electronic door to almost everything anyone could possibly want to know about every publicly traded company in the country—every financial record it has ever filed with the Securities and Exchange Commission, its complete stock trading history, and almost every news story ever written about it.

"Couldn't you get all that from the Internet?"

"It's not the same. Bloombergs have two monitors with unique software and a special keyboard. Graph days or years of stock trading on one monitor, display news and analysis on the other, and a company's history unfolds in ways that single-source machines can never duplicate."

"Where can you get them?"

"Almost any local brokerage office will have several."

"But they're all closed. This is Sunday."

"I heard you say that a minute ago," Maureen said. "But if you try hard enough, you can do great things."

Outside the restaurant, Maureen asked Gregory to give her a few minutes alone to make some calls. He said he'd read the rest of the *Herald* in the car. She walked around the parking lot with her cell, phoning ten people in New York or New Jersey, finding only three, two at home and one at his office. I need some help, she told them, and each said, "Anything," just as she knew they would. They might need a copy of one of her stock reports someday.

Our firm doesn't have branches in Florida, Maureen told them, something they probably knew but it wouldn't hurt to remind them. Could you arrange for me to use the research facilities at your Lauderdale office? Particularly your Bloomberg.

On a Sunday?

Yep, right now this morning.

Each of them said they'd see what they could do, then asked the same question, word for word: What are you working on?

Nothing, Maureen said. But of course none of them believed her. So she said, I'll let you know if I find anything good. That satisfied them. She didn't tell them she wasn't looking for something good. She wanted to find some dirt, things Pettigrew had done that analysts had overlooked, secrets that would persuade Gregory and the nuns to stay away from Pettigrew and his money.

They all asked about the weather "down there," so she gave them a climate report, toning it down a notch. They said it wasn't so bad in New York, which to them meant it wasn't raining, wasn't snowing, and wasn't below freezing. Then, to a person, they made a crack about wishing they didn't have to work for a living and could spend the winter in Florida. You could, Maureen thought as she stood in the warmth of the sun. You've made so much money you don't have to work another day. But you're all addicted to the market. You won't let go until it kills you.

About this point in the conversations, these good friends started making excuses. Their branch offices in Lauderdale would be closed, and they didn't know if they could find the managers. Maureen persisted. "I can't wait until Monday."

Finally the one at his office said, "Hell, if I have to work on Sunday, our local guy does, too. I'll get him off the golf course if necessary." He gave her the office address and suggested she wait an hour before arriving. Maureen told this to Gregory, who said she could borrow the rental car. He'd spend the afternoon reading or something.

Maureen expected to find a gray-haired, pot-bellied branch manager still in his golfing outfit, most likely in yellow pants and a St. Patrick's Day green knit shirt. Surprise. The manager was a woman her age, maybe a little younger, in tennis togs. Maureen apologized for bringing her in on a Sunday and heard her say she didn't mind.

Briefly Maureen wondered why everybody lies about what they mind and what they don't, but said, "Tell me about Pettigrew." Just like that. No buildup. She didn't believe in wasting time.

"Our local Midas Man. Everything he touches—"

"Everything?"

"He's had a few clunkers, but when he gets one, he unloads it quickly."

Maureen waited.

"I know what you're thinking. You can't justify the multiples and share prices of his companies by any of the usual yardsticks. But he's got a following, and to them he can do no wrong."

"Like the Pied Piper?"

"He hasn't led them astray yet."

"Maybe he's like the Wizard of Oz," Maureen said. "He hasn't been exposed yet."

"He has more than smoke and mirrors going for him."

Enough, Maureen thought. Local brokers are never objective about companies in their backyards. Either they root for the home team or wonder how anyone could rate the bum so highly. "Where's your Bloomberg?"

"Down the hall. New York said to let you use whatever you want."

Maureen followed her down a corridor between glass-enclosed cubicles, the boxes new salesmen sat in while they made call after call to strangers and friends, speaking softly into their mouth pieces, caressing, beguiling, enticing, anything to get prospects to buy something, sell something, trade something, anything that would create a commission. She'd never had to do that and never would.

A Bloomberg, her old friend, sat against a wall.

"Have at it," the manager said. "Let me know if you find anything good."

Again. That's all they look for.

Maureen sat down and went to work.

Chapter Fourteen

The sky was dark when Maureen got back to Gregory's apartment.

"Find anything?"

"Sit down. This will take a while."

Again Gregory took the shell-shaped chair; Maureen sat on the sofa.

"It's as I told you," she said. "Midas Man is a shrinker."

"Everybody shrinks a bit as they get older."

Maureen knew Go was grinning inside, but she wasn't going to get sidetracked. "He shrinks companies."

"I never said he was a Bill Gates or Wayne Huizenga. But almost every stock he touches goes up."

"But you don't know why."

"Don't have to. A man as prominent as Pettigrew couldn't have any secrets."

'That's what you think," Maureen said.

"How could he?"

It occurred to Maureen that they were talking like little kids. Felt good. Like the long conversations in Go's bedroom when he was recovering from polio. She always tried to keep a step ahead of him then, and now she was ready for his question.

"It has to do with history. For most of the last century, company officials could do almost anything—smart, stupid, selfish, or silly—and the government didn't care as long as they reported it to the Securities and Exchange Commission. The idea was markets would be fair and honest if everybody had the same information."

She looked to see if Gregory was paying attention. So far, yes.

"It didn't work. Some corporate executives lied outright, and some of these got caught and went to jail. Not nearly enough, of course. But almost as damaging—at least to people who invested in the company's stock—prominent stock analysts became cheerleaders for the companies they covered. Their firms wanted to get the company's underwriting business and—" She saw Gregory frown. "They wanted to sell new stock and bonds for the companies and receive big commissions."

"I knew that."

Maureen tried not to smile. "So most analysts sucked up to companies and didn't ask tough questions. Everybody—brokerage houses, big institutions and retail customers—was happy with all this until The Bubble burst and shareholders lost billions. Then last year Congress passed a new law cracking down on both company execs and brokerage firms."

"What's all this got to do with—"

"The point is that SEC records have gobs and gobs of information Pettigrew filed before the Sarbanes-Oxley Act was passed. Nobody has ever really studied it."

"Except for you."

Maureen shook her head. "There's such a stink about him that I knew I'd never recommend one of his companies to my clients."

"But you told me that just Friday morning you—"

"That was for a short-term trade."

"Not much of a distinction."

Again, Maureen wasn't going to be diverted. "It took a long time to go through thirty years of records on the Bloomberg."

"And you found...."

"Let me tell this my own way."

Gregory pulled back. "Touché."

Maureen began her report, not needing to look at notes. All the information she'd found on the Bloomberg was stored in short-term memory, just like information she'd discovered in years of newspaper reporting. A week later she would have forgotten most of it, but by then the story would have been written or the stock report sent to clients. But it was all there now, and she gave it to Gregory, almost word for word at times, staring at the floor to concentrate.

"Over the years Pettigrew has controlled more than thirty corporations, but now he or the Trust own only nine. Three medium-sized manufacturing plants. An aging retail chain. A regional insurance firm and a small paper company. A finance company specializing in second mortgages. A chain of boat dealers. And a gun manufacturer. That was a surprise."

"I never said he was a liberal."

"Notice anything about them?"

Gregory shook his head.

"The companies have almost nothing in common. Even the manufacturers are in such different lines that there's no chance for synergy." She looked up to see if Gregory understood but couldn't tell. "There's no way they can help each other. No way for two and two to make five."

Gregory grinned. "Yes, teach."

Darn his sarcasm. OK, no more coaching. "They have nothing in common except that each is losing money and sales are stagnant. The same with the other twenty companies he's controlled over the years."

Gregory leaned back in his chair.

"There are many ways to increase profits, but Pettigrew used only one: Cut costs. He fired most executives and middle management, laid off hundreds or thousands of workers, slashed research and development budgets, and sold corporate real estate. In each and every case, Wall Street was delighted. The price of stock in the companies doubled, tripled, or quadrupled. The market loves nothing better than a turnaround story with the prospect of big profits just over the horizon."

Gregory pretended to yawn.

"Most people on The Street didn't care that Pettigrew was cannibalizing the companies for the sake of increasing profits every quarter. And nobody objected when Pettigrew appointed himself and a few cronies corporate officers, then awarded themselves options to buy stock at pre-turnaround prices. Everybody was making money, so who wanted to quibble?"

"You, apparently."

"I told you," Maureen said. "Before this weekend, I had no reason to dig into any of this."

Gregory nodded.. She plunged ahead.

"It was the same pattern over and over—a slash-and-burn operation eventually followed by a sale or merger after profits improved. Years and years later, the company would fail or file for bankruptcy protection, but the new management always got the blame. Pettigrew had moved on to other things."

"Anything illegal about that?"

She shook him off. "Maybe this will interest you. Pettigrew used small companies to take over much larger ones. The way Wall Street works, a minnow can swallow a whale if the minnow's P-E is high enough." She decided against trying to explain price-earnings ratios. "Nothing illegal about that. But Pettigrew inflated stock prices of his minnows by selling companies to himself."

"Sold companies to himself?" Gregory said. Maureen knew she had his attention now.

"No one ever used those words, of course, but selling companies to himself is exactly what he did. He and a few cronies would buy or start a small company. They'd give it a fancy name—they called one of them First National Travel USA—and sell a few shares at an initial public offering. Pettigrew's name alone was enough to bring exorbitant prices for the stock. Then— and this is where it got interesting—with its value inflated beyond all reason, they sold the little company to a much larger public company Pettigrew controlled through the Trust. All legal, because it was all disclosed, and some whore of a brokerage firm would write a report saying the deal was fair."

Maureen paused to study Gregory's face, but he didn't have a comment or question.

"Of course, the brokerage house would write in its statement that it hadn't done any independent research, that it was relying solely on Pettigrew's figures, and that it had worked for firms affiliated with Pettigrew on other deals," she continued. "For multi-million dollar fees, it turns out. But I doubt if anyone bothered to check then."

"Legal?"

"Probably at the time. It wouldn't be now."

"Anything else?"

"Pettigrew had another tactic," she said. "He and his cronies would buy an interest in a half dozen money-losing companies, then package them with one that was profitable and had a sexy image. They'd issue stock in the new corporation and watch it rise until people realized what a dog it was."

"Sounds absolutely legal."

"Oh yes. Pettigrew and his lawyers were very careful. He never sold his stock before it was legal to do so, and when he did unload it, everybody believed his explanation that he was diversifying his holdings."

"So what you're saying is that you spent all this time and—" Gregory started to get up.

"Grace Pettigrew."

Gregory's body seemed to freeze. "What about her?"

"Grace Pettigrew's name was all over those documents. She was usually an officer of Pettigrew's little companies and owned big chunks of stock in them."

Gregory was staring now.

"Pettigrew always disavowed beneficial ownership of her stock, of course, but I doubt if anyone believed the disclaimer for a moment."

"Anything illegal about that?"

Maureen sighed. "I'm trying to tell you everything I found. Do you want to hear the rest of it, or not?"

He nodded.

"By this time, my eyes were tired and I was flipping through documents so fast I almost passed by the name. Then all of a sudden, there it was." Maureen paused for effect. "Melody Pettigrew."

"Who?"

"I wondered the same thing, at first. She was an initial shareholder of one of Pettigrew's smaller companies, with Pettigrew disclaiming beneficial interest. Then her name appeared over and over again, as stockholder or officer of Pettigrew's other companies. She was just as prominent early on as Grace Pettigrew was later."

"But who is she?"

"And then I remembered what Kennedy told me. Pettigrew had a first wife who's now living in Santa Fe."

"I didn't know that."

"But then I got to wondering. How do I know she's in Santa Fe? How do I know she's even alive?"

Gregory said, "So you checked to find out?"

"Couldn't run a web search on the Bloomberg. After dinner maybe."

Gregory was silent now, looking up at Gandhi, then back at her.

Maureen said, "I keep wondering if Pettigrew's wives had short lives."

"Now you may be on to something."

Chapter Fifteen

They walked to the beach and ate hamburgers at a pub called The Quarterdeck. When they returned, Maureen phoned information for the number of any Melody or M. Pettigrew in Santa Fe, but there was no Pettigrew of any kind with a listed number.

"She could have changed her last name," Gregory said.

"She could have done a lot of things. I'll do a computer search in the morning."

Neither said anything for minutes, the awkward silence getting to Maureen. So she said, "If you don't mind sleeping on the sofa again, I'd like to stay here again tonight. Or I'll switch with you and sleep in here."

"No way. You can use the bedroom as long as you want. Use whatever you want in there."

For reasons she didn't completely understand, Maureen decided to put on a pair of his pajamas, red with a white pattern, and was wearing them when she stood in the door between the living room and the bedroom and asked, "Go why did you ask me to come here?"

"I told you. To tell me if Pettigrew is legit."

"I could have told you that from New York."

Go looked around the room, then back at her. "I guess you could have."

Maureen wanted to say something then, even more felt like doing something, rushing across the room maybe, hugging him, and telling him the way she felt. But it was too late for that. Almost twenty years too late.

She turned and went back into the bedroom.

In the morning, Gregory said, "Think of it this way. This is Monday, but you don't have to go to work."

Maureen knew he was trying to get her mind off the suspension but wished he wouldn't bother. "I've got to move to a hotel today," she said, expecting Go to ask Why? or something. But he didn't. All he said when he looked up from the shell chair, a mug of coffee in his hand, was "OK."

It seemed too easy.

Then he said, "Where?"

"Kennedy told me Roland Pettigrew lives in a penthouse at a hotel on the beach. I want to stay there."

Gregory hesitated but finally told her the name of the hotel. "It's new and probably has some vacancies."

Something was wrong. Gregory was being too casual about this, acting as if he didn't care. "Something's bothering you. Out with it."

Gregory looked away, then back. "You know that boy I told you about?"

"The one who killed himself."

Gregory closed his eyes, bowed his head, and told her the whole story then, the words coming out in a low monotone at first, louder, more intense as he went on. It had happened at his last job, when he was working at a low-budget, United Fund-supported agency in Bethesda, Maryland. The boy was fifteen years old, an only child, the son of a neurologist who worked at one of the Institutes of Health and a career bureaucrat who'd found employment over the years in a half dozen federal departments. His mother was the physician.

At first, the boy didn't seem much different than many of the children who lived in the rich satellite of Washington D.C. "Those kids lived in seven-hundred-fifty-thousand-dollar-homes and their parents pulled in six-figure salaries, but emotionally they were the poorest kids I've ever seen. Nobody paid attention to them."

The boy stole things. Shoplifting was the least of it. He picked up things from school, from neighbor's houses, from the playground, from any place he went. "Same old thing. He didn't need the stuff. He wanted attention."

Gregory began twice-a-week counseling sessions with the boy, bi-weekly talks with his teachers, and monthly conferences with his parents. When he could get them to show up, that is. The boy started studying, even got involved in some clubs at school. His parents said they were grateful. No more cop cars in their driveway. No telephone calls from the school while they were at work. No court appearances.

But then the boy's mother and father changed. Not a surprise. When one member of a family changes, the others change, too, Gregory explained. And not always for the better. The parents began talking about their son, then started blaming each other, then arguing about everything else that had gone wrong between them. Their marriage, fragile before, fell apart. They decided to divorce and send their son to boarding school.

The boy was stunned. He didn't want to leave, wouldn't go to some damn boarding school. He begged and pleaded but his parents were adamant.

"Then he wanted to come live with me," Gregory said. "I couldn't let him do that. It was out of the question. Against all the rules."

After Gregory turned him down the third time, the boy said, "I'm not going." Just that, nothing else. Two days later a maid found his body in the basement of his parents' house, his wrists slashed, his stomach full of every drug in his parents' medicine cabinet, a two-word note beside his body. "Goodbye, Go."

Gregory looked up at Maureen now, his eyes begging for understanding. She put her left hand on his shoulder.

"He took the pills sometime around midnight and then slashed his wrists. He didn't die until dawn. His parents didn't notice he was missing. If only somebody— "

"Then you began drinking. Again."

"Yes."

"It's in the past, Go."

"No."

"What?"

Gregory looked out the window, his eyes following a flock of green parrots. He turned to Maureen. "Because now Bridget wants to come live with me."

Maureen felt as though someone had tossed an explosive into the living room, and it took her a while to get over the blinding flash. Bridget live with him? Live with Gregory? Sleep with him? No, Maureen told herself. Go wouldn't do that. She had a dozen questions in her head, and the first one that came out wasn't necessarily the most important.

"Why you?"

"I must remind her of some man in her past. It'd take counseling to find out."

"You've never counseled her?"

"No."

"What's wrong with Providence Place?"

"She calls it puke house. And, in truth, she's a bit old for it."

"When? When did she ask you?"

"She came by yesterday afternoon. When you were in the broker's office."

"And you didn't tell me."

Gregory looked away, then back at her. "I needed to think it through."

Maureen almost didn't ask the next question. A part of her didn't want to hear the answer. But she needed to know.

"Are you going to let her? Let her move in?"

"Of course not."

"But you needed to 'think it through'."

"Because of what happened to the boy."

Maybe, maybe that made some sense, Maureen thought. Or maybe it didn't. "But why— We're suspects in a murder. What a time to be even thinking such thoughts."

"I think about Providence Place," Gregory said. "Giving Bridget and kids like her a place to stay, is why it's necessary to expand the work there. Pettigrew's offer makes that possible."

"It's blood money. What he's offering you."

Gregory shook his head. "Name one thing he's ever done that was illegal."

The question again. This time it was Maureen who looked away. Gandhi's face stared at her from the poster.

"You tried, and you couldn't find a damn thing."

"Not yet." She took a deep breath. "But I'll bet I can."

Chapter Sixteen

Maureen sat in the apartment wondering what to do next. Gregory had left saying he needed to go to Providence House. "To talk to Bridget?" she'd asked. And he said, "Bridget said she wasn't going back there even if I wouldn't let her stay with me." She wondered now if she should have asked more questions, but it was too late for that. Like a lot of other things. Now what? She'd gone for her morning run and made a hotel reservation for that night, but it was too early to check in. And she couldn't stand the thought of reading another newspaper.

The *Times* had run another brief. Her firm announced she was taking an "indefinite leave," and the paper said she couldn't be reached for comment. The Florida newspapers ran follow-up stories about Grace's murder, but Maureen's suspension was mentioned only near the bottom of what were essentially recaps. If there had been any significant developments in the investigation, the papers had not discovered them.

Maureen missed Go already. Strange. They hadn't seen each other for months, and there'd been days, sometimes weeks, when she didn't think about him at all. Now, two hours and—

Already she regretted her braggadocio, her "I'll bet I can." It was the sort of thing she and others in the newsroom used to say back in her days as an investigative reporter. The good old days, she thought of them now, exposing corrupt politicians, corporate shenanigans, and judicial malfeasance. The trouble usually began where money met politics, and she loved finding hidden connections. She'd won a passel of prizes for her work, accepting but not much caring about them as she moved from small newspapers to larger ones in the mid-Atlantic, each job giving her greater independence and clout.

But gradually she'd become disillusioned with newspapers. Big chains and conglomerates had bought up most of the papers in the country, and they were run like any other corporation—make the biggest short-term profit this month, this quarter, this year, and to hell with the future. Worse, they imposed more and more restrictions on what she could investigate and gave her less and less time and money to do it.

About the point her faith in newspapers slumped to its nadir, many of men and women she'd graduated with began bragging about all the money they were making in the stock market, particular small tech stocks listed on the NASDAQ. Curious, she did some research. Even a perfunctory investigation made the situation clear. What some people had already begun calling The Bubble was all hype and mirrors, a crash in the making. She found a small firm in Baltimore where people at the top had the same feeling, and they put her on the payroll.

There she learned how to research a company, determine what earnings were real and which suspect, what enterprises could continue growing and which ones had peaked. She discovered that working as an analyst paid better and required the same skills she'd used as an investigative reporter. At least the way she did it. Double and triple check everything. Don't take anybody's word for anything. Using those simple tools, she'd helped clients make a lot of money and, just as frequently, saved them from making bad investments.

When the small Baltimore partnership merged with a larger one in New York, she moved to the city. Wall Street paid huge salaries and bonuses, and she made more money than anyone working for a newspaper could dream of. Even if it wasn't as much fun. Then Gregory wanted her to tell the nuns that Pettigrew was all right—that they could accept his money. She was still sure they'd be absolutely crazy to let this man get involved with Providence Place, but it was clear now she'd need to dig much deeper. Was it worth the effort?

Maybe, she thought, just maybe doing the outside research would help get the magic back—the way she felt when she was a reporter hot on the trail of corruption. In those days she'd thought of herself as being on a holy mission. But since she'd began working on Wall Street—working with people like Pettigrew— she'd felt flat, without a real purpose in life. Maybe she could recapture the old feeling.

She'd start with the Pettigrew Trust reports Luther gave her. Where did she put them? She remembered setting them on the floor of the Mustang, later bringing them upstairs, then putting them— On the black sofa table, the one behind the cream leather love seat. She found them there now and spread them out on Gregory's little dining table. More than a dozen in the stack, each printed on thick glossy paper like corporations use for annual reports to stockholders, hoping the medium conveyed feelings of success and prosperity no matter what the numbers inside might say.

The cover of each Pettigrew Trust report displayed a color photograph of a hospital, a residence for youngsters like Providence Place, or the headquarters building of other organizations the Trust had donated money to. Then, on every inside first page, every report reproduced the same faded, formal black-and-white photograph of Reginald and Sara Pettigrew, the old man three decades older than his bride. Easy to see him as a cantankerous S.O.B., standing there so stiffly, a vaguely Edwardian presence about him. But young Sara, with her round cheeks and strands of hair that wouldn't stay in place, wasn't having any of it. Her expression said, Let's get this over with and go have some fun.

Maureen started with the oldest report, vowing to study them all, read them word-for-word if necessary. She flipped to the back pages, looking for the financial statements. Nothing there. But somewhere there had to be a balance sheet, something that showed assets and liabilities, income and expenses. She looked at every page, but it was all photographs and words. She tossed the report away, grabbed another, and looked through it. Nothing there either. Quickly she leafed through the others. None there either.

The only dollar signs she could find in any of the reports were in front of rounded off totals of the Trust's assets ($1.8 billion according to the last report) and the amounts of a few relatively small contributions referred to in photo captions. Relatively small? Yep, she told herself. When you're dealing with a billion dollars, contributions of a million or two were relatively small.

Junk. For her purposes, the reports were junk, a waste of time, the texts nothing but pretty words without substance. Did Luther think she'd be satisfied with these? She was looking for figures she could dig into. What stocks did the Trust buy and sell? When? Bonds, too. What firms did the Trust do business with? And where were the footnotes? That's where corporations hide the dirt. Maybe Trusts do too.

Why do any of those things matter? She could almost hear Gregory's voice asking the question. Well, Go, she'd say, I want to see if Pettigrew uses the Trust for personal gain. Did the Trust ever loan money to Pettigrew or his friends? Did it buy stock in Pettigrew's companies? Or their bonds? Or loan them money?

Come to think of it, if Martha Stewart could be sent to jail for a relatively minor infraction of insider trading laws, wasn't Pettigrew more vulnerable? As a corporate officer he knew information about a company before the news was made public. If he used that information to benefit the Trust, wouldn't that be illegal? And, more to the point, what if he used inside knowledge of the Trust's planned stock purchases to buy it for himself or his companies? A guaranteed profit—and maybe a ticket to jail.

These thoughts made Maureen more determined than ever to see some real financial reports filed by the Trust. What had Luther said? *We file more detailed reports with the clerk of the court.* To hell with you, Luther. The stuff you gave me is worthless, but you couldn't file trash like that with a court. I'll see what you're telling them.

Maureen walked through an older section of the Broward County Courthouse, the marble floor scratched and dull from wear, the ceilings low and the lighting poor. After phoning for directions, she'd decided to walk—straight down Las Olas past the restaurants and shops, then left and over the Third Avenue bridge On Las Olas she'd noticed a building with a small discreet sign that said, Pettigrew Enterprises.

Finding what she wanted was difficult, hardly any signs pointing the way to departments, the courthouse hallways crowded, uniformed deputies and citizens mingling together as if they'd been pals forever. Maureen wondered how many would be on opposing sides when they got into courtrooms. Finally she found a cluster of computer monitors on the second floor, Broward County's civil and criminal court records, even property appraisal data, all indexed and accessible in the same place.

Maureen sat down at a monitor and read the instructions. In the civil system index, push the PF10 key to move forward, the PF11 key to go back, one said. On the other hand in the criminal system, pushing ENTER moved things forward, but— Jesus! Typical of a government system cobbled together over many years.

But research is never easy, she reminded herself. Someone said it's a process of going up alleys to see if they're blind. Or as Einstein put it: If we knew what we were doing, it wouldn't be called research, would it?

Maureen keyed in the words "Pettigrew Trust." Nothing. She punched in "Reginald Pettigrew Trust." Another blank. She tried Sara Pettigrew, Reginald Pettigrew, the Sara and Reginald Pettigrew Trust and every other combination she could think of. Nothing connected in the civil system. No criminal charges against anyone named Pettigrew, either.

Then she saw a little notice saying circuit court records were electronically indexed only back to 1987 and county court records only after 1990. Could the latest Pettigrew Trust reports be that old? Shouldn't be, but more than once Maureen had discovered secrets by pursuing improbable leads. She found the handwritten index books in another section of the courthouse and searched indexes in each volume. It was slower, more laborious work than using the computer, and the longer she was at it the stronger her suspicion grew that there wasn't anything to find.

Two hours later it was a firm conclusion: If the indexes were accurate, the Pettigrew Trust hadn't filed a single report with any court in Broward County. Luther had lied to her. And he'd seemed so straight up. What had he said? Remember. *Everything I've told you is true.* Every word of it. No, Luther. It wasn't. Maybe none of it. You lied.

Finding the secrets of the Pettigrew Trust was going to take more than checking records. She'd have to go to Plan B—talking to anyone who might know anything. Who would that be? Pettigrew? Sure. But would he be anymore truthful than Luther? Would he even talk with her now? Did she really want to talk with to Midas Man again? Did she have any other choice?

Chapter Seventeen

Walking back over the Third Avenue Bridge, Maureen saw a water taxi pass by in the New River, then stop on the south side of the Pettigrew Enterprises building to load and unload passengers. Nice. A person could board one of those funky little boats and go almost anywhere in town.

OK, now do it, she thought. Midas Man will either talk to me again or he won't. She got out her cell, pushed in the number for Pettigrew Enterprises, cradled it to her ear with her right hand, and put her left over the other ear to shut out traffic noise. The bastard must be up there in his office, probably on the top floor. Now put me through to him, damn it.

The switchboard operator connected her to a man who said he was Pettigrew's special assistant. "I've been expecting your call. Can you see him about two o'clock this afternoon?"

"I'll be there."

"Not at the office. His yacht."

"What?"

"Mr. Pettigrew meets people there when he wants absolute privacy." He gave her directions.

They sat in the cabin of Pettigrew's yacht, dozens of boats as big and bigger in the marina around them, Pettigrew in a chair, Maureen on the sofa, the brass around them gleaming, the teak smelling of fresh oil. Midas Man had taken off his dark gray suit coat and loosened his maroon tie, but once again he seemed ill at ease, fidgeting and touching things around him. Again Maureen wondered why. She'd been around many powerful men, and all the others had more self confidence.

"This is a Bertram, the best made," Pettigrew said. "Of course some people prefer a Hatteras. It's like, do you prefer a Mercedes or BMW?"

He paused, waiting as if Maureen might have an opinion about brands of expensive boats. Or maybe cars. She preferred a fancy truck, an SUV with all-time four-wheel drive, but didn't waste time telling him that.

"Forty-three feet long, almost a half-million dollars new. Probably worth more now." Pettigrew rubbed his hand over the seat's white leather. "Twin Detroit diesels, more than five hundred horsepower each. Makes almost thirty knots when it runs full-out."

Pettigrew stopped, again waiting for comment or question, but Maureen had decided not to help him.

"Two staterooms below, one with a double bed, the other with two single bunks. Two heads. A full galley up there." He pointed to the front of the cabin.

"A tiny apartment that floats and goes fast." Maureen said.

"I suppose you could look at it that way." Pettigrew's face showed he didn't like the comparison.

"A person could hide out in a place like this." That should irritate him even more.

"Hadn't thought of that." Pettigrew looked around the boat's interior as if seeing it for the first time. "I gave considerable thought to what I'd name it. In the end, I chose *Sybarite*. Pursuit of the best is the way I mean it."

Not comfort? Maureen wondered, not really caring. Her thoughts had moved on. She was trying to figure if Pettigrew really reminded her of her father. Had Gregory been right?

"I could afford a bigger one," Pettigrew said, "but this is about as large as one person can comfortably handle. I want to be able to take it out to sea and back by myself. Even in and out of the marina single-handed."

He looked and acted like her father. The mustache, the nervousness, the smoothness in his voice. About the same weight and height, too.

"I've kept it pretty much like I bought it. Upgraded the locks and made it more secure, but the engines and interior didn't need any work.

Why change the locks?

"Safety." Pettigrew answering her question before she asked it. "You'd be surprised at the cheap locks they put on expensive boats."

Maureen remembered her father having bars installed on the first story windows of their Maryland house after hearing of a neighborhood break-in.

"While I was at it, I had unbreakable glass installed throughout the cabin, fixed the forward hatch so it could be locked from either inside or out, and reinforced the stateroom doors. Now nobody can get in unless I want them to."

"Or out," Maureen said.

"Hadn't thought of that." Pettigrew smiled again. "But you didn't come here to talk about boats. I hear you and your friend visited Luther."

Maureen had decided on making a direct accusation. No hesitation. No waffling. No hinting around. "Luther lied to me."

"Oh?" Pettigrew pursed his lips. "Luther's always been a very truthful person.."

"He told me the Pettigrew Trust files a report with a local court."

"It does."

"I spent three hours at the Broward County Courthouse this morning. The Trust hasn't filed anything there."

Pettigrew put a hand over his mouth, then moved it away. "Did Luther say we filed it in Broward County?"

"Where else?" A sliver of doubt crept into her mind.

"When Reginald Pettigrew died, he was a resident of Palm Beach. The reports are filed in the Palm Beach County Courthouse."

Of course. Luther had said Reginald retired to Palm Beach. That's where his will would have been filed for probate and where the trust would have been established. Score another point for Midas Man. Maureen felt she'd been tricked. Like her father used to do.

Pettigrew said, "What do you want the reports for?"

"I'm doing some research on you and your companies."

"The companies report to the SEC."

"I go beyond the corporate filings."

"So I've heard." Pettigrew rubbed his cheek. "Well, research away. I've got nothing to hide."

Oh yes, you do, she thought. There isn't a man in business, certainly not one as successful as you, who doesn't have many things to hide. When they say they don't, it's all the more reason to keep digging. She'd try a different approach.

"Do you have any idea who killed your wife?"

"Former wife."

"Your second wife."

"No matter what you call her, I have no idea who killed her. But I read you and your friend Gregory are suspects."

"That's absurd." The word came out without thought, and Maureen told herself to quit using it.

"I'm inclined to think so, too," Pettigrew said. "But your firm doesn't."

So he knew she'd been suspended, Maureen thought. Score another one for this bastard. But he was talking with her. Why?

"In town less than forty-eight hours and already you're a local celebrity," Pettigrew said.

"Why did you agree to see me?"

"I spoke to you much too harshly the other night at the party. I apologize for that now, and I hope Kennedy conveyed that message to you earlier."

Maureen kept her expression blank.

"I wasn't myself that night. Even lost my temper when that girl ran away with the silver tray. One that wasn't worth piss." Pettigrew stood, walked to the galley, and opened a little refrigerator. "I invited you here in the hope that we might become friends. A drink?"

"Never in the afternoon."

"I meant a Coke." The no-carat smile again.

There's one difference between the two men, Maureen thought. Her father was a lush. She'd bet Pettigrew didn't have two drinks a week. If that. Had she seen him even sip from his champagne glass at the party? Not that she could remember. She watched him put ice in two glasses, open a large Coke and fill each.

"Ever since my initial reaction, which I've apologized for, I've been trying to make things as easy for you as possible." Pettigrew held out a glass. "That's why I arranged for Luther to stay at Trust House all day Saturday and Sunday, waiting for you to call."

Maureen took the glass, realizing a second later that the way Pettigrew passed it was exactly how her father used to hand out drinks.

"Your reputation and my money," Pettigrew said. "We'd make a formidable team."

The thought was so absurd—that word again—that she didn't answer.

"I'm not without influence in this town. I could put in a word with the police to go easy on you and your friend."

"Forget it."

"We're very much alike."

"I doubt it." Not only does everything I touch not turn to gold, but I don't want it to, Maureen thought.

"We both know the importance of research and information," Pettigrew sat down in the chair. "With me, it goes back to high school. I was on a debating team, and we went to Deland for a competition. After it was over, I walked around the campus of Stetson University. I saw a slogan carved above the entrance to the library. Knowledge is Power."

So what? But Maureen had resolved to listen away. Eventually these guys usually give away something.

"Those three words changed my life. I realized then, and believe now, that if you know enough about a situation, you can control it."

"That's not been my experience." But Maureen admitted to herself that her views weren't much different. Hadn't she said she could move the market when she knew something others didn't—and then made it public?

"When I got back to Palm Beach, I pressured the old man to send me to college. He agreed, probably to get rid of me as much as anything else." Pettigrew began talking faster. "I wanted to go to Harvard right away, but my high school grades weren't good enough. So I enrolled in a state university, graduated the equivalent of Magna Cum Laude, then went to Harvard. Top of my class when I got the MBA."

"You must tell that story to every reporter who interviews you."

Pettigrew gave her that stupid smile.

"They've written a lot about you," Maureen said. "But I don't think you're the man everybody thinks you are."

Did Pettigrew flinch? She thought so. But what he said was, "Maybe not."

She waited now, almost able to see Pettigrew's mind processing something, eventually reaching a conclusion.

"There's something to what you say," he said. "For instance, did you know I grew up poor?"

"I don't think so."

"Oh, we lived in a fine mansion in Palm Beach, and there were servants and plenty to eat. But I felt poor. Reginald and Sara Pettigrew paid no attention to me."

Maureen didn't believe it. A father and mother ignoring their son?

"I went to private school, but I was never invited to the homes of other students, and none of them could come home with me. Their parents didn't want them to have anything to do with the old man or Sara."

Maureen said, "You were lonely. Not poor." But what he was saying matched the facts Luther had supplied. The cantankerous Reginald Pettigrew and his much younger bride were ostracized by Palm Beach society.

Pettigrew said, "Let me tell you a story," and Maureen knew he would whether she was interested or not. "One day when I was about twelve years old, I saw the old man and Sara getting ready to go on a boat trip with some of their friends. They'd been drinking heavily, but that never stopped them. The paid a captain who was always sober. I begged to go along. Finally, they agreed." Pettigrew stared out a window. "They had a cabin cruiser, something like this, but of an older design with engines not nearly as powerful."

From this point on, Pettigrew wasn't talking to her. His mind was somewhere deep in the past. He tried to help cast off the lines, but Sara yelled, "Don't let the boy do that!" She was always shrill. So when they got away from the dock he went up to the bow and walked out on the bow pulpit, as far away from them as he could get.

It was glorious up there. He could see everything. Then the boat turned into the Palm Beach Inlet and the big waves rolling in from the Atlantic. The bow became a bucking bronco. He loved it at first, but when they reached the ocean, the waves grew taller and taller and the bow pitched higher and higher, five, maybe ten feet into the air.

Fun for a while, then scary. He almost lost his grip. The bow crashed down again, harder than ever. The force pushed him forward, the top of his body lurching beyond the railing. He looked down. Gray water swirled below. He just knew he was going to fall in and drown.

A wave tossed the bow upward again, throwing him high into the air, pushing him back. He couldn't hold on. His body smashed into the deck. He reached out for something to grab, finally getting his fingers around the anchor line. Then it slipped away. The boat bucked again, slammed him back, then pushed him forward. This time he knew he was going overboard. He made his back rigid, hoping his body would be too stiff to slip beneath the bow rail. It worked but—

Pettigrew turned toward Maureen. Tears formed in his eyes. He looked away. "It worked, but then I saw Sara and the others in the cabin, looking through the windshield. They were laughing at me. Sara more than any of the others."

A tear rolled down his cheek. "I couldn't stand it. I turned away, determined not to let them see how scared I was."

Would a mother and father torture their son this way? Maureen was wondering. Why?

Pettigrew kept talking. The bow lurched again, throwing his body back into the windshield, all the while people in the cabin looking down, laughing at his misery. He held one leg tight to get some traction and pushed the other one against the deck, trying to get to the side of the boat. Another wave came along and threw his body forward, but not straight ahead. He hit the railing at the side of the boat, the port side.

Pettigrew remembered thinking, This is the last chance I'll ever have. He forced his fingers around the railing and held on as tightly as he could. When the boat lunged up again, he used its force to push himself along the railing toward the stern. The bow bucked again. He held tight, then edged back when the boat leaped upward. Slowly, three or four feet at a time, he made his way along the side of the boat. Finally, he reached the cockpit. He wanted to scream, wanted to get inside to the warmth of the cabin, but most of all he didn't want them see him cry. He sat in a corner of the cockpit, his body shaking, the inside of his head exploding.

The cabin door opened. Sara stood there, Reginald and their friends behind her. "Little man," she said. "Where have you been?" Pettigrew could still hear Sara's voice today. He pushed himself up and ran screaming toward her. He meant to destroy them all, get his revenge. Sara stepped back, and one of the young men grabbed Pettigrew. Another hit him in the face.

"Don't hurt the little man," Sara said, making it worse. Her friend held Pettigrew so tight he couldn't move. Finally, Sara told the boy, You'd better go below. He stared at her, still furious but defeated. The little stairway leading to the cabin beckoned. The man released his grip. He went below. There was nothing else he could do.

Now Pettigrew turned to Maureen, his checks moist, his eyes fixing on hers. She couldn't tell if his feelings were real or if he was putting on a show. But in spite of her earlier reservations, Maureen felt herself almost drawn to the man. If a child was treated badly, emotionally and physically abused, he'd grow up cold and manipulating, not giving a damn about the feelings or welfare of others. Did that explain this cruel man?

"I didn't go to sea again for more than twenty years," Pettigrew said. "But when I could afford to, I bought myself a yacht, one only a little smaller than this one, hired a captain and had him take me out every day. We started when the Atlantic was smooth, then built up to the roughest seas the boat could take. Even went out when the Coast Guard posted storm warnings.

"I learned to pilot a big boat single-handed in any sort of weather. I conquered my childhood fear through sheer force of will. Now I feel completely confident and safe in any storm."

Pettigrew paused, looking at Maureen, almost begging for a reaction. Conflicting thoughts and feelings ran around her mind. Pettigrew's recollection of the incident was so vivid that there might be something to it. Or maybe it was completely fabricated. Almost a coin toss. Maybe it told her something about this man, maybe not.

She said, "Why have you told me this story?"

"To show you that I can overcome any adversity. They licked me when I was a child. As an adult, I beat them all."

Maureen stared at him thinking, No, there was another reason, something more. All those details, the emotions, his memory like it happened yesterday. But something was missing.

"Now," Pettigrew said, "you know something about me nobody else knows. And why I take such pride in taking Sybarite to sea. I could afford a much larger yacht, but this is the largest a person can mange single-handed."

That helped her, saying he could afford a larger yacht. Yes, you could buy a much larger boat, one as big as a cruise ship. But look how you got the money. The millions, the billions, from walking over others, all in the name of charity.

No. Maureen wouldn't fall for it. Follow first principles. Pay attention to what they do, not what they say. It didn't matter if Pettigrew reminded Maureen of her father, or not. She'd do her job. She wouldn't be swayed by emotions. He didn't deserve pity. He's a bastard.

"Francis Bacon," she said, pushing herself off the coach.

Pettigrew stared.

"Francis Bacon said it first."

"What?"

"Knowledge is power. But get the words right, the whole thing. What he wrote was, 'For knowledge, too, is itself power.'"

She walked away, leaving Pettigrew standing there staring at her back as she climbed up to the dock, not all that proud of her parting shot, but thinking, Damned Harvard MBA's think they know everything. *Sybarite*, the best. My foot. Greed is what motivates this man, and a hard luck story about something that may or may not have happened to him as a kid wasn't going to change her mind.

Chapter Eighteen

Maureen was halfway up the stairs to Gregory's apartment when she heard the voice.

"Hey lady."

She looked down. Bridget stood below almost hidden in the big leaves of a clump of sea grapes, wearing the same outfit as at the party, the T-shirt with the big P turned inside out, dirty like the shorts, but her face scrubbed clean and her hair combed and tied into a neat pony tail.

Maureen yelled, "Come on up."

"No."

"Then I'll meet you at the bottom of the stairs."

"First, I've got a question," Bridget said.

"Ask it."

"Whose side are you on?"

The same question no matter where Maureen went. Corporate presidents asked it when she was investigating a merger and acquisition offer or simply finding out about a company. She always gave them the same answer.

"I'm on my side." Now to Bridget she added, "And I'm not going to stand here shouting all day."

The girl emerged from the leaves and walked to the bottom of the stairs. "I mean are you on Pettigrew's side or ours?"

Slowly, so she wouldn't frighten Bridget away, Maureen walked down the stairs until she was eight to ten feet from the bottom, the closest she'd ever been to this girl-woman. Now she could figure Bridget's age better than the other night. Sixteen, seventeen, eighteen at the most, but with the poise of someone older.

"Who's 'our side?'"

"Us," Bridget said. "The girls and boys at Providence Place."

"Why are you so opposed to him?"

"He's a bad man. Evil."

"I don't believe that's your main reason." Maureen folded her arms in front of her.

"It is."

"No. I think you and your friends don't want to leave the beach."

Bridget opened her mouth, closed it, and looked away.

Maureen knew she was onto something. "Pettigrew said his fifty-million dollar gift would allow Providence Place to move to a much larger building on the mainland."

"Nobody down here calls it the mainland," Bridget said.

"OK. Farther west. 'Away from tourist activity,' he said. That means away from the beach."

"Why? So he can buy the property and build a big hotel on it?"

Maureen stopped. It was a possibility. "Do you know that for a fact?"

"I know some things," Bridget said. "I know a lot."

"What?"

"They're my secrets until I decide what side you're on."

Maureen lowered herself to the step. "Sit down with me."

"No."

"Suit yourself. I'll tell you exactly where I stand in all this."

Beginning with Go's phone call, Maureen told Bridget why she'd come to Florida, about seeing Grace's body floating in the lagoon, the encounter with Lt. Detective Fourquet, and then getting stabbed in the back by her partners. "Now that I'm involved, I've got to find out who killed Grace."

"Fourquet's an asshole."

"You know him?"

"He's always trying to bust us. Says we're prostitutes and thieves."

"He's in homicide."

"Tell him that."

Interesting, but beside the point. "Bridget, if you know anything that would help us find out who murdered Grace, tell me. It might help you, too."

Maureen could almost read Bridget's mind. What did she know about this woman from New York? I mean, really know. Test her somehow.

Bridget said, "You really like him a lot, don't you."

"Who?"

"Gregory. The one you called Go when you were telling why you came down here."

"We're just—" No, she wasn't going to say it again. "Yeah, I like him a lot."

"I like him, too," Bridget said. "What little I've seen of him."

It came to Maureen to ask how much time she'd spent with Gregory and exactly why she wanted to move in with him, but the analyst in Maureen made her stick to priorities. "Tell me what you know about Grace."

Bridget seemed to have made a decision about Maureen. She said, "There's a hole in the fence between Providence Place and the Pettigrew Trust headquarters."

"I've seen it."

"Sometimes I go though the hole and hang out in the garden."

Maureen waited.

"Usually there's nobody in there. But one time I found Grace Pettigrew sitting on a bench, staring at the mansion."

Maureen remembered the bench, wrought iron with wood slats, on the far side of the lagoon, almost under the bamboo hedge. "How did she get in?"

"The guards liked her. So did Kennedy and Luther, and Pettigrew was almost never there." Bridget eased her body down and sat four steps below Maureen.

"Go on."

"At first I started to run away, but I had a feeling about her. So I stayed and we talked." In those talks, Bridget learned Grace Pettigrew had two passions. The first was to help Providence

Place residents. "She'd do almost anything for homeless kids. She said she was almost one herself."

"And the other passion?"

"Revenge." In Grace's eyes Roland Pettigrew, the son of a bitch, was the scum of the earth, a person you couldn't believe a word he said, a bastard who'd tricked her into signing documents she shouldn't have, who'd promised her the world and gave her almost nothing, not even Trust House and the garden, which he'd assured her she would own no matter what, not to mention that he was the most sexually fucked up man she'd ever known. She hated him and would do anything she could to destroy him.

Bridget looked up, smiling. "You get the idea?"

Maureen smiled back. "Just about."

"I really liked her. She felt just like we did."

"I understand."

"We met there almost every afternoon just to talk," Bridget said. "If one of us had to leave before the other got there, we'd tape a note to the bottom of the seat."

Maureen could see it, a young woman and an older one, both outsiders, both feeling they'd been treated unfairly by the world, their conversations providing enough strength to get through another day. Probably neither one thinking others might be watching, that someone might see one of them taping something under the bench.

"Eventually," Bridget said, "she told me there were some secret papers that could destroy Pettigrew. She said she knew where they were."

"What papers?"

"I don't know. Something she was going to turn over to authorities."

"Documents about his companies?"

"Something about the companies or the stocks he bought and sold."

How could that be? When Maureen dug through SEC filings at the broker's office Saturday, she found Pettigrew filed every document required for his corporations exactly on time and with all the specificity anyone could ask. The same for his personal filings, the ones that reported his personal purchases and sales of stock. But now that she thought about it, neither she nor anyone else could imagine all the things they didn't know to look for. Nobody could tell what information he didn't report

"Where are they? The documents."

Bridget shrugged. "Grace said her husband moved them around like a shell game."

"Did she have any idea?"

"She said they might be in the safe in Luther's office upstairs, but what really turned her on was the idea that they were in the bow of his boat. One time she saw a locked storage compartment up there."

Maureen remembered Pettigrew talking about installing new locks on his yacht, inside and out. It sounded strange then; it made sense now. And she was sure there were documents hidden somewhere that could hurt Pettigrew. A wife would know.

"What else did she tell you?"

"That's all," Bridget said.

"I don't think so."

"It is. That's all I know."

"No," Maureen said. "I think you intentionally drew everyone's attention to the boathouse while Grace was being killed. Maybe you knew she'd be killed."

"No!" Bridget closed her eyes and shook her head, her blond pony tail wagging. "It wasn't like that."

"What was it like then?"

Bridget pushed herself up. "You still haven't told me what side you're on."

Maureen's turn to make a decision, and it took no time. "Bridget, if there really are secret documents that would have an effect on Pettigrew and his corporations, I'm on your side. But before I can decide about that, you have to tell me the complete truth."

Bridget stood still, everything about her body signaling she didn't know whether to stay or run. A minute, maybe more, passed. Maureen knew better than to say anything.

"OK. But promise you won't tell anybody else."

Maureen choose her next words carefully. "People in business tell me many secrets. I tell them what I'll tell you. I'll use the information, but I won't tell anybody who told me."

"Even the cops?"

This was tricky. "Even the cops. But I won't lie to them, and if I'm ever called before a Grand Jury or something like that, I may have to reveal what you tell me." Maureen knew the situation wasn't that simple, that in certain instances law officers had the same powers as a Grand Jury. But what she told Bridget was close enough.

Bridget took a deep breath. "Grace and I made a deal. I'd get the attention of the crowd while she'd go somewhere and get the papers."

"Was she going to the boat or the penthouse?"

Bridget shrugged again. "I heard her shouting at Pettigrew when he was behind the microphone, but I didn't talk to her up close that evening."

"Even if she got to where the papers were hidden, how could she get in?"

"She had keys. She said she even knew combinations of all the safes."

They could have changed locks and combinations, Maureen realized, but that wouldn't matter if Grace hadn't thought it.

Bridget's head dropped, her shoulders slouched forward. "And now she's dead."

Maureen stood, put her arms around Bridget and pulled the girl to her. Bridget began to cry. Maureen rubbed her back, understanding now why Bridget revealed what Grace had told her. She felt guilty about Grace's death. She had to tell someone. She'd came to tell Gregory, and not finding Go at home, she'd told his friend.

Maureen understood, too, what happened on the night of the party. Grace started things, drawing attention to herself and away from Pettigrew. Bridget and the gang from Providence Place joined in, grabbing the spotlight. Then, while Bridget put on her show, Grace walked away from the stage area, probably intent on going to her car. Maybe she'd parked somewhere she wouldn't need to use valet service and could slip away unnoticed. Not that it mattered, the way things turned out. She got only as far as the lagoon. Someone stopped her there. And killed her.

Who? Pettigrew. Who else?

Chapter Nineteen

When Bridget left, promising to go straight to Providence Place and check herself in, Maureen fired up Gregory's personal computer and looked for Melody Pettigrew's telephone number. She couldn't find one listed anywhere, but several vendors offered to sell her an unlisted number for a M. Pettigrew in Santa Fe, saying they got the information from "utility records." Maureen had a dozen questions and qualms but punched in a credit card number anyway.

Melody picked up on the second ring, her voice strong but friendly. She listened while Maureen explained the reason for her call. "Tell me again who you are."

Maureen described her job.

"I own some stocks," Melody said. "But why—"

"I was at the party when Grace Pettigrew was killed."

"She was killed?"

Maureen gave her the short version.

"I've heard about Grace but never met her," Melody said. "What did she look like?"

Maureen told her, leaving out the ruddy complexion and wobbly walk.

"A good looking woman. That's all he wants us for, you know."

"No, I don't."

"He can't do anything. In bed, you know. All he wanted me for was a showpiece."

Interesting, Maureen thought, but no help. "I'm surprised the papers out there didn't run a story about the murder."

"I don't read newspapers, or watch television news. I'm too busy with important things like playing tennis." Melody laughed. "First things first."

Maureen waited, wondering if Melody was putting her on.

"In fact, my doubles partner is picking me up soon."

Six o'clock in Lauderdale, three in Santa Fe.

Melody asked, "What were you doing at the party?"

"A friend asked me to come."

"You said you worked in New York."

"Less than three hours from Lauderdale by plane."

"You must like your friend very much," Melody said.

No, Maureen thought. That's not what this is about. Melody is stalling, buying time to decide whether to talk to a stranger. Get her back to the subject. "Melody, I saw you were a stockholder in many of Pettigrew's companies."

"Oh, that was just for show. Back then I signed whatever he handed me."

"So you trusted him."

"Not anymore."

"What happened?"

"You know that mansion on the Intracoastal?"

"Yes."

"Pettigrew and I used to live there," Melody said. "I thought we owned it jointly. When we broke up, he said I'd get it, but after I filed for divorce, my attorney discovered it was owned by the Pettigrew Trust."

Grace thought she'd get the house, too, Maureen remembered.

She said, "Do you know anything about Pettigrew's stock trading?"

"No."

"There's a guy here named Kennedy. How'd he get so close to Pettigrew?"

"Jesus," Melody said. "Don't you know?"

"No."

"All you have to do is check birth certificates."

"For what?"

A long paused now. "I'm sorry. My ride's here and I've got to go." The connection clicked off.

Maureen felt she'd been slapped. Melody had hung up on her deliberately, using the tennis ride as an excuse. Maybe she'd remembered she had no idea who she was talking with. Maybe she felt she'd said too much. About what? Pettigrew's impotence? Hardly. An ex-wife would delight in revealing that.

But what did she mean about checking birth certificates. Whose? Where? Maureen would call her back tomorrow.

Chapter Twenty

The plan came to Maureen as she was packing to go the hotel. She could carry it out by herself, of course, but it would be better to have someone along. And that meant waiting until the next day to check into the hotel. She didn't cancel the reservation, though. She couldn't be sure about Gregory's reaction.

When he got back to the apartment and they were sitting in his living room, she asked him, "What do you know about Luther?"

"The same as you. He's a high-profile bookkeeper who runs the Pettigrew Trust."

"I mean as a person."

Gregory shook his head. "Nothing. Why?"

"There's something about him. Pride bordering on arrogance. Something inside him wants us to know he isn't Pettigrew's lackey. He almost said he was telling us things Pettigrew wouldn't want him to."

"So?"

"Why did he do it?" Maureen said. "He depends on Pettigrew for his livelihood."

Gregory shook his head. "Does it matter?"

"I've learned that when something doesn't make sense, it could matter a lot."

Gregory stood up. "There's more ice cream in the freezer."

"Not now." Time to tell him. "I want to borrow your car again. Or rent one of my own."

"Sure. Mine is yours."

She smiled at that and stood up.

"Is it OK to ask why?" Go said. "Or where you're going?"

"I'm going to tail Luther," she said.

Gregory was halfway to the kitchen when Maureen said it. He turned, disbelief on his face. "Aren't you taking this detective stuff a little far?"

"I don't know how to find out about what Luther does after work without following him. You don't have to come with me."

"You couldn't keep me away with dynamite."

Gregory said they should trade the Mustang for something less conspicuous, something like a gray Taurus, but Maureen said there wasn't time and besides it was almost dark. She thought about asking to drive but decided she might see more from the passenger seat.

Gregory eased into a parking space on Birch Road, the street connecting Trust House to Sunrise Boulevard. "I'll bet Luther drives that big Lincoln Town Car we saw the other day."

"No bet," Maureen said, thinking the car went with the strangely proud and aloof old man.

They waited in the Mustang, talking a little but content to stay silent for long periods. It was after six when the Lincoln came by, Luther driving. Gregory followed at a distance, scrambling to keep up as they crossed the Intracoastal. A mile or so down the road Luther turned left, a sign saying, *Welcome to Victoria Park.*

"He's trying to shake us," Gregory said.

"Now you've read too many detective novels. This is reality, Greg."

"OK. OK."

Victoria Park didn't look like the rest of Lauderdale, at least the part Maureen had seen. Mostly modest homes and townhouses with manicured hedges, a few apartment buildings, some of each being demolished to make way for new townhouses. No glitz, just pure Americana almost in the shadow of downtown. Luther pulled the Lincoln into a driveway in front of a Colonial two story, the only one in the neighborhood but somehow fitting right in.

Gregory drove past it, turned around, and parked a quarter block away. "How long are we going to wait?"

"As long as it takes."

Twenty minutes into their vigil, Pettigrew's black Mercedes crept up the road, Kennedy at the wheel, and pulled into the driveway next to Luther's Lincoln.

"The boss visiting the help?" Gregory said.

"Nobody's in the back seat."

"So Kennedy's on his own."

"Privileges of a chauffeur," Maureen said.

Kennedy emerged wearing a black suit and walked toward the front door. Before he got there, Luther came out, hugged him, walked to the Mercedes, the two men laughing about something.

"They hugged?" Maureen said, not believing what she'd seen.

When they got in the car, Kennedy drove, Luther sat in the passenger seat. Gregory pulled out behind them, leaving about a half block between the Mustang and the Lincoln, closing closer at intersections. From Sunrise they turned left onto Andrews Avenue, then made a right. Soon the Mercedes stopped in front of a large white building. *The New Church of Today*, said a sign out front.

Kennedy parked next to the church. Gregory drove past, and by the time he could turn the car around all Maureen could see was Kennedy and Luther walking up the stairs and into the building.

"Let's go in," Maureen said.

"We're going to church?"

"Do you good," she said.

Chapter Twenty-One

The faithful entered the church singly and in pairs, a few in larger groups, the street well enough lit to see the congregation was about half white, half black, all young. An organ began playing inside, loud and lively.

Maureen said, "Let's wait outside until they begin singing the first hymn."

"Sit together or separately?" Gregory asked.

"Whichever seems practical."

When the hymn ended, an usher handed them hymnals and pointed toward a rear pew. A rough cross made of dark wood, thirty to thirty-five feet high, hung above a white altar, dominating the auditorium. The room was bigger than it seemed from the outside, seats for three or four hundred, about half filled this night, the worshipers mostly in their teens and twenties, only a few as old as thirty. Maureen wondered what brought them to church on a weekday night.

The congregation finished the second hymn. The minister had some announcements. Maureen sat higher in the pew, searching for Luther and Kennedy. She spotted Luther sitting by himself in a pew near the front, but Kennedy was nowhere in sight. The announcements stopped. Gradually the coughing, talking, and restless rustling ceased, and the church became quiet.

"And now the man I know you've come to hear," the minister began, "my assistant and guest preacher—"

"Yo," cried a male voice. Laughter erupted throughout the hall. Maureen couldn't hear the rest of what the preacher said, the shouts and yells drowning him out. He stepped back and looked toward a door on his left. It opened. A man in robes bounced out.

Kennedy. No mistaking him, even in the purple robes, his hair slicked down more than usual, a huge smile on his face and looking even more confidant than at the party, looking in fact like he'd been on stage all his life.

The clapping and cheering grew louder. Kennedy walked to the lectern and raised his hands. Instant silence. He started talking, quietly and slowly at first, then faster and louder. He began with the story of Jesus and Mary Magdalene, a message of forgiveness, healing and redemption. He said there were some Mary Magdalenes here in South Florida, maybe here in the congregation tonight, or maybe people who felt like her. Many want to condemn them and the brothers who associate with them. But this is not the charitable view, the Christian approach that we can learn from the Bible.

"No, friends, Christians are not against sex," Kennedy said, his voice loud and confident. "It's lust that's the enemy." He paused. Murmurs echoed around the hall. "You know the difference between sex and lust?"

Dead silence.

"Well, I'll tell you." Kennedy looked to each side, to the seats in the front and to the seats at the back, stretching out the silence. Maureen wondered if he could see her from where he stood. She started to scrunch down, decided not to, on reflection realizing it might not be bad if Kennedy spotted her now.

"I'll tell you," he said. "Sex is when you do it with one person, one person with whom you are acquainted, one who in ideal circumstances you have some emotional relationship with, and it-is-to-be-hoped whose name you can remember the next morning."

Giggles and laugher spread through the auditorium, stopping when Kennedy raised his hand.

"That's sex," he said. "Now lust, that's another matter. Lust is when you're walking down the street, and you want to do it with anything that wiggles."

More giggles, more laughter.

"Lord, help you—" Kennedy pushed his voice louder. "Lord help you if a horse comes wiggling down the street."

He stepped back and let the laughter explode. "Go brother," somebody yelled and others took up the cry.

Corny, corny, corny, Maureen thought, but these youngsters loved it.

When the hall was silent again, Kennedy went back to scripture, then sex, back and forth, scripture and sex for thirty minutes, every soul in the hall his. They laughed, they applauded, and they turned silent at his bidding. Maureen was impressed. What he said didn't make sense, in fact wouldn't survive two seconds scrutiny, but the congregation didn't care. A man able to manipulate people like this could go far. She wondered how long he'd been practicing.

Kennedy ended with a plea for money "for God's work and for our work," and when the deep bronze plates reached the back pews, they were filled so high the bills almost spilled out. Maureen and Gregory tossed in five bucks each. The show had been worth it.

Chapter Twenty-Two

Maureen stood on the passenger side of the black Mercedes, Gregory on the driver's. She said, "They can't drive home without talking to us."

"Unless we die of starvation, first."

He had a point. It was taking Kennedy and Luther forever to come out of the church. Three young guys in their teens, attitude showing in every movement, walked up to them. Maureen said, "Waiting for Kennedy," and they left.

Kennedy came down the church steps first, Luther following, both working the crowd, but only Kennedy managing to shake two hands at once. They got ten or twelve feet from the driver's side of the Mercedes before they stopped

"My favorite gimp," Kennedy said.

Maureen lobbed her words over the car's roof, hoping they'd hit like a grenade. "Pettigrew doesn't know."

Luther put a hand on Kennedy's shoulder and stepped forward. "Let me handle this."

"Pettigrew doesn't know," Maureen said again, determined to repeat the phrase as often as necessary. She knew in her gut that what she was saying was absolutely true. And important. Soon or later they'd understand.

Luther walked around the front of the car, stopping in front of Maureen. Kennedy positioned himself next to Gregory.

"Pettigrew doesn't know," she repeated.

Luther said, "I heard you the first time," his voice soft. "It doesn't mean anything."

"Pettigrew doesn't know that his chauffeur and personal trainer preaches sex and salvation before a congregation of young people," Maureen said. "He doesn't know his trusted bookkeeper and confidant goes with him."

"Assuming what you say is true, what difference does it make?" Luther's tone said he'd reason with her. "None. Absolutely none."

Maureen knew then that she had him. *Assuming what you say is true*. When corporate executives told her that, she could bet it was true. "It makes a difference, and I think you know it. When Pettigrew finds out about this, he won't like it."

Luther shrugged. "I don't see why."

"Trust me," she said. "He'll hate it."

"There is nothing for Mr. Pettigrew to like or not like. Kennedy is an unpaid, part-time preacher at this church. It's an opportunity for him to polish his oratorical skills. Skills, I shouldn't have to say, that will be useful to him in the practice of law."

"You saying you cleared all this with Pettigrew?"

"Mr. Pettigrew knows Kennedy is a law student. In fact, the man is financing his legal education."

"For reasons you can try to explain some other time," Maureen said. "But Midas Man does not know that Kennedy is down here preaching."

Kennedy, the object of the debate, was standing on the other side of the Mercedes looking back and forth between them, as if watching a tennis match. Now he said, "So the man gets a surprise. Do him good."

Luther frowned at Kennedy. "I said I would—"

"OK. OK."

"Kennedy is half right," Maureen said. "Pettigrew will be surprised. And a man like Pettigrew doesn't like to be surprised. He'll be angry."

Kennedy looked at Luther, clearly asking what he thought.

"If there's one thing Pettigrew reveres, it's information," Maureen said. "He calls it knowledge. He believes if he knows everything about a situation, he can control it."

Luther nodded involuntarily. A beat later, Kennedy did the same.

"Conversely, if he doesn't know something important, he'll think he's not in control," Maureen said. "He worships control. It's his religion. And now this—this secret Pettigrew doesn't know about the man who drives him around, the man who probably visits his penthouse regularly as his personal trainer, the man he's paying law school tuition for."

Kennedy looked as if all of this was occurring to him for the first time. Luther remained expressionless, Maureen, sure that Luther knew from the beginning exactly what she was talking about, turned and looked over the car to Kennedy.

"What do you suppose your boss will do when he finds out?"

"He'll shit in his pants," Kennedy said.

"And you," Maureen said to Luther. "You, a man he trusts more than any other, aiding and abetting. Keeping it a secret from him."

"I don't believe—" Luther started, but Maureen could see his heart wasn't in it.

"Pettigrew will be frightened," she said. "He'll lash out at both of you."

Luther said nothing, and Maureen knew better than to interrupt his thoughts. It took two minutes, maybe, but when Luther made up his mind he surrendered with dignity. "I would be honored if the two of you would join us for a cup of coffee. We have a lot to discuss."

Maureen looked toward Gregory, who nodded.

"You can ride with us." Luther gestured toward the Mercedes.

Maureen shook her head. "We'll follow you in our pretty Mustang. You two may have things to talk about."

Chapter Twenty-Three

Maureen and Gregory followed the Mercedes to the Peter Pan, a twenty-four-hour restaurant on Oakland Park Boulevard. "Why here?" she asked as they pulled into the parking lot.

"Probably no one here will recognize them."

Ever since she'd seen the two men enter the church, Maureen had been thinking about something that struck her when she first saw Luther. "Have you noticed that except for the difference in age Luther and Kennedy look very much alike? Their mannerisms are the same, too. Like the way they hold their hands out, or look upward when there're thinking."

"Mannerisms, yes. Looks? It's a stretch."

"Make allowance for their ages."

"Kennedy's skin is so much lighter."

Yes but…. There was probably a reason, even if Maureen couldn't think of it now.

They went into the restaurant and sat opposite Luther and Kennedy, the men already sitting in a booth. Coffee only, Luther told the waitress, but Gregory ordered apple pie with vanilla ice cream and whipped cream on top. "Ice cream without the pie," Maureen said. And Kennedy said, "I'll have what the gimp is having."

When the waitress left, Luther said, "Exactly what do you want of us, Ms. O'Neal?"

"I want to know everything you know about Pettigrew."

Luther smiled. "That again."

"I understand there are some documents relating to Pettigrew's companies that he keeps secret."

"Who told you that?"

That came out too quickly, Maureen thought, too sharp, too surprised. Luther was truly apprehensive for the first time since they'd started talking. "You know a good stock analyst doesn't reveal her sources."

"Ridiculous," Luther said. "Mr. Overman here is the prime suspect in the murder of Mr. Pettigrew's former wife. The police are treating you as an accomplice. And you're trying to blackmail us."

"I don't like the term blackmail."

"Neither do I, but you—"

"If you want to complain to the police, feel free. We'll tell what we saw tonight and the police will tell Pettigrew." Maureen wasn't sure of this last and waited to see if Luther or Kennedy would challenge her.

Kennedy said, "You're all over the TV."

Luther said, "Kennedy, *please*."

Kennedy shook him off, keeping his eyes on Maureen. "The TV reporters say you aren't registered at any of our major hotels. They say you may have left town."

That was news to Maureen, but she said, "You forget why we're here. We know something you don't want Pettigrew to know."

Kennedy said, "We can just tell you to go to hell."

Luther nodded, giving in to the younger man now.

"And we can drop Pettigrew a letter," Maureen said. "Better yet, we could tell him about it face to face. On that boat he likes to show off."

Luther studied his coffee cup. Kennedy looked at a red-haired waitress. Nobody said anything for minutes. Finally, Luther said, "I apologize for Kennedy's rudeness."

"And you'll cooperate with us?" Maureen said.

"I need some time to think."

"Me too," Kennedy said.

"And check with Pettigrew?" Maureen fixed her eyes on Luther's.

"Obviously not," he said. "Under the circumstances."

"How long do you want?"

"Two or three days."

"Forty-eight hours," Maureen said. "Max."

"You sure push," Kennedy said.

"Agreed." Luther stood up. "I cannot say this has been pleasant."

Kennedy got up, too, looking at Gregory. "Keep this up, and you're not gonna be my favorite gimp anymore."

"You'll always be my favorite preacher."

All during the conversation, Maureen had been thinking about what Melody Pettigrew said. *All you have to do is check birth certificates.* Now, with Luther and Kennedy standing side by side, their mannerisms and style so much alike, she decided to go for it.

"You and your father here can be of great help to me," she said, looking at Kennedy.

Luther, already turning to leave, swirled around. "Father? That's ridiculous."

"Yeah," Kennedy said.

"If you could see yourselves," Maureen said. "You both run your fingers through your hair the same way. You shrug your shoulders the same. You even smile alike."

Luther sat down and leaned across the table. "I'll tell you what. The two of us will submit to DNA tests. If we're father and son, you win whatever it is you want. If we're not, you'll forget you ever saw us at the church tonight."

Never accept a bet proposed by someone else, Maureen said to herself. "I'll think about it."

Luther smiled. "So now we both have something to think about."

"Think, think, think," Kennedy said, still standing. "Life's a bitch."

Luther stood up straight. "Goodbye, Ms. O'Neal. Goodbye Mr. Overman. I'll phone you soon. Or you can phone me."

Kennedy followed him out. Maureen looked at Gregory, giving him plenty of time to say whatever he had to say. She knew she'd messed up, that she shouldn't have brought up her suspicion that Luther and Kennedy were father and son. Finally, when Go didn't say anything, she said, "It seemed like a good idea."

"Wasn't like you," he said. "You usually get the facts first."

"The Florida air must be addling my brain."

Back at Gregory's apartment, finishing a bowl of Phish Food, Maureen said, "OK, so I jumped to a conclusion. But what did Melody mean about birth certificates?"

"Maybe she was blowing smoke," Gregory said.

"Why? What motive would she have?"

"What motives do any of these people have?"

They were silent.

Finally Gregory said, "I don't think you should move into Pettigrew's hotel."

"Why?"

"It's a bad idea."

"Why?"

"It just is."

Maureen smiled. "I'll think about it."

"Tonight you might as well sleep here."

"Right." Maureen walked into the bedroom, closing the door behind her. Something was happening to Gregory, but she was too tired to think about it.

Chapter Twenty-Four

The next morning, after Gregory left the apartment saying he had to do something at Providence Place, Maureen made enough phone calls to find out that if she wanted to learn about birth certificates she needed to phone the State Department of Health in Jacksonville. She did so, and after going through an automated maze reached a woman with a friendly voice, one she pictured as gray-haired and matronly. Watch it, she said to herself, remembering how wrong she'd been about Luther and the local brokerage manger. This woman could have flaming red hair and three-inch heels.

"How can I look at some birth certificates?" Maureen asked her.

"Honey, you can't."

"How about copies?"

"You asking about yours or a child's?"

"Not mine. Someone else's child."

"You can't do it. Not without a court order."

Maureen inhaled. "Aren't they public records?"

"They're protected under Florida confidentiality laws."

Maureen paused.

"Only three exceptions," the woman said. "People over eighteen can get copies of their own certificates. Parents can get copies of their children's. Or a court could order us to provide a copy to someone. That's rare."

A dead-end.

"I forgot. There's another exception," she said. "If a person is deceased or over a hundred years old, anybody can get their certificates. Is this person you're interested in dead?"

"No." Maureen was about to thank the woman and hang up when another question occurred to her. "Can a mother list anyone she wants as the father of her baby?"

"Certainly not. A married woman has to name her husband as the father of her child—no matter who he may be in fact." The woman giggled. "If she's not married, she can't list the father's name unless he signs something acknowledging paternity."

"And if they don't know the father's identity?"

"They leave it blank."

So Melody Pettigrew didn't know what she was talking about. She couldn't have seen anyone's birth certificate. That was clear enough. Why did Pettigrew's first wife want to mislead her? Didn't matter. Melody was unreliable. Maureen decided against phoning her again.

Now what? Maureen's trip to the courthouse produced zip. Likewise her confrontation with Pettigrew. Even the information she and Gregory got from Luther was suspect now. Three strikes. No. Three tries, no results. Not yet. Sooner or later, she could visit the Palm Beach County Courthouse and read copies of the Pettigrew Trust's official reports. And maybe there was something valuable in the shaggy dog story Luther told them about the Lolita of her time and all that. As for Pettigrew's story about being scared at sea, it just didn't make sense that parents would treat a son the way Pettigrew described. But if it happened, no wonder Midas Man was such a cruel bastard. Or was he? This last question, completely unconnected to anything she'd learned, popped out of nowhere. What'd it mean? She'd learned to consider such thoughts, but nothing came to mind. Maybe later.

And what was Maureen to make of Bridget? Maybe her story about the secret documents and making a deal with Grace was a fabrication. But one part of it was true. She had distracted almost everybody at the party long enough for somebody to hold Grace Pettigrew's head under water and terminate her lifelong tenure as trustee of Providence Place. Who benefited from that? Pettigrew.

But he had an alibi. Didn't he? Fourquet's teeth, flashing confidence beneath the mustache, filled her mind. He'd said it'd been established that Pettigrew had left the party when Grace was killed. By whom? Fourquet hadn't said. A smart-ass cop, trying to throw his weight around. Gregory and her drown Grace Pettigrew? Fourquet must know better than that. They'd just met the woman. But someone killed her. Who? She'd eliminated Luther as a suspect. There wasn't enough time for him to run down the stairs at Trust House, drown Grace, and get back upstairs before the body was discovered. But he could have seen something. Something he didn't tell Gregory and her or the police. What?

Who could she trust? Kennedy, maybe. He told her Pettigrew's first wife was in Santa Fe, and she was there just as advertised. She was no help, though. What about Kennedy as a suspect? He'd certainly shown up at the lagoon soon enough. She hadn't noticed if his trousers were already wet when he splashed into the water to help Gregory. It they were, it could mean.... Ludicrous, every single bit of it. Pettigrew was the only logical suspect. As far as Maureen knew, Pettigrew's alibi was unconfirmed, he had a motive, and he was probably strong enough to hold his ex-wife under water. But how could she prove it? She closed her eyes.

The ring of Maureen's cell phone woke her.

"There's something I want you to hear," Gregory said. "Some information."

"Well, come back here and tell me about it."

"I want you to hear it from the source."

"Who?"

Gregory paused a few seconds. "Tell you later."

"Where are you?"

"The International Swimming Hall of Fame."

"Sounds like something out of an old Esther Williams movie," Maureen said. "Is it in black and white?"

"This is serious."

He sounded gruff, but she knew he must be grinning. "Come pick me up then."

"You can walk here."

"Why?"

"I shouldn't leave. You'll understand when you get here."

Maureen agreed to walk, and Gregory gave her directions. Only after she clicked off did it occur to her that Gregory was being just as mysterious as when he phoned her in New York. She wondered if he'd do this if they were really a team.

Chapter Twenty-Five

It was a short walk, east on Las Olas, over the bridge, and then a right turn. "How much?" Maureen asked the guy in the booth at the gate to the pool.

"Two dollars if you live in Lauderdale. Three bucks if you don't."

She paid three dollars.

"Lockers over there." He pointed with a shoulder. "Open swimming between the bleachers."

The pools glistened in the midday sun, two Olympic-sized near the entrance, another—deeper and with higher diving boards—over at the Intracoastal. Maureen counted the swim lanes, automatic calculation a habit she hadn't tried to break. Ten in each pool, the chlorinated water looking artificial but still more inviting than the gray gunk of the Intracoastal It was a wonder Bridget didn't catch something when she dived in.

Gregory stood at the top of one of the spectator bleachers, waving for her to come up, Bridget sitting next to him in a one-piece bathing suit, tall and slim. Go hadn't mentioned her when he called.

Maureen climbed the bleacher seats and when she reached them said, "You could have told me to bring a bathing suit."

Bridget said, "Hi."

Gregory said, "When I got to Providence Place, they told me I could find Bridget down here swimming laps. I walked down and we started talking."

"You two are quite chummy," Maureen said.

Gregory frowned.

Bridget said, "I was almost finished anyway."

"Bridget told me a story I thought you should hear," Gregory said, standing up. "Look over there." He pointed to the opposite side of the pool, toward the marina behind the hotel where Pettigrew stayed. "You see Pettigrew's boat?"

"I've been on it," Maureen said.

"Well, Bridget has, too," Gregory said.

Maureen looked back toward the girl. Bridget shrugged, a crooked smile on her face saying she didn't know whether to brag or what. Maureen had a zillion questions, but she knew to let Gregory direct this play.

He sat down next to Maureen. "Bridget, tell her about it."

The girl put her feet on the seat in front of her, spread a towel over her legs, and looked at Maureen. "Did you ever wonder where I stayed after I put on my show and left the party?"

"I wondered."

Bridget said, "I stayed on Pettigrew's yacht."

"How did you get in?"

"I have a key."

"Where did you—"

"Grace gave it to me. She had it made when she was about to leave Pettigrew."

Gregory said, "Pettigrew didn't know that and didn't change the lock. You see, this wasn't the first time Bridget stayed on the boat."

A tiny apartment that floats and goes fast, Maureen remembered telling Pettigrew. But she knew a prompt when she heard one and followed Gregory's lead. "I'd like to hear about those times, Bridget."

"I stayed there off and on for weeks," the girl said. "Whenever I got disgusted with Providence Place. Then something happened to scare me away."

"What?"

"One night I woke up and heard somebody walking on the deck. It was spooky. I looked out the windows, but I couldn't see anything. Then the footsteps stopped. I waited a couple of minutes before I opened the hatch."

"And?"

"Pettigrew was sitting in the cockpit, looking toward the cabin. He saw me. I didn't know what to do."

"How was he dressed?"

"Tan pants. A blue coat like Kennedy wears."

"A blazer?"

"I guess." Bridget nodded. "He said, 'Don't be afraid,' and I got the idea he was scareder than I was. I closed the hatch and locked it behind me. Eventually I heard footsteps leaving."

"So you didn't stay on the boat anymore?"

"I wasn't afraid. I stayed right there. " Bridget stared across the pool toward Pettigrew's yacht. "Pettigrew was back the next night, and this time he knocked on the cabin door."

"What did you do?"

"He said he wanted to talk, so I let him in."

"Why?"

"I told you, I thought he was more afraid than me," Bridget said. "And I could use the company."

"Reckless," Gregory said, speaking for the first time since he'd turned the girl over to Maureen. "But people Bridget's age have more self-confidence than fear."

Maureen kept her eyes on Bridget, who was still staring at the yacht. "Go on."

"He went directly to a chair and sat down," she said. "I sat on one of the soft seats at the table. Then he started talking and didn't stop for the longest time."

"About what?"

"He said he was lonely. I told him I didn't see how he could be lonely with all his money. He said had been lonely all his life, starting when he was a kid."

Maureen knew what was coming.

"He told me about how he grew up in a big house in Palm Beach. He said his sister had married an old man and they didn't have any time for him. He said they were mean to him."

"Not his sister, Bridget. His mother."

"Whatever," Bridget shrugged. "But he told me sister."

Bells went off in Maureen's head, but she didn't know what they were telling her, and this wasn't the time to figure it out.

"He told me about going out to sea with them and nearly drowning." Bridget looked toward Gregory. "He told me that's the reason he bought this boat. To get over being afraid."

"Did he cry?" Maureen asked.

Bridget jerked around. "How'd you know?"

"Go on."

"He got a real odd look in his eyes. He told me his sister was a lot younger than her husband when she married him. He said I looked something like her when she was young."

Maureen felt her neck muscles tighten.

Bridget closed her eyes as if to remember better. "He said a lot of people thought it was peculiar she'd marry a man so much older. But she got the last laugh. That's what he said. The 'last laugh.' She ended up being the richest woman in Florida."

"What else?"

"He kept looking at me funny, and saying the same things over and over again. How much I looked like his sister. And how rich she became."

"Did you feel in danger?"

"He didn't touch me," Bridget said. "He didn't even come close to me. But wait until you hear the last."

"Tell."

"He asked me if I'd consider marrying him."

"Really?"

"He sure did. You know what I told him?"

"What?"

"I lied and told him I was only fifteen years old."

"What'd he say?"

"He said that was all right. He said his sister was only fifteen when she met the rich man she married."

That son of a bitch, Maureen thought. A man with all his money could have his pick of many women, but there he was trying to entice a girl who he thought was only fifteen years old.

"That's when I decided to move off the boat." Bridget sought Maureen's eyes, looking for understanding. "I only went there one more time. The night I dove into the Intracoastal and we ruined Pettigrew's party."

"Did he bother you then?"

"He didn't show up." Bridget looked from Gregory to Maureen and back again. "But he might have known I was there."

"How?" Maureen said.

"I tried to get in the secret compartment in the bow," Bridget said. "The one I told you about. The one with the papers."

"Did you?"

"I couldn't. I banged it and tried to pry it open, but all I managed to do was mess up everything around the lock. The hinges and stuff."

Maureen looked at Gregory. "Bridget shouldn't go anywhere close to the marina or Pettigrew's hotel again."

"She won't. Will you Bridget?"

The girl shook her head.

"She's going back to Providence Place," Go said.

Maureen said, "Do you remember anything else?"

"That's all I remember."

"Think," Go said. "Any little thing might help us."

Bridget looked around the pool, shaking her head. Then she stopped. "One thing. There was a pamphlet there from a bank. It was in Costa Rica. I thought that was odd."

Costa Rica! He's moving money. Maureen put a hand on Bridget's shoulder. "Thank you Bridget. You've been more help than you'll ever know."

Chapter Twenty-Six

Back at Gregory's apartment, after they walked Bridget to Providence Place and picked up the rented Mustang, Maureen and Gregory fell into one of their silences, Gregory staring at the Gandhi poster, Maureen thinking there wasn't enough time to get to the courthouse in West Palm Beach and accomplish anything before it closed. She'd drive there tomorrow.

Her mind dredged up loose ends. "Go, is Pettigrew strong enough to hold Grace under water long enough to drown her?"

"Can't tell. We've only seen him with a shirt and coat on."

"Kennedy said he's Pettigrew's personal trainer."

"If Pettigrew works out regularly, maybe he could hold Grace down."

Neither said anything for a while, Maureen wondering why Gregory kept staring at the poster. Finally she said, "Go, what sort of name is Fritz?"

"Fritz is a nickname for Frederick."

"Could Luther have said Fitz when he told us about Pettigrew's boyhood?"

"I thought he said Fritz."

No help, she thought.

Gregory got out of his chair, stood before her, and said, "Mo, I'm sorry."

"For what?"

"For getting you into this mess."

"Go, that's silly." She took his hand. "I haven't felt this alive since we spent all that time together as kids."

"But you've been suspended from your job and the police think you're an accomplice in a murder."

She patted the sofa beside her. "Sit down."

He did as instructed.

Maureen said, "For the last nine years, everything I've done has been about money. Making it, conserving it, allocating it. All for other people. None of them cared about me as a person. I was just an instrument." She looked into his eyes, hoping for some flicker of understanding. Nothing came back. She tried again. "Go, I like being with you."

"I don't know why. I've been such a fuck-up."

"Oh, Go no—."

"You know why people become therapists and counselors?" Go said. "Nine times out of ten they're trying to answer the question, 'What's wrong with me?' Then they realize the issue is much more complicated than that and decide to study more. Soon psychology is all they know, so they take it up as an occupation."

This was new. Until now Go had hidden this side of himself from her, the vulnerable, unsure of himself, dark side. She said, "All this will work out all right."

"I swear, before this is over I'll make it up to you."

Maureen moved closer to Gregory on the sofa, her body touching his now. She wanted to comfort him, maybe wanted him to comfort her, too, to get rid of the barrier that had separated them for so long. Gregory turned toward her, the expression on his face puzzled, as if physical closeness was the last thing in the world he expected. He stood up and walked toward the kitchen. Halfway there, he said, "What can I get you?"

"You mean, what can I do for you?"

He stopped and turned. "Yeah."

"Leave the freaking ice cream alone and take me to a good restaurant."

Maureen went into the bedroom to shower and change, pausing to really look around for the first time. Books were everywhere. Books on the washed-oak dressers, books on the matching bedside tables, and books on shelves. Titles like *The Spirituality of Silence, Getting in Touch with Your Spiritual Self, How to Understand Your Spiritual Life*. Gregory had changed. Maureen could remember when Go's library consisted solely of psychology books and sex manuals.

She'd changed, too. The platinum angel on her necklace was just the part that showed. Long before the television shows and the movies came along, Mo began collecting angels. She had them all over her apartment in New York. Ceramic angels mostly, tall ones, miniatures, a few made of bronze, a couple of dozen at least. She kept them to remind herself there were some things in life you can't see, feel, hear, smell, or even measure. Maybe she was the only person on Wall Street who believed that. Didn't matter. She'd often wondered if those feelings in the back of her neck were touches of an angel. More likely her intuition at work, perhaps a message from her subconscious. Angels. Intuition. Subconscious. Maybe they were all the same thing.

The Street would never learn about her angels. Or the underwear she bought from Victoria's Secret. Oh, she owned some sex manuals, too, but it seemed to her that the physical side of things was the easy part. Finding the right man was— Well, that was impossible.

They ate at the Café de Paris on Las Olas, and by the time they reached it Maureen had calmed down. A nice place. White tablecloths, wine glasses and good china on the tables, the waiters authentically French and haughty, the awning out front properly red, white, and blue.

"Beats the hell out of those diners you've been taking me to," Maureen said as they walked to the bar at the back.

"I didn't pick Peter Pan," Gregory said. "Luther did."

Maureen ordered red wine, Gregory a bottle of still water, the bartender eager to chat between drink orders. "You are not bad for a new country," he said. "But for real civilization, you must go to Paris."

Maureen knew the line was probably one he used on every customer but decided to play along. "I like your attitude."

Gregory said, "The French have always been a modest people."

Maureen smiled. The bartender frowned and walked to the other end of the bar.

Soon they were led to a table close to the window, heads turning as they passed just as at the Floridian, Maureen again wearing nothing special, tan slacks, tight on her hips but loose in the legs, and a frilly dark green blouse.

She ordered lamb, Gregory the sautéed snapper, and when the food came Maureen asked for another glass of wine. "Yes. This is more like it."

"The rolls were spectacularly good," Gregory said, starting on the snapper. "Crunchy on the surface, deliciously soft inside."

Maureen wondered if they were going to keep up this inane small talk all evening. If so, she wasn't going to try to stop it. She'd done her best earlier. They talked of old times, of Maureen going off to the University of Missouri and then straight to work, Gregory doing his undergraduate work at George Washington University and going on to Johns Hopkins in Baltimore, neither far from their parents' homes in Sumner, Maryland. He'd moved into the District of Columbia, up Wisconsin Avenue, commuting backwards into Maryland when he took the counseling job.

"I thought you liked nursing," Maureen said.

"I did," Gregory said. "But patients came and went so fast I never got to know any of them."

"What about hospital administration?"

"The whole idea is supposed to be helping people get well, but that seemed to be the furthest thing from anyone's mind. It was all about money and politics. And power."

Sometimes Gregory could be so naïve. Almost everything is about money and power when you get down to the roots. "Counseling children is better for you."

"Yeah, but—"

"Yeah but, yeah but, yeah but," Maureen said. "You won't let me do that."

He laughed and the rest of the meal was fun. They shared cheese cake for dessert and Maureen had a glass of port. Gregory finished what must have been his fourth cup of coffee. Walking home, Maureen thought about holding Go's hand but decided against it. Not after what had happened earlier. She felt good anyway. All was well in the world, God in her heaven, things getting better and better, even here on this stupid Isle of Venice.

"Look ," Gregory said when they reached his apartment.

"Where?"

"Up on the stairs. Something—" He began running, bobbing back and forth like he always did, like a crab Maureen thought but had never told him. Then she saw it, too, and ran after him.

Gregory got there first, almost jumping up the stairs until he got to the body lying at the top, a rag doll wearing a blue T-shirt and white shorts, eyes open, legs collapsed underneath her. He picked up an arm and felt for pulse, then tried to detect any flicker of breath.

He turned to Maureen. "Call 9-1-1. Ask for a medic and an ambulance. I'll work on her, but I think it's too late. Bridget's dead."

Chapter Twenty-Seven

Maureen sat on a green metal chair at a table in a small room inside the Lauderdale police station, the hard vinyl seat already feeling uncomfortable, the air conditioning turned down low, too low. Fourquet and a detective who hadn't introduced herself sat across the table, a video camera behind them.

"The girl probably died of strangulation," Fourquet said. "Of course we won't know that until the medical examiner makes his report."

"I've heard that before." Maureen gave him a smile, one much like she'd give a company executive she didn't know whether to believe. She'd decided to make a game of this, pretend Fourquet was just some other corporate bozo so the time would pass sooner. "Where's Gregory?"

"He's in another room."

"I'd like to see him." The police had taken the two of them to the station in separate squad cars.

"All in good time." Fourquet's white teeth flashed below his damn mustache, just as at their first encounter. He thought a lot of himself.

Maureen looked around the room again, trying to find a one-way mirror. If there was one, it wasn't being used. A Venetian blind covered the single opening.

Fourquet said, "Mind if we tape your statement?"

"I mind," Maureen said.

"You got something to hide?"

She didn't answer.

"I've got to read you this." Fourquet pulled a card from his wallet. "You have the right to remain silent, you have the right...." The familiar language of the Miranda warning oozed from his lips, soft and fast, barely audible. Anything she said could and would be used against her in a court of law. If she couldn't afford a lawyer, one would be appointed to represent her. She had the right to remain silent, of course, but the way Fourquet read it, to do so would be tantamount to pleading guilty.

"Am I suspected of committing a crime?" Maureen said.

"We just want to find out what happened."

"Turn the video camera on and let's start over."

Fourquet looked at the other detective. She sighted through the camera and pushed a button, the red light clicking on.

"Now," Maureen said. "Let's run through this again, starting at the top."

"What do you mean?"

"Let's hear you mumble through the Miranda warning on tape."

Fourquet pursed his lips, then recited the warning, clearer and louder this time, not looking once at the card. The business about reading it had been an act, something designed to make it seem unimportant and foreign.

Again Maureen said, "Am I suspected of committing a crime?"

"At this time, we don't know what to suspect."

"That's not my question. Am I suspected of committing a crime?"

"We always suspect everybody."

Maureen knew he'd keep weaseling for as long as she could ask questions, so she had a decision to make. Refuse to talk or go along? If she didn't cooperate, news of her refusal would be on front pages tomorrow. Not only would her partners in New York become even more enraged, but her clients—probably already beginning to have doubts about her—would conclude they had misplaced their faith.

"Ask your questions," she said.

Fourquet pulled a cigar from his shirt pocket. "Start at the beginning. Describe what happened before you found Bridget's body."

Maureen told him about walking to and from the Café de Paris, not being able to resist saying, "You want to know what we ate?"

The cop shook his head, then asked how much they had to drink. She told him.

He said, "Who saw the body first?"

"Gregory."

"And you say he outran you to the bottom of the stairs and got up to the top before you could?"

"Yes."

"You had only two glasses of red wine and the glass of port?"

"Yes." Now Maureen realized the drinks were a bit of information Fourquet could leak to reporters and make it sound any way he wanted. She said she had only three drinks, but we haven't talked to the waiters.

"You run or jog?"

She nodded.

"I thought so. It just seems so strange that with his bad leg and all— He's a cripple and you're a jogger and he got there before you."

"What are you getting at?"

Fourquet held the unlit cigar in his hand. "Everything seems so remarkable. You arrive in town and within four days there are two murders. Both times your friend Gregory Overman was found hunched over the body."

"Not hunched," Maureen said. "He was trying to help them."

"So you say." Fourquet ran the cigar back and forth under his nose, making no move to light it. "It's just so remarkable."

"Do I need a lawyer?"

"I read you your rights. When was the last time you were in Lauderdale?"

"More than twenty years ago."

"We can check that." Fourquet smiled. "And why did you come here this time?"

"I told you that Saturday night."

"Tell me again."

"All right," Maureen said. "But after that, charge me or let me leave."

She went through the story again, Gregory's phone call, flying down to Lauderdale and going straight to Pettigrew's party, all the while Fourquet staring at his cigar as if it had all the answers. When she finished, Fourquet shook his head. "Strains belief, you know, you having to come down here and check up on our most prominent citizen."

Maureen didn't reply. The way she told it to Fourquet, leaving out the most important part, her story did sound strange. What he didn't know and Maureen wasn't going to tell him was she wouldn't have made the trip for just anybody. Only Go. Fourquet wouldn't understand that, so why bother telling him?

"Where are you staying?" Fourquet said.

"At Gregory's. At Mr. Overman's apartment."

"How long have you two been sleeping together?"

"We haven't, and we aren't."

"Stranger and stranger," Fourquet said.

Maureen didn't say anything to that.

Fourquet stood up, turned off the video camera, and went to the door. "Stay here. I'll be right back."

Minutes passed. Maureen looked at her watch. Almost midnight.

"He can be a real pain in the ass," the female detective said.

Maureen smiled, glad someone saw Fourquet the way she did.

"Guess you didn't know what you were getting into when you came down here?" she said.

Then Maureen understood. "You're the good cop."

The woman frowned.

"Forget it," Maureen said.

Fourquet came back about forty-five minutes later. "You know a man named Kennedy?"

"You know I do."

"Kennedy told another officer you were harassing him and Luther last night."

"Not true," Maureen said.

"He says you were threatening to expose them for doing something you thought they didn't want Mr. Pettigrew to know about."

Maureen knew Kennedy was talking about his preaching at the church, but she couldn't imagine Kennedy telling Fourquet about it and risking it getting back to Pettigrew. She said, "And what was that?"

"He won't say."

"So there's nothing for me to rebut."

Fourquet frowned. "He also says you think Luther is his father."

Maureen lifted a shoulder. "It's a theory."

"He said those beliefs might give you and Gregory Overman a motive to murder Grace or Bridget or both of them."

"Absurd." Maureen waited for Fourquet to follow up, but he'd apparently decided to outwait her. They could sit this way for hours. "What does Luther say?"

Fourquet had the cigar out again, studying its tip. "Luther won't discuss it."

"So there isn't anything to what Kennedy said."

"Ms. O'Neal." Fourquet's words grew loud, his tone gruff. "I don't think you realize the seriousness of your situation."

Finally, Maureen thought. Finally we're down to it.

"I can keep you here overnight," Fourquet said, "until you decide to discuss these matters with more candor than you've shown so far."

Good! When corporate executives threatened her, it meant they'd run out of things of substance to say. Fourquet was just like them. "I've got nothing better to do."

"But I've got more important things on my plate." Fourquet stood up and walked out without saying another word. The good cop turned off the camera.

Maureen felt her momentary elation drain away, the balloon collapsing. Damn. This could go on forever.

Almost two a.m., according to Maureen's watch. Still no word from or about Gregory. For the first time, Maureen began to think the situation was more serious than she'd admitted to herself so far. Her innocence—and Go's—didn't matter now. It was the appearance of things that counted. She'd been in denial. And now it had stopped working.

One phone call. That's what she'd always heard. You get one phone call. What criminal defense attorneys did she know? She dug into her memory, trying to remember all the attorneys she met at parties, all those men and women in thousand dollar suits standing there with drinks in hand, smiles on their faces, business cards ready for a quick draw. Not one practiced criminal law. None. Zip. The only attorneys she knew specialized in securities law, and she only had their phone numbers at work. Maybe their home phones were listed, maybe not. Even if she could get to one, how would he—or she—react if she woke them at two o'clock in the morning?

"I'm ready to leave," she told the good cop.

"Just a few more minutes."

"What if I just walked out of here?"

"There's a couple of guys a lot bigger than me who'd stop you."

At ten to four, Fourquet returned. His cigar was gone, but the smile was back. "There's good news and bad news," he said.

"The good news is I'm leaving," Maureen said.

"Yep."

She started to stand but stopped when she realized Fourquet had another card to play.

"The bad news is that your friend is not leaving," he said. "Now that we've had a chance to think about it, Mr. Overman's story sounds ever stranger than yours."

"How could it possibly—"

"Listen to this as if you're hearing it for the first time." Fourquet pulled a cigar from his shirt pocket and held it loosely in his left hand, his arm casually extended to one side. "Until recently Gregory Overman, known as Go to you and some of his associates, was working as a child counselor in the suburbs of

Washington at less than one-third of the salary he made as a hospital administrator. A boy who came to him for counseling killed himself. Your friend got drunk and stayed that way for six weeks."

"Off and on," Maureen said.

"Whatever. So he comes to Lauderdale to get sober. Before he's in rehab six months, he's hired by the nuns at Providence Place to counsel children with the provision—get this—that he treats only the boys."

"A common arrangement, I'm sure."

"We're not. Within twenty-four hours we'll know a lot more."

"Twenty-four hours?"

"At least." Fourquet smiled. "Listen to the rest of the story. Even with that understanding, that he'd counsel only boys, Mr. Overman became good friends with a sixteen-year-old girl who's been in and out of Providence Place for years."

"They've seen each other, that's all."

"He may have told you that," Fourquet said. "But she came to his apartment early yesterday afternoon. He's admitted to that."

"She came to see me," Maureen said. "She didn't come inside. She left before Gregory got there."

Fourquet ignored her. "Later Gregory took the girl to a swimming pool and phoned you. Then, still later, she's found dead on his stairway. You can see how it looks?"

"No."

"You wouldn't. You're too involved."

Maureen waited.

Fourquet said, "Maybe Mr. Overman had a relationship with the girl we don't know about. Maybe she knew too much."

He let the thought lay there, Maureen knowing he'd used the word "relationship" deliberately, letting it mean anything a listener wanted to hear. She didn't respond. She wasn't going to tell Fourquet the things Bridget told her. For all she knew, the bastard might pass them on to Pettigrew.

"Anyway," Fourquet said now, "we're going to hold your friend overnight. You can leave."

"You bast—" The word was halfway out of Maureen's mouth before she stopped. "What are his legal options?"

"Nothing until the morning. They'll be a preliminary hearing and then we'll see what's what."

"Has he been charged with anything?"

"Not yet."

"Can't he put up a bond or something?"

"In the morning. Maybe. But it'll be substantial. A judge is not likely to put a lot of trust in a person whose nickname is 'Go'." Fourquet smiled as if he'd made a joke.

"I named him that."

"He says that, too."

Maureen inhaled and looked slowly around the room, taking in every detail. She expected to find the female detective smirking, but she sat stone-faced, staring into Maureen's eyes. Damn, maybe I should have talked with her, tried to warm her up, Maureen realized.

Fourquet said, "So you can leave. Your friend stays here."

"What more could you possibly want to know about him?"

"How he's treated every female client he's ever had. Have there been any complaints? That sort of thing."

"But that'll take days."

"Exactly," Fourquet said. "But we've had two murders, and body strength may have been an important factor in both killings. Your friend's a strong guy, easily capable of strangling Bridget and holding Grace Pettigrew under water."

"He's not unusual. Many cripples—" Maureen caught herself. "Many handicapped people build up their arms and shoulders."

"But none of those others were found with dead bodies in their hands."

"I was there," she said, almost yelling now. "He didn't kill anybody."

Fourquet folded his arms and stared, every muscle in his face saying, Exactly what we'd expect you to say.

Maureen lowered her voice. "What in the world do you think his motive for killing Grace was? Or Bridget?"

"Grace was standing in the way of something Mr. Overman wanted—for Pettigrew to make a huge donation to Providence Place. Someone could have seen him kill Grace and told Bridget about it."

"Someone like who? Who could have seen Grace's death?"

"Luther, for example."

"Luther couldn't have seen the murder from his window."

"Oh?"

Maureen knew she'd screwed up.

"You know something you didn't tell us?" Fourquet said.

"You didn't ask me about it." Briefly Maureen told him about going to Luther's office with Gregory and discovering that palm tree fronds blocked Luther's view of the lagoon.

"So Mr. Overman even took you downstairs to make sure Luther couldn't have seen him?"

"That's not what I said." Maureen looked at the good cop, then back at Fourquet. "If you keep twisting my words, I'll quit talking."

"Who's to say Luther couldn't have gone to another part of the house and seen what happened from there?"

"What does Luther say?"

Fourquet patted his shirt pocket as if looking for a cigar, then saw it in his other hand. "He's not talking."

At that moment Maureen understood. Luther and Kennedy didn't like her attempt to pressure them the night before. Now they were getting their revenge. Both men were withholding information that would help Gregory and her. What had she learned in college physics? A Newtonian law: Every action produces an equal and opposite reaction. Yes. That's what was happening.

"What about Pettigrew? He could have killed Grace and Bridget."

"No motive to kill Bridget," Fourquet said. "And no opportunity to kill his ex-wife."

"Who says?"

"He says." Fourquet turned his back. "And that's good enough for me."

Thirty minutes later Maureen had run out of things to try. She'd threatened, cajoled and pleaded.

Fourquet said, "His attorney can try all that. Now get out of here."

"When and where is Gregory's preliminary hearing?"

"We usually do it by closed circuit television. The judge and the lawyers are in the courthouse, the prisoner stays in jail."

"I want to be with him."

"No way," Fourquet said.

Maureen paused, trying to find the right words. Then she said, "Someday things are going to be different. You're going to want something from me."

"That a threat?"

"No. A prediction."

Chapter Twenty-Eight

Now Maureen stood on the sidewalk outside the police station, wide awake and still angry, cars rushing by on Broward Boulevard, the morning commuting rush already started. She looked at her watch. Almost nine hours since she'd been brought to the station, the first time since college she'd pulled an all-nighter. Fourquet had said an officer would take her back to Gregory's apartment, but she'd said, No-Thank-You-Very-Much-I'd-Rather-Get-Home-On-My-Own.

She started walking east not caring that the Isle of Venice was something like thirty blocks away, a distance she'd managed several times in Manhattan but not in these shoes, the ones she'd worn to the Café de Paris, even if the heels were only moderately high. It was going to be a rough trek. Only now did she remember she hadn't asked Fourquet why, if Gregory was going to be charged, she wasn't charged as an accomplice. Nothing Fourquet had done made sense, but who was she to judge? She didn't know anything about police procedure.

Ten blocks east of the police station, Maureen saw the county bus station. It was after five o'clock, so the buses had started running. Some form of Goodness must be with her. She caught one that took her out Las Olas to the Isle of Venice. The name was beginning to grow on her.

No time to sleep. She showered, fixed herself some toast with the bread Gregory had in his refrigerator, not exactly fresh but edible, found the keys to the rented Mustang and drove to the courthouse. Inside the building was a confusing mess, even more deputies and cops than she seen there during her previous visit, more civilians, too, but finally she found the room where they were conducting preliminary hearings. She sat down and waited.

Drunks, petty thieves, assailants, then a stalker whose ex- had gotten a court order earlier, a possible armed robbery and a disputed rape, everything handled quickly. Shouldn't be long before they called Gregory's case. But after an hour or so they still hadn't called his name. She asked a female deputy who looked like she knew what was going on when they would hear charges against a Gregory Overman. The woman looked through papers on a clipboard and said Gregory's name wasn't on the list. Damn!

Angry again, Maureen drove back to the police station where the traffic on Broward was even heavier than before, every car and truck going more than the speed limit, not giving a damn they were passing the hub of Lauderdale law enforcement. She saw Fourquet walking out of the station toward a lot where civilian cars were parked.

"Your friend's not here," he said when she got close enough to hear him.

"Where is he?"

"I don't know. He didn't want a ride either."

"I just spent two hours at the courthouse. They never did arraign him."

"We released him," Fourquet said.

Maureen stood still, the anger rising again. "Why didn't you phone me?"

"We released him to one of Mr. Pettigrew's attorneys." Fourquet yawned. "He said he would drive your friend to his apartment."

"Why? How?"

"Pettigrew's attorney talked to someone at City Hall who talked to the chief who suggested I didn't have sufficient grounds to charge him."

Pettigrew? Why would he arrange to have Gregory released? What possible motives…. Maureen wanted to ask those questions and more but didn't. Fourquet probably didn't know the answers either.

"I didn't argue," Fourquet said. "I'm not going to be a cop all my life."

A strange remark. Maureen resolved to remember it, maybe process it later, but this wasn't the time.

"Now, I'm going to go home and get some sleep," Fourquet said. "I suggest you do the same." He walked to a red Mazda Miata, got in, and drove away.

Maureen watched him thinking Gregory would be home by now. She caught herself. Not home, not our home. His home, his apartment. He was probably sleeping, but Maureen knew she couldn't. She was too amped up. Just like college, when she finished a test after an all-nighter, she couldn't go to bed, even if it was noon. It took hours to decompress. Back then, she went to a pool and swam laps. Same thing today? No. She had work to do.

Chapter Twenty-Nine

Maureen's anger, barely under control before, exploded as she passed through Pompano Beach, traffic on Ninety-Five a bitch already, only the so-called high-occupancy lane less than bumper to bumper. Bridget. Murdered. Why, of all people, Bridget? Who had she ever hurt? All she wanted was to keep Pettigrew from moving her and her friends away from the beach. Grace's plan might have been crazy, but could a sixteen-year-old know that? Surely not a sin punishable by death. Damn them. Damn them all. Pettigrew, Fourquet, Kennedy, Luther, everyone who was responsible. Even Gregory.

Her self-righteousness began to fade in Boca Raton, and by the time she got to Delray Beach it turned inward. Maybe she was to blame. Maybe she should have spent more time with Bridget. Maybe she should have done a lot of things differently. Just like her screwed up relationship with Gregory. Go had every reason to stand back after what she did to him in high school. But she'd done it for his own good. At least she thought so then. Now she wondered if anyone ever did anything totally for someone's else's benefit?

Maureen knew she couldn't change the past, but her mind insisted on replaying the scene over and over—what she'd said, what Gregory said, what…and on and on. More than twenty years ago. No, twenty-five. After all these thousands of days, the words in her memory couldn't be exact. But they were close enough. She still thought she'd been right. Most days.

After Go recovered from polio and entered grammar school, Maureen was ready for middle school so they rode on different buses and spent most of the day apart. But every afternoon when she got home, he was waiting on the front steps of her home. She'd invite him in, and they'd talk and study together. It was fun, exactly as it had been at his house. More than that, Maureen felt warm and good when he was around, an inner glow she had no desire to analyze. Eventually, though, she realized she might be doing him harm. Go wasn't spending any time with anybody else. And neither was she.

Maureen started rationing the hours she spent with Gregory and told him he had to start being with other kids, too. He agreed, but only in principle. He never had any of his classmates over to his house, never went to theirs. And often, when she got home late, she saw him looking out his front window toward her house.

So one afternoon Maureen told him, "Go, I can't see you anymore. You've got to get some new friends."

Even now she could see the shock on his face. "No," he yelled, "you're the only friend I ever want."

"You need male friends," she said, "and you need to meet other girls."

Gregory argued, he protested, he even looked as if he were about to cry, but nothing would change her mind. He ran from her then, and years later he told her about the pain he'd felt, the torment excruciating. He couldn't read, couldn't write, couldn't do anything. Every cell of his body yelled out that he wanted to die. Life wasn't worth living without her.

So one day Gregory skipped his school and went over to hers, the high school. He planned to ambush her during lunch break, he confided long afterward, but a teacher saw him wandering around the halls and told him to go back where he belonged. He left the building but hid in a parking lot where he could see the front entrance.

Hours later Maureen came out, a boy on either side of her, three or four others trailing behind, all of them laughing, kidding around. She saw Go immediately but decided to pretend she didn't. Without thinking she put her hand on the shoulder of one of the guys.

Gregory came at them, running faster than she'd ever seen him move.

"I told you to stay away," she said, the first thing that came to her mind.

"Leave her alone," shouted the tall guy on her right. "You heard her," said the plump guy on the other side. "Get lost!" one of the others yelled.

Maureen wanted to reach out to Go then, maybe even hug him, but she knew she couldn't. If he was to make friends of his own, they'd have to separate. "Please leave," she said. Gregory stood there, numb and speechless. "Please!" she shouted.

Finally he turned away.

Variations of the same scene played out during the next few weeks, the details different but the result always the same. Eventually Gregory learned his lesson. If he wanted to avoid pain he needed to stay away from her. So he did.

Later, out of loneliness if nothing else, he began hanging out with kids his age. Some of the guys tried to teach him football and basketball, but with his legs like they were, he was too slow and clumsy. Try softball, someone said, and he wasn't bad at that as long as he played catcher. At first someone ran the bases for him, but later he insisted on running them himself, the extra distance of his hits compensating for lack of speed. Already he'd begun to work out.

A girl developed a crush on Gregory, gimpy leg and all. Soon he became interested in other girls, too. His life went on, as did Maureen's. She heard about his activities from a discreet distance, mutual friends filling her in, happy that her gamble had paid off.

Years later, when Mo returned from college during her freshman year, she made a point of seeking him out at the high school, beginning from the same spot in the parking lot where he'd hid before. He was in a group, another guy and a couple of girls, walking and talking.

"Go," Maureen shouted. He saw her, turned away, took a step, then stopped. She walked to him. "It's time for our separation to end," she said when he turned around. His face betrayed so many feelings she could read only half of them. Anger. Puzzlement. Delight. He didn't say a thing, didn't even say goodbye to his buddies, just walked with Mo to her car. She drove them to a diner (maybe that's why he liked diners so much, even now) and over hamburgers and fries they had their reconciliation.

Reconciliation? No, that wasn't the right word, Maureen thought later. To reconcile, two people must be separated, and although they were physically apart he'd never been far from her thoughts. Nor, Gregory confessed at that diner, she from his.

"I did it for your own good," she said. "Can you see that now?"

Go didn't answer for the longest while. Then he said, "But it's over, isn't it?"

Mo reached across the table and squeezed his hand. "Sure it is."

And that was that. But they were never as close as before. And except for a few years later when Gregory's parents were in London, they saw each other only on weekends and even then not on weekend nights she had a date, and especially not the times she stayed overnight at a date's apartment. He'd never told her how he felt about those nights, and she'd never asked him.

Now, more than two decades later, Maureen realized she and Go hadn't really put this high school history behind them. He was being standoffish and aloof, a little boy who'd had his fingers burned and wasn't going to get close to the heat again. Twice since she'd come to Lauderdale, they'd been physically close. Twice he'd pulled back. Was there anyway to bust through that barrier?

There wasn't time to figure it out now. The West Palm exit was just ahead.

Chapter Thirty

The Palm Beach County Courthouse matched Maureen's mood. Gray. The ceilings gray. The carpeting a gray-brown. The desktops and counters a black and gray laminate, the computer terminals in light gray cases. Architects for the Palm Beach County Courthouse must have been told: No colors. No bright colors, no muted colors, no color at all. Even the marble floor and walls of the hallways were black and white.

At least there's some clarity with black and white, Maureen thought as she sat down in front of one of the black-on-gray monitor screens in the public records room. She didn't want any more ambiguity about Pettigrew; she wanted something solid, something she could hang the man with.

Her mood hadn't been helped when a clerk told her most of the information filed with the county could be accessed through home computers, knowledge that might have saved her this trip. She'd been impetuous, not checking the web first. But now that she was here, she'd see what was available

Warming up, Maureen punched commands into the keyboard, learning the system. Not bad. Damn good in fact, a computer index that catalogued all public records back to 1909 when the county was founded. Criminal, civil, real estate, and other records all on the same system, even old handwritten entries converted to digital data—so much better than the system in Broward County. One flaw, though. If she wanted images of documents filed before 1990, she'd have to use one of the microfilm readers that lined the office walls. Maureen hated the things.

She set to work. It took a bit of experimenting—learning she had to key in TRUSTREGINALD with no comma in between the words, for example—but she soon found seven indexed entries for the Reginald Pettigrew Trust, each filed five years apart starting in 1972. She pulled up images of the 1992 report. Short, only five pages, the first page declaring the document was filed in accordance with a Florida statue, which it named, and a court ruling (it listed the style of the case) that required the trust to make a public accounting of its stewardship every five years.

Wow! she thought. What a great deal for Pettigrew. He and the other trustees controlled almost two billion dollars but had to reveal the Trust's holdings only twice a decade. Assuming the other trustees were rubber stamps, a probability, Pettigrew could do almost anything with the money between reports, then clean things up just before filings. The possibilities for self-dealing were boundless.

Maureen felt excitement welling up inside, the thrill starting in her gut and spreading to the tips of her arms and legs, then rising to her brain. She was onto something big. Pettigrew loaning Trust money to himself or his friends was only one possibility. He could use Trust money to fund his start-up companies. He could buy stock just before the Trust purchased it. Maybe he pledged the Trust's securities as collateral for loans to his companies. And insider trading? She was sure he'd done it.

But who would catch him? Who would think of checking? The Securities and Exchange Commission regulated corporations and markets. The Internal Revenue Service collected taxes, auditing only for compliance with revenue laws. And the Florida Circuit Court's function seemed limited to receiving reports. Any illegality by Pettigrew would fall through the cracks.

Maureen clicked the next image onto the screen. It contained a list of stock and bond holdings, their value itemized in the right-hand column. Nothing unusual, the companies good, solid names, neither particularly risky nor conservative, their total worth in 1992 just above a billion dollars. She marked the pages to get photocopies later and went to the next report. The Trust had grown to more than two billion since then, a superficially impressive performance. But was it really? She didn't think so. The Trust's worth might not have even kept up with market averages for the go-go period. She'd do the math later, but she knew there were many ten-year periods when any portfolio that didn't triple or quadruple was being poorly managed.

Maureen stretched her arms high, then rolled her neck, trying to ease the tightness in her shoulders. She knew fatigue would set in soon. In college when she reached this point after an all-nighter, she'd go to bed and sleep. But not today. She couldn't stop until she'd looked at the microfilm, at the material not available on the web.

She found the blue microfilm cartridges for 1972 and stuck one into a reader, fortunately one powered by electricity, not the old-fashioned kind where she'd have to turn a crank. Images blurred as she ran the film through the machine and stopped at the page listed in the index.

The Trust's first report, filed a year after the elder Pettigrew died, was short, only four pages, all that was needed to show the dozen or so stocks the old man held at his death. General Motors, Ford, General Electric, Dupont, the old Standard of New Jersey, IBM, AT&T, and half a dozen other Blue Chips. Who could have guessed then that some of them, A&T for example, would fall on hard times, supplanted as market favorites by Microsoft, Intel, Dell, and the like? Still, the old warhorses were worth several hundred million dollars when the report was filed, a spectacular amount of money in the nineteen seventies, and still impressive today to anyone but billionaires. The report was signed by Sara Pettigrew, the woman Luther said had become a merry widow; a bank official whose name didn't matter, and someone named Fitzgerald, probably some friend of Sara's, maybe one of her boating pals.

Now to see how well they managed the Trust's wealth. Maureen switched microfilm rolls and reeled to the Trust's second report. The Trust had sold all of old man's Pettigrew's holdings and invested the money in equities of more speculative companies. Its value had grown, but not by much, maybe not anyone's fault, the market such a treacherous beast in the seventies.

The signatures at the bottom had changed from the original report. Sara Pettigrew was gone. So was the bank officer; a different bank had taken over and a different man represented it. And Fitzgerald had been replaced by Roland Pettigrew. He'd moved in quickly.

Maureen yawned. God, she was tired. She thought about quitting. Surely the other reports wouldn't tell her much more. She could be in Lauderdale and in bed in a hour. No. She'd come this far. She'd finish.

The reports filed in the eighties showed an enlarged stock portfolio, one that grew steadily more valuable, and greater diversification of stock holdings, standard practice for big money managers. Maureen went through the list looking for companies Pettigrew had been involved in. She didn't see any she recognized offhand, but she was dealing with corporations in existence a long time ago. She'd check them later. Again, she marked pages for photocopying.

Maureen reached the signature page of the 1987 report, the last one she needed from microfilm. The trustees hadn't changed, and she hadn't expected them to. Once Pettigrew installed a friendly bank and a pliable second trustee, he wouldn't need to change anything. Her hand moved forward to the rewind knob, but before it got there she felt a pain in her neck. Something stuck in her mind. A fuzzy vision. What? From when? Another page from an earlier report.

Rushing now, the haste backfiring and slowing her down, she found the signature page of the first report. Just what she thought. Fitzgerald's signature was almost the same as Roland Pettigrew's, the same first name, too, the big R in the front, a bold beginning shrinking to tiny letters at the end. She wasn't a handwriting expert, but she was sure the same person wrote both names. Later she could get a professional to confirm her impression.

Why? That was a more important question now. Why did the same man use two different names to sign the documents. Was one of the signatures fraudulent? The situation would make sense only if…. He couldn't have. Could he?

Heart beating almost as fast as her brain was racing, Maureen pushed herself away from the microfilm and rushed to a computer terminal. She keyed in FITZGERALD ROLAND. Only two entries, a petition and a court order. She copied the page numbers and went back to the microfilm. Insert, scan— There it was. *Fitzgerald --Petition to Change Name.*

Now to the order. *Petition granted to change name from Roland Fitzgerald to Roland Pettigrew.*

The scoundrel. He changed his name. The scoundrel changed his name. Maureen's mind kept repeating the phrases. And I caught him. I caught him. The fatigue vanished. She'd found the Rosetta Stone of the puzzle.

Luther hadn't told her about the name change. He'd lied to her. He'd told her Roland was Reginald and Sara's son, Maureen thought. But again an ache in her neck signaled to her. Had Luther really said Sara was Roland's mother? She dredged deep into her memory and remembered exactly what he said. *Sara Fitzgerald must have been the Lolita of her time. When Reginald first met her she was fifteen or sixteen. He was visiting the Eastern Shore of Maryland on a hunting trip. She lived there with her little brother. Dirt poor, but she must have been something to see.*

Her little brother. Yes. That's what Luther had said. Maureen had missed it because she focused on what he'd said later. *After he divorced his second wife he married Sara, sold all his companies and moved to Palm Beach. He bought her a mansion, one of the biggest on the island. They lived there, just the two of them and their servants, and eventually little Roland.*

She'd jumped to the conclusion Roland was their son, not Sara's brother. Luther had been misleading, maybe, but he hadn't lied, not about this anyway. Even what Roland Pettigrew said about himself, the story he told Maureen first and later repeated to Bridget made sense now. Pettigrew had said, *Did you know I grew up poor?* Lonely, she understood at the time, Sara and Reginald ignoring him. But he and Sara were poor before Reginald Pettigrew came along, and afterward was worse. Sara and Reginald were cruel to him. Little Fritz was a nuisance, the little brother Sara had to take care of but resented and Reginald felt obliged to support. Now Maureen believed the story about Sara and Reginald treating Roland so vilely on their boat. *I saw Sara and the others in the cabin, looking through the windshield. They were laughing at me. Sara more than any of the others.* It all made sense.

And Bridget had been right. She said Pettigrew talked about his sister. *He told me about how he grew up in a big house in Palm Beach. He said his sister had married an old man and they didn't have any time for him. He said they were mean to him.* Not his sister, Maureen said then, his mother. *Whatever. But he told me sister.*

Bells had gone off in Maureen's head then, but she had more pressing questions to consider. Damn. Both Luther and Pettigrew had toyed with her, telling her the truth but knowing she wouldn't understand it. The fault was hers, though. She'd made some bonehead assumptions. It didn't help that many people made the same mistakes. All the stock analysts, all those hotshot business reporters who wrote so much about Pettigrew and his companies, all the attorneys who'd vetted the stock offerings, none of them had ever unearthed this truth.

Enough, Maureen told herself. She'd found the truth now. She'd discovered it using nothing but old-fashioned patience and persistence She felt like running around the room like a happy puppy, rolling around on the floor, jumping over the counter, and congratulating the Clerk's wonderful employees for their fine record-keeping. What kind of a man would take the name of his brother-in-law and let the world think he was his son and heir? Surely not a man to be trusted.

She could hardly wait until she got back to Lauderdale and told Gregory what she'd found. This would convince him, if anything would. Roland Pettigrew was a fake, an imposter, a charlatan—exactly what her instincts told her from the beginning.

Chapter Thirty-One

Go stood above her, his image blurry and distorted. Where was she? Go's bedroom. How did she get there? Maureen remembered driving on I-95, passing through Boca and.... Nothing after that. But she must have made it to Lauderdale. She closed her eyes again.

"You've been out for at least ten hours," Gregory said.

"How? When?"

"When I got back, I found you on the living room floor. Your vital signs were OK so I carried you in here."

Now she remembered. Fading in and out of consciousness on the highway, finally pulling off at Broward Boulevard and making her way to Las Olas. Thank God, thank Goodness, thank her angels, thank whatever.

She went back to sleep without asking why it was dark outside.

When Maureen woke again, she could see faint light in the window, edges of clouds turning pink, the dawn so quiet she could hardly hear Gregory's heavy breathing in the other room. The digital clock beside the bed read 5:16. She'd slept at least fourteen hours, probably more. One all-nighter deserves another. Of sleep.

She let herself lay there until she heard wild parrots squawking somewhere out the window. Gradually the events and discoveries of the day before came back to her, especially the revelation that Pettigrew had changed his name and kept the switch a secret for so many years. Now to figure out how to use the information. She eased out of bed a few inches at a time, every movement a challenge, flesh and bones still tired, not like the quick rejuvenation she'd experienced in college. With effort, she took a shower and dressed, clean underwear but the same jeans she'd almost lived in since Saturday.

By then she had a plan. She packed her other clothes in the suitcase and maneuvered her way through the living room, careful not to wake Gregory, opened the refrigerator, poured and drank a glass of milk, then a second. No time to eat anything. She had work to do.

Suitcase in hand, Maureen once again walked to the beach, but this time when she got to the Swimming Hall of Fame complex she kept going until she reached Pettigrew's hotel. Correct that, said the editor in her brain. Make it the hotel Pettigrew stayed at, the new one right next to the Radisson Bahia Mar. Maybe he did own it. Or the Trust. So much to find out.

Minutes later, Maureen walked though glass doors into the hotel lobby. Huge and ornate, exactly what she'd expect from a five-star hotel, but something was amiss. What? Big glass chandeliers hung from the ceiling above a huge expanse of beige marble speckled with insets of dark coral and jade shaped like diamonds. Fancy enough. Nothing wrong, either, with the black and tan leather furniture sitting around the glass-topped tables, their marble bases resting on rugs that repeated the accent colors.

The scene should have looked stunning, but someone had crisscrossed the floor with black rubber runners everywhere people might walk when they came in from the beach wearing wet bathing suits. Architects and interior designers must have been told to replicate the Taj Mahal, then lawyers came along and said, "Hey, somebody could fall down and sue." So the lobby looked junky.

Maureen walked to the desk clerk, explained she'd had a reservation a day or so before but was delayed and hoped she could still get a room. The guy pushed buttons on a keyboard and said her reservation had expired but he had another room available. She was lucky, he said, they were filling up quickly.

"Kennedy around?" she asked.

"Who?"

"Mr. Pettigrew's chauffeur."

The clerk's attitude changed. He studied Maureen now, looking at her as if she might be somebody important. Or a threat. "He's around here someplace."

"If I leave a message, will you make sure either he or Roland Pettigrew gets it?"

The clerk shook his head. "Strict instructions. Everything regarding Mr. Pettigrew must be taken to his office."

Maureen shrugged and took the elevator up to her room, her eyes scanning the lobby through the round glass cage, memorizing locations of stairs and the hallway to the parking garage. Before she got off, she had a plan and knew how to carry it out.

Inside her room, Maureen wrote on a hotel letterhead, glad that at least this hotel hadn't dropped the tradition of stashing stationery in room desks. For an instant she wished she could write the message in red ink, then concluded it would be dramatic enough in plain black. She sealed the sheet of paper in an envelope and wrote one word on the outside. "Pettigrew." Would he understand the significance of the quotation marks? Maybe, but probably not.

Maureen left her room, walked down the hotel's stairwell to the lobby, and crossed into the hallway leading to the parking garage. She was almost certain the desk clerk hadn't seen her, his view blocked by an expanse of foliage near the elevators. She saw Pettigrew's Mercedes parked in a reserved spot less than twenty feet away, the closest space to the lobby entrance. He must be upstairs in his suite. Kennedy wasn't in sight.

For an instant, Maureen wished she had some red lipstick with her. She wanted to scrawl a message across the windshield. *Killer! Or You Killed Them!* Yes, them. She knew in her gut that Pettigrew had killed both Grace and Bridget, even if she didn't know exactly why. She looked around the garage to make sure no one was watching, put the envelope under the car's windshield wiper, and walked away, confident her message would scare the bastard into making a mistake.

Your name isn't Pettigrew.
You are not a real Pettigrew.
How will the market react to the news?

At the bottom she'd written her room number, nothing else. Your move, you son-of-a-bitch, she thought. Any other time news of your name change would be considered ancient history. But coming after two deaths springing from a party you gave, the market will react with shock now. The stratospheric price-earnings ratios of your stock will tumble. If you're deeply margined, your shares will be sold. You could go broke.

Pettigrew would grasp all that in an instant. Now all she had to do was wait.

Back in her room, Maureen ordered breakfast from room service and asked if they could bring up copies of the *Wall Street Journal*, the *Times*, and the *Miami Herald*. They could. Waiting, she read the free copy of *USA Today* she found outside the door, settling down to digest the first business and market news she'd seen in days. With everything that had happened, she'd been ignoring both the market and her own portfolio, always dangerous. Time to catch up.

She'd been right about Qualflex. It was in freefall. If Rebecca had followed her partners instructions, they'd missed an enormous profit by covering her short. Monday's rise had been a dead cat bounce.

The rest of the market seemed strong enough, having more than recovered from Friday's downdraft. Charts of major indexes continued to move sideways, but that didn't mean anything. The market churns along in an almost a flat line at both bottoms and tops, building bases or topping off, something most pros forgot at the top of The Bubble. She hadn't.

Was the market now in the midst of Irrational Exuberance II? The touts were saying last Friday's sell-off was just a pause in the action, but Maureen wasn't so sure. She wished she'd brought her notebook computer to Lauderdale. Sometimes a chart is worth a thousand words and figures. She usually traveled with a laptop, but this time she'd thought she'd be away only for the weekend.

Or had she been fooling herself? If Go had asked her, she might have stayed for weeks, murder or no murder. If….

A knock on the door. Good. She didn't want to go down that road again. Maybe later she'd use a computer at the hotel's business center off the lobby. She opened the door and a waiter rolled in a cart with her breakfast. Poached eggs again, but this time she allowed herself some bacon.

Now to the *Journal* and the *Times*. All the lessons that should have been learned in the aftermath of The Bubble boiled down to one. The market doesn't go up forever, and anyone who thought it did lost money. But people kept doing the same things, over and over. Maureen felt something touch the back of her neck, a reminder she was sure, that she repeated mistakes, too. OK, OK, she vowed. This time when I confront Pettigrew, I won't make the same mistake again. I'll listen, not accuse.

She went back to market statistics in the *Journal*. Not a cloud in sight, in the United States at least. But something overseas was worrisome. The LIBOR—The London Interbank Offered Rate— was inching upward. When this international trading market for dollars went up, could U.S. rates be far behind, taking the stock market down? Thinking about these things was such a relief, almost a vacation. So much easier than dealing with Pettigrew. And Gregory.

The phone call came about an hour later, again from the man who described himself as Pettigrew's administrative assistant.

"Mr. Pettigrew would appreciate the pleasure of your company for lunch."

"On his boat?"

"In his dining room at our offices. Would twelve thirty be convenient?"

Chapter Thirty-Two

Maureen had eaten in executive dining rooms in New York, Chicago, and San Francisco, but she'd never seen one as self-indulgent as Pettigrew's. A large room, maybe forty by forty, furnished with heavy Edwardian furniture. Not the usual heavy dark woods though, these pieces made of pecan, oak, and ash more fitting to Florida. Massive china chests and green leather sofas lined the walls, but only three tables sat in the middle— small, medium, and large, settings for two, four or fourteen. Three computer monitors glowed in a corner. The aroma of oranges hung in the air.

Dressed in the same black suit she'd worn at the office Friday but wearing dress shoes and a different blouse, Maureen felt comfortable. She'd taken a taxi to the building to look her confident best. Pettigrew motioned her to the smallest of the tables, the one next to a window. No one will sit at the others, she figured. Pettigrew was a man who demanded privacy. And control.

"That's Port Everglades." He pointed out the window. "Over there is the airport."

Maureen knew the etiquette of dining rooms like this. Postpone business talk until after they ordered food. But Pettigrew went on forever, talking about new construction at the airport, the convention center near Seventeenth Street, cruise ships at Port Everglades.

Finally a waiter presented a little menu, the choices prime rib, broiled snapper or steamed chicken in some fancy sauce. Pettigrew ordered the beef, Maureen said she'd try the fish and didn't care which vegetables went with it. By the time the waiter left, her patience had drained to zero. She locked on Pettigrew's eyes.

"You've been deceiving people."

He didn't blink. "Not that I'm aware of."

"You changed your name."

"Oh, everybody knows that."

Maureen hadn't expected this response, but when Pettigrew said it she knew she was on solid ground. More than one corporate executive had tried to belittle her findings by saying they were common knowledge.

"Not everybody," she said. "Certainly not the people who've written stories about you."

"Perhaps," Pettigrew said. "But they don't matter."

"Reputations matter. You know that."

"It's old news. I had good and sufficient reasons to change."

The waiter entered with salads. Maureen took a deep breath, Gregory's trick. She'd violated her resolution. She'd led with an accusation. Now what? She looked out the window. A white cruise ship plowed toward the Atlantic, smaller boats darting around it. Heavy cranes unloaded cargo carriers at the docks. An older Southwest Airlines' 737, mustard and orange in the sunlight, flew over gasoline storage tanks. OK, she told herself. There's nothing to do now but plunge ahead.

"How do you think The Street will take the news that you've been living under what amounts to a false identity all these years?" she asked Pettigrew when the waiter left.

"The Street cares about results, not names."

"Unless the name is fraudulent."

"It's not fraudulent," Pettigrew said. "It's my name."

"But it covers a fraud. People think you're Reginald Pettigrew's son. You aren't."

"Everybody close to the situation knows about the name change. You can ask Luther."

"Interesting choice of a confidant."

Pettigrew waited.

Should she go for it? Yes, but cautiously, testing the water. Maureen said, "Until recently I was convinced Luther was Kennedy's father."

Pettigrew jerked his hand to his mustache.

A flinch? Merely a harrumph? Hard to tell.

He switched to his no-caret smile "A most interesting but radically wrong theory."

"How do you know its wrong?"

Again Pettigrew flashed the smile, and this time Maureen knew how to read it. He was deciding how to respond, which of two or more paths to take. He made his choice.

"I would know," he said. "They've both been with me for some time."

"Just as people would know you've changed your name?"

"Feel free to tell that to anyone you want. In fact, this is an excellent time for that information to come out."

"Why?"

"Because you're the source. You, someone whose best friend is suspected of killing two women. You, a person who may have witnessed both killings."

Damn, Maureen thought. She hadn't anticipated this response, either.

"You'd be ridiculed," Pettigrew said. "Everybody would see your 'revelation' as an attempt to draw attention away from the plight of your boyfriend."

"Not so," Maureen said. That wouldn't be her motive. And Go wasn't her boyfriend. But Pettigrew might have a point. Maybe no one would take her seriously. She tried another approach. "Maybe the information could come out some other way. From a third party, someone not connected with any of this."

"If that happened, I'd merely explain the business reasons for the name change."

The waiter returned, placed plates before them, and refilled their glasses. Pettigrew waved him away.

"What 'business' reason?" Maureen said.

"When Reginald Pettigrew died, Sara didn't know what to do and she turned to me."

"You and your sister weren't friendly. You told me about the incident on the boat."

"That all changed when the old man died." Pettigrew cut into his prime rib. "The will named me and Sara and a bank as trustees of the trust it created. She didn't understand any of it and didn't want to be bothered, but I'd just come home with my Harvard MBA."

Luther had said Sara liked to party. But with the age difference, wouldn't the young bride have learned something about her husband's affairs? She must have known....

"The old man's lawyers thought we'd be rubber stamps," Pettigrew said. "That was a big mistake. They treated us like children. Or, as Sara said, like dirt."

Maureen nodded, all the while wondering if she could believe a word of it.

"Eventually Sara started drinking heavily, but before she did, she asked me to get the lawyers out of her life. I went to Miami—" Pettigrew looked out the window to the south. "—and found some lawyers who would be absolutely delighted to show us both considerable respect. So we switched law firms."

Pettigrew looked up, trying to see if she'd bought his story so far. Maureen didn't show him anything.

"The Palm Beach bank named in the old man's will objected to the change in lawyers, but we outvoted them. Then the new lawyers recommended we switch banks to the old First National in Miami. I wouldn't go along until they agreed I would have to approve all investment decisions."

"You didn't need to change your name for that."

"Just wait. As soon as we switched lawyers and banks, I started going to Miami almost every other day. I couldn't move there, because I needed to watch Sara."

"And get her signature on papers."

"Of course. I moved to Fort Lauderdale so I could be between Miami and Palm Beach." Pettigrew put a napkin to his mouth. "Not long afterward I realized I needed to change my name."

"I don't see why."

"The Miami bank treated me well. But I soon learned that if I wanted to be taken seriously on Wall Street, I needed more clout. Changing my name to Pettigrew gave me instant name recognition."

Maureen ran Pettigrew's story through her mind to see if it held together. It did, in a sick MBA-way. Often when one company buys another, it's buying brand names as much as anything else. In taking his brother-in-law's name, Pettigrew got himself an established brand name. Maureen might have recommended something similar to a client. She decided to ask Gregory what he thought of Pettigrew's explanation. Then it occurred to her that she could do something for Go. Now. Here.

"OK," she said.

Pettigrew frowned. "OK, what?"

"I'll trade."

"Trade what?"

"I won't tell the Street what I've found, not today anyway, if you won't hold up your contribution to Providence Place."

Pettigrew smiled broadly, the first genuine smile she had seen on him since they'd met. "You drive a tough bargain."

"It's not much to ask. These deaths have nothing to do with the kids there."

Pettigrew put his hand forward. "A deal."

The instant he stuck the hand out, Maureen knew something was wrong. But she took it, his shake more enthusiastic than hers.

"Already done," Pettigrew said. "I signed an agreement with the nuns this morning. The first installment will be wired to their bank this afternoon."

Maureen dropped his hand. Damn. She'd traded something for nothing. Some days you do your best, but nothing works.

Chapter Thirty-Three

S o Midas Man won again," Maureen told Gregory as they sat in his living room that night, each with a bowl of Ben & Jerry's Chocolate Chip Cookie Dough. Maureen planned to return to her hotel room later, but now she wanted to be near her pal. She'd given him an almost verbatim account of how she discovered Pettigrew's name change and then confronted the man.

Go listened in silence, nodding his head from time to time. When Maureen finished, she expected questions or criticism or something, but he didn't say a word. They sat in silence for minutes. Then Maureen surprised herself, saying something she hadn't planned.

"I get so tired of doing all this alone."

Gregory looked from across the room. "You don't have to, you know."

"But there's no one—"

"I'm available," he said.

Maureen pulled back, the words sounding strange, almost frightening.

"You're working alone by choice," Go said. "You went off to the Broward Courthouse by yourself. You decided to phone Melody and the State Health Department on your own. You drove up to West Palm by yourself. Then you confronted Pettigrew alone."

"But that's the way I always work."

"You don't have to this time. We're in this together."

"But you—"

"I don't have anything to do that's more important than helping you."

Maureen stared at Go, waiting. Next would come the qualification. Or a retraction. Or the cost. Ever since she was a kid, when her mother and father finally bought her the bicycle she wanted, she'd known to be on guard when she started feeling good. They even put on a birthday party, inviting all the neighborhood kids, and Maureen felt like the most important person in the world. The euphoria lasted until that night, when her parents told her they'd be leaving the country for a couple of years, but she'd stay behind in someone's care.

Gregory said, "You keep treating me like the kid next door with polio. Someone who has to be taken care of."

Yes. But he did need—

"I've been a big boy for some time."

But not then. Not then.

"Until you came down here, I didn't realize you'd become such a loner."

True, Maureen had to concede. Her occupations—newspaper reporting and stock trading—were among the most competitive in the country, and she'd let the trait spill over into her personal life. Or maybe she'd never been a team player. There were people on Wall Street who spent the whole day on the phone, exchanging gossip and rumors. But not her. She was proud to be a maverick, no matter how much it might cost in personal friendships. Her reputation as a lone wolf made her recommendations more valuable. But....

"So now," Go said. "Why don't you let me help you?"

Maureen felt confused, and as always when she felt that way she didn't say anything for a while. Could she risk it? When the answer finally came, she didn't waste words.

"OK."

Gregory got up from the shell-shaped chair and sat on the sofa beside her, not saying anything. She looked at him, wondering. He picked up her right hand with his left, then put both hands around hers. She moved closer, not conscious of what she was doing.

More minutes passed. Or so it seemed. Finally, Maureen said, "Do I have to tell you to kiss me?"

It was a gentle kiss, hesitant and experimental, one that didn't last long. She put her head on his shoulder.

"Go, I've missed you."

"I've always been here."

They kissed again, mouths warm and eager this time, lips expressing things they'd never been able to say, minds shutting down. Maureen felt Gregory's tongue on her neck and pulled his hand to her breast, the thought coming to her that this may be their last chance—ever—and she wasn't going to lose it.

"Let me do this," Maureen said, and from then on she took the lead, unfastening her bra, feeling his mouth on each breast, his tongue circling her nipples, then kissing her body lower, pulling his pants off, her mouth on him, eventually her body on top, bending to put him inside, hands on his chest, pushing him higher, leaning back, then forward, taking her time, riding, riding, on and on, letting it happen. "Now switch," she said, pulling him on top, pushing up to meet him, her hands on his shoulders, arching up to him, their bodies melding, rhythm matching, and finally, finally, the sweet release.

Together now. At last.

Chapter Thirty-Four

In the morning they made love again, and afterward Maureen said, "Why did it take us so long?"

Gregory said, "We weren't ready."

"What does that mean?"

"Time takes time," he said. "There's no substitute for it."

She picked up a pillow and hit him on the head. "Don't tease me with those rehab slogans."

"If you don't believe me, go out and try to buy some time."

Maureen was already out of bed now, looking in Go's closet for a robe, something she hadn't done when she slept in the room alone.

"On the far right," he said. "See if you like the one with green and white stripes."

"Do you have any decent food in this place?"

"Ice cream. Cashews. Cream soda. What more could you want?"

"Breakfast food," Maureen said, knowing he understood what she was talking about from the beginning.

"Toast and jelly."

"I saw those."

"Isn't that enough?"

She headed toward the kitchen feeling good. Already things were different between them, easier, as if they'd been living together forever.

After Maureen fixed the toast and yelled for Gregory to come get it, she watched him limp across the room in shorts, the first time in years she'd seen his twisted leg. She didn't care about the leg, but she knew he did, that he must think about it every day. Their new closeness gave her courage to bring it up again.

"I still blame your mother for what happened."

"Nobody's perfect," he said.

"But some are better than others."

"Depends on the category."

What categories? Decency? Honesty? Taking good care of your children? The questions came to her, but she told herself to be cautious. She knew his story by heart—the story which had became part of her story, too.

Both their fathers, hers and Gregory's, had been in the U.S. Foreign Service, which requires its officers to work two to four years overseas, two to four years in the States, again rotate to another country, then come back home, then leave again, over and over until they finally retire or leave the service. This nomadic life is rough on parents—alcoholism, adultery, and emotional collapse are common—and children pay a bigger price. Maureen and Gregory had been hauled overseas periodically, gone to different military or foreign schools every few years, hung around too many embassy parties, and, like their parents, relied on embassy, military, or foreign physicians for medical care.

When Gregory's mother became pregnant, she and his father were stationed in Saudi Arabia. Instead of going back to Washington immediately, she decided to stay in Riyadh for most of her term and fly to a military base in Germany to give birth. All went well except for one thing. The military doctors at Landstuhl thought the embassy physician would give Gregory all necessary inoculations and vaccinations. The embassy doctor, neither an obstetrician nor pediatrician, assumed those routines had been taken care of in Germany. Gregory's mother was supposed to remind the doctor but didn't. Later she said her to-do list got lost.

It'd been terrible timing, perhaps the worst possible point in medical science for something like that to happen. Albert Sabin had perfected his oral vaccine for polio, but it wasn't widely available throughout the world so either the military doctors or the embassy physician should have given Gregory the Salk vaccine. The oversight wasn't found until Gregory's parents were transferred back to the states, and by then he'd already been infected with the polio virus.

Now, sitting at the kitchen counter in his apartment, Maureen said, "One bad assumption, and your whole life was screwed up."

"Skewed is a better word," Gregory said. "I made peace with it long ago,"

"But don't you—"

"I could have an operation to fix my leg, but the limp is so much a part of me that I don't want to."

"But the ghost—" Maureen started, then stopped, sorry she'd raised the subject.

"Go ahead and say it. Post-polio syndrome. PPS as it's so inelegantly called. Only one chance in five I'll get it, and I consider those pretty good odds."

"All because of one bonehead assumption by your mother."

Gregory looked at her. "Not like your bonehead assumptions."

Maureen felt the sting. "Like what?"

"Like assuming that Pettigrew was Reginald and Sara's son. Or assuming that the Trust reports were in Fort Lauderdale."

"I've done everything I could." Maureen didn't like the sound of her voice. Too sharp. Too defensive.

Gregory said, "Have you checked the clips?"

Damn, she hadn't.

"When you worked at newspapers, you were always talking about looking at clips."

Maureen thought about it. "You're right. I'll do it now."

"Not without me," Go said. "Remember, you don't have to do everything alone."

Could that be true? she wondered.

Chapter Thirty-Five

They rode north on Interstate 95, Gregory at the wheel this time, Maureen in the passenger seat, Mo saying, "The main Palm Beach County library has the *Palm Beach Post* on microfilm all the way back to 1916. That's what the woman who answered the phone said."

"Why not go directly to the newspaper office?"

"I phoned them. They won't let outsiders use their morgue." She didn't like having to explain herself. It felt weird. "Besides, I wouldn't want to risk someone there seeing what we were doing."

They rode in silence then, Mo glad for a chance to think, her mind turning cartwheels, alternately wondering about this new relationship with Go and kicking herself for forgetting to check clips on Pettigrew.

Are they still called clips? she wondered. Probably not a major newspaper in the country cuts out stories and files them in envelopes anymore, everything digital these days, the original keystrokes of reporters preserved on computer discs. But when she worked at newspapers, editors still asked, "Have you checked the clips?" Old news brings perspective to the new. How could she have forgotten?

More important, Why hadn't she and Go hooked up earlier? Why hadn't she forced the issue? His almost avoiding any physical contact with her all these years, ever since she'd rebuffed him so long ago. Wasted years. Too damn many distractions. Earning a living and all. Same excuse about the clips. Too damn many distractions, the murders and all. What a ridiculous comparison.

"What are you laughing about?" Go said.

"Nothing. Nothing really."

"When people say 'nothing' there's usually a lot going on in their heads."

She reached over and put her hand on his shoulder. "The next exit is Forest Hill Boulevard. We drive west to South Congress, then make a right on Summit."

"Not a very graceful way to change the subject...."

"I want to say so much, but I don't want to say anything."

"OK," he said. "Maybe later."

The Palm Beach County Library turned out to be a large, single-story structure that looked as much like an airport passenger terminal as a book center—a wide glass front, polished marble floors, and big empty spaces. Maureen and Gregory found the microfilm and microfiche machines at one side of the main room, next to the file cabinets holding celluloid rolls of the Post's back editions.

"Where do we start?" he said.

"You begin in the fifties when Reginald Pettigrew moved to Palm Beach. I'll start in the seventies after the old man died. When Roland's last name was still Fitzgerald."

They worked side by side in silence, grinding cranks slowly enough to skim headlines, each looking at every section except sports, stopping whenever they found a story about the Pettigrews. They had to sit too far away to touch each other, but Maureen kept glancing over at Go, and twice she caught him staring at her.

Finally Maureen found what she was looking for, something even better than she could have imagined, and said, "Go, let's go outside and talk." He nodded.

Standing in the parking lot, Maureen stretched her arms high into the air. "Haven't gone through that kind of torture since college."

"Me neither." Gregory stretched, too. "My eyes ache, and my shoulders muscles are so tight I can barely turn."

"A sadist must have designed these machines."

They moved closer, shy as grade school kids, almost touching, until Mo pulled back, thinking, No, work now. "What'd you find?"

"In my batch, only the society pages were useful," Gregory said. "During January, they're filled with accounts and photographs of lavish New Year's parties in Palm Beach. No mention of any party given by the Pettigrews, though. And neither the old man nor his wife are in photographs or even mentioned in the stories about parties given by others."

"That matches what Luther told us." Maureen remembered it word-for-word. *They threw big parties, but the 'A' list never came. To Palm Beach Society, the Pettigrews were nobodies.*

"I learned about a lot of other things, though, especially toward the end." Gregory was smiling. "George McGovern said he'd end the Vietnam War if elected. A survey showed almost one-third of all college students used pot."

"Go, be serious."

"Lt. Calley got a life sentence for his role in the Mylai massacre and Charles Manson was sentenced to death. I guess you know those sentences got changed, but not in the newspapers I read."

"Gregory, stop it."

"OK." Gregory's face became more serious. "There was almost nothing about Pettigrew except for one mention of a new hospital wing named for him and a short story about a political contribution that exceeded legal limits. Once he came to Florida, the old man couldn't do anything right."

Maureen nodded.

"Every May the Palm Beach social season died. For most rich people on that little island, the season lasts only a few months—January, February and March, with December and April optional. Seems many of them would rather spend Christmas and Easter—or, alternately, Chanukah and Passover—up North."

Maureen licked her lips, saying to herself, Just wait.

"Nobody of any importance stays in Palm Beach beyond May. Old man Pettigrew did, though. He was on the island in June when he died," Go said.

"The *Post* ran a seventeen-inch obit, slightly larger than average. For the most part it was a straight account of Reginald's government and business activities before 1955, when he moved to Palm Beach. He was survived by his widow, Sara. No mention of Roland."

"Of course not," Maureen said, thinking his name wasn't Roland Pettigrew then, and Sara wouldn't want her brother mentioned.

"Now it's your turn," Gregory said. "What'd you find?"

Maureen was ready. She'd do to him what he'd done to her. "In August, 1971 President Nixon imposed a ninety-day freeze on wages and prices, suspended conversion of dollars into gold, and proposed a ten percent import surcharge on automobiles and other goods—all ostensibly to fight inflation. In fact, it was to win the next election."

"Wait a minute," Go said.

"Wall Street was ecstatic. Wild trading pushed the Dow Jones Industrial Average up 32 points, a record one-day jump at the time, on volume of almost 32 million shares, another record. At the end of the day the Dow stood at 888."

Gregory said, "You knew all that before you read the papers."

Maureen ignored him. "Think about it. The Dow at 888. You realize it went above 12,000 before The Bubble burst? Nowadays a 32-point jump is a little hiccup. And daily volume always exceeds a billion shares, often it's above two billion."

"Now you stop it." Go's voice was sharp. "Did you learn anything about Roland Pettigrew?"

"Just following your example." But she knew it was time to get on with it. "Yes. I did."

"What, for Christ's sake?"

"Not much. Except that he probably killed Sara."

Gregory stared.

"Drowned her in the Atlantic, as a matter of fact."

"You're kidding."

"Come back inside and I'll show you."

Chapter Thirty-Six

Maureen motioned for Gregory to sit in front of one of the machines, pulled a chair beside him, and put in a roll of microfilm. She turned the crank to the first of the *Post* stories she'd found, gave Go enough time to read it, then moved on to the next.

Sara Pettigrew emerged from mourning the November after Pettigrew died and held an afternoon tea for a dozen women described as close friends. In December, she was listed among prominent guests at dozens of holiday parties, always escorted by one of three men—a banker, a lawyer, or a guy identified as a "socialite and financier."

"Probably trying to get their hands on the Pettigrew Trust," Maureen whispered. "Or maybe they already had it and were romancing Sara to make sure they kept it."

"Maybe they wanted her, too," Gregory said. "The photographs show a very good looking woman."

Maureen changed the roll of microfilm, pushing in one for 1972. The society pages began exactly as the previous year—the same parties, the same hostesses, the same guests and the same photographs—with one exception: Sara Pettigrew had become a star. She was at every party and in many of the photographs with one of her three escorts. Palm Beach Society shunned the cantankerous Reginald Pettigrew, but it held no grudge against his widow.

"Now we skip to July." Maureen ran the roll forward, stopped at a page and pointed.

TRAGEDY AT SEA, shouted a front page banner. Below it were a two-column photograph of Sara and a larger picture of a yacht. The story, written in a style that combined police-beat facts and society-page gush, said the popular Sara Fitzgerald Pettigrew, so active in the Palm Beach social scene, fell from her yacht and drowned in the Atlantic the day before. Her many friends were shocked by her untimely death.

Sara had gone to sea with her brother, Roland Fitzgerald, who recently earned a MBA from Harvard and had just returned to Palm Beach. No one else was aboard. They'd reached the Gulf Stream and the waves were choppy, he was quoted as saying. Sara had been at the bow leaning over the railing, watching the wake. A big wave, fifteen feet tall Roland estimated, higher than any he'd ever seen, hit the bow of the boat and lifted it up. Frightened, Sara let go of the railing and turned to walk back to the cockpit. The wave passed and the boat fell back into a trough and threw Sara forward. Her body flew across the railing and dropped into the sea, disappearing in seconds.

"It was awful," Roland said. "One second she was there, and the next she was gone." He threw a life preserver overboard, turned the yacht around, and returned to the spot. No sign of Sara. With difficulty, he unhooked a life raft and tossed it in the water, all the time trying to keep the boat close to the preserver. The floatation devices drifted northward, Roland following, figuring Sara would emerge near them. He circled for thirty minutes, but there was no sign of his sister. Finally he remembered the radio and called for help.

"The son-of-a-bitch," Gregory said. "He could handle a yacht then." Maureen nodded. Now, Roland Pettigrew was saying he'd learned to pilot a boat only years later, needing lessons and perseverance. Claimed, in fact that he'd only recently overcome his fear of the water. Bull.

"Two people aboard the boat and only one survived," Go said. "No one could challenge his version of what happened."

"Notice how much Pettigrew's story is like the one he told me about almost drowning when he was a kid," Maureen said.

"Sara was at the bow looking down at the water. The wave was the highest he had ever seen. She fell over the railing. Exactly what Pettigrew told me he was afraid would happen to him."

Gregory agreed. "He told you her story as if it were his own."

"More likely, he repeated the one he made up back then."

"And everyone believed it."

"Read the rest of the story."

Prominent Palm Beach socialites were uniform in their praise of Sara. She was so charming, so effervescent, so exuberant. Such a shame she hadn't participated in Palm Beach society earlier. The late Reginald Pettigrew, identified as a philanthropist and retired business leader, was mentioned in the story but not by any of Sara's mourners.

"Now look at the jump." Maureen scrolled forward. Above the continuation was a single-column photograph of an attractive young black woman. "She remind you of anyone?"

"Vaguely. Who?"

"Later. Look at the rest of the story.

The young woman was identified as Evelyn Washington, a recent graduate of Bethune Cookman College in Daytona Beach working temporarily as a maid at the Pettigrew Estate, the only servant who would speak to the press. She said she'd liked them both, Sara and Roland. "How sad."

They scrolled through the next few editions. Sara's body was never found but there was a well-attended memorial service at Bethesda-by-the-Sea, the Episcopal church in Palm Beach. The Coast Guard conducted an investigation but found there was nothing in the circumstances of the drowning that would contradict Roland's account. The report was critical of his waiting thirty minutes to call for help but said the delay could have been caused by inexperience

Maureen said, "We know everything now. How Roland Pettigrew got control of his brother-in-law's fortune and the real reason he moved away from Palm Beach to Lauderdale. It was to get away from people who knew about the drowning."

"And we know the man who killed Grace and Bridget."

"Probably," she said. "But how can we prove it?"

Chapter Thirty-Seven

On the ride back from West Palm, the afternoon traffic worse than the morning's, Maureen said, "What I can't figure is why people in Fort Lauderdale don't know all about Sara's drowning."

Gregory, in the passenger seat this time, said, "Back then, West Palm and Lauderdale were two separate worlds. Lauderdale was almost a suburb of Miami, and West Palm just an adjunct to Palm Beach."

"But—"

"That's changed, but the division between the two places remains. There's an imaginary line that cuts through Delray Beach. The cities south of it face Lauderdale, the ones on the north are aligned with West Palm. The two areas have different newspapers, different television stations. They're almost different countries—different average ages, ethnic mixes, economic status, everything."

"Still, there must have been stories in the papers."

"Sure, but I'll bet they weren't discussed much in Lauderdale then. Like stories out of Afghanistan back in the last century. Who knew then what we know now?"

"If you say so." Maureen wasn't convinced, but there were more important things to think about.

When they passed through Boca Raton, Gregory said, "What do we do now? Do we confront Pettigrew with what we know?"

Maureen shook her head. "I've tried that twice. It was a rout both times."

"What then?"

"I think I'd like to talk with Luther again."

"Why?"

"I need to check my memory on something."

Gregory didn't say anything to that, didn't ask "why" or "what," and Maureen knew he was trying to understand the boundaries of their new partnership. She was, too.

Too much to think about. Two murders since Maureen had arrived in Florida. Pettigrew's sister drowning years ago, probably another murder. Her partners in New York suspending her. The stock market. Her father. The ideas churned in Maureen's head. She needed to lighten the load.

She pulled off the Interstate at Deerfield Beach and stopped the car at a shopping center. "Go, before we do anything else, I've got to get out of the market. You drive the rest of the way."

"Are stock prices going down?"

"I don't know. Nobody does. But I haven't been paying attention, and for me, that's dangerous. I used to know what was going on in the market every hour, almost every minute. Now days go by while I'm absorbed in this Lauderdale mess."

Maureen got out her cell phone and called Rebecca, using the direct number to her desk. Two rings, then she heard the call being automatically transferred to another extension.

Rebecca picked up, her voice brisk and confident as she announced her name. Maureen asked how she was doing, what was going on in the office, and what the partners were saying about her.

"I haven't heard anybody talking about you," Rebecca said.

"Is that good or bad?"

No answer.

Maureen said, "You still have authority to trade for my account, don't you?"

"Yes."

"I want to sell everything."

"What?"

"I'm getting out. Completely out."

"Do you think—"

"I don't know any more than anyone else, but I don't have time to pay attention."

"OK," Rebecca said. "But I think you're making a mistake."

"Maybe, but sell it all right away. You know your Shakespeare. *If it were done when 'tis done, then 't were well it was done quickly.* Shop the big blocks around, sell the small holdings at market."

"I know how to do it."

Young people are always so confident, Maureen thought. And defensive. Change the subject. "I tried to get you at your desk. You didn't answer."

"I'm working out of your old office now."

This time Maureen kept silent.

"They're talking about giving me your old job."

When Maureen told Gregory what Rebecca told her, he said, "If you don't get stabbed in the back by the people you mentor, what good are they?"

"You didn't always used to be so cynical."

"Better to laugh about it than cry."

She touched his arm. "You don't suppose Rebecca's been working against me from the start?"

"Could be. Those things happen."

"But that would mean the partners knew they were going to suspend me even before I left New York."

"Mo, you said you wanted to talk to Luther."

"Right."

She phoned Luther, and he said to come on over, he almost never left Trust House in the daytime. Surprisingly cordial, for a man who thought they were blackmailing him. Or did he just want to know if they'd found out anything?

Chapter Thirty-Eight

The black and white photographs still hung on the wall behind Luther exactly as Maureen remembered, to his left near the window, so she sat in the wing chair closest to them. Luther, sitting behind the big desk, looked at Gregory, then at her.

"What brings you here today?"

Maureen knew Go wouldn't say anything. They'd agreed on that beforehand. And she thought it would be unwise to start with the photographs. So she said, "Did you see who killed Grace Pettigrew?"

"You know I couldn't see the lagoon from the window."

"The police are speculating you could have gone to another part of the house and seen the murder."

Luther picked up the ball-shaped cigarette lighter. "Let them speculate."

"They think Gregory killed Grace, and that someone saw him and told Bridget. They say that's the reason he killed Bridget."

"Then why isn't he in jail?" Luther moved the lighter into his other hand.

"They claim your boss used his influence to get him out."

"Doesn't that strike you as preposterous?" He put a hand inside his vest and pulled out a pack of Camel Lights.

"Everything about this is preposterous."

Luther laid the cigarettes on his desk and folded his hands in his lap. Maureen stood and walked toward the black and white photos on the wall. Luther swiveled his chair to follow her.

Slowly, making enough of a show of it so Luther couldn't miss what she was doing, Maureen studied the pictures, the one of the young women by herself and the one with a baby. She'd been right.

She turned and fixed her eyes on Luther. "How do you know this girl?"

It caught Luther by surprise. Maureen could tell that by the way he took so long to say, "Why do you ask?"

"She worked for Sara Pettigrew in the nineteen seventies."

Luther's body froze, hands squeezing together, a deer in headlights.

"Who was she?" Maureen said. "Your mother? Your daughter? Who?"

Now everything depended on what happened in the next sixty seconds, two minutes at most. Maureen figured it could go either way. She'd done her best.

Luther unclasped his hands and swiveled his chair to face the desk. He took a cigarette from the pack and picked up the lighter. He looked at Gregory. He pivoted the chair back toward Maureen, stared at her, then turned back to his desk. He flipped the lighter, watching the flame erupt as if he'd never seen fire before, then lit the cigarette and inhaled deeply. He held the smoke in his lungs, then blew it out fast, the fumes spilling into the air between Gregory and Maureen. Finally he put the lighter on the desk and turned back to her.

"That's Evelyn. My sister."

Fact? Fiction? Half-truth? Maureen couldn't process it. "And what was she doing working at the Pettigrews?"

"It's a long story."

"Give us the short version."

Luther's face, stone since Maureen asked him about the photograph, relaxed, a flicker of a smile crossing it. "I don't have to, you know."

"But you will," Maureen said, not sure why but knowing Luther would, just as he told them so much about old man Pettigrew. Reginald.

"Why?"

"Because we know Pettigrew changed his name. And we know—"

"No," Gregory said, but Maureen finished the sentence.

"—and we know Roland Pettigrew murdered his sister."

The instant it was out, Maureen wondered if she'd gone too far. She could tell by the expression on Gregory's face that he thought so.

"Interesting," Luther said.

That was all, nothing more. A cool son-of-a-bitch, Maureen thought. "So what was your sister doing working in Palm Beach?"

"Half sister, actually." Luther stubbed the cigarette out in the ash tray. "And much younger."

Maureen knew then that Luther had decided to tell them something. Now all she had to do was listen.

"When I went to college, public education was still segregated in Florida. I had only one choice." Luther pointed up and behind him to the Florida A&M diploma. "A pretty good school then, not a bad school now." He shook his head, as if clearing away thoughts of the past. "But when Evelyn reached seventeen, she could go to any school in the state. I wanted her to go to Florida State or Gainesville."

"FSU in Tallahassee or the University of Florida at Gainesville," Gregory said, looking at Maureen. She nodded, appreciating of the assist.

"But Evelyn insisted on Bethune Cookman," Luther said. "She said it was a black pride thing, attending a predominately black school. I thought she was avoiding confrontation, but eventually I gave in."

He looked straight at Maureen now, his expression defiant. "A year before she was to graduate, she got a strange idea. She said she wanted to find out how wealthy people lived. She was going to write an exposé, an article or a book titled 'The Foolish Filthy Rich,' something like that."

Maureen nodded.

"She had an aunt, my mother's sister, who lived in West Palm Beach and worked as a maid in Palm Beach. She got her aunt to help her get a job working at the same place. To my surprise, she liked the experience. She went back the following summer." Luther picked up the cigarettes and put the pack inside his vest. "That's all there was to it."

"Where is she now?" Maureen said.

"I don't know."

"Hard to believe."

"Well, believe it or not, that's the truth." Luther stood up. "And that's all the time for I have for you."

His reaction was so quick and harsh that Maureen suspected two things: Luther was telling the truth about not knowing where Evelyn lived now and something about that truth was very painful. She had to make a quick decision. Should she push Luther more now? Or leave and try again later?

Luther came around the desk and held out a hand to Gregory, who said, "All she asked was, 'Where is Evelyn now?'"

"No," Luther said. "Your friend said what I told her was hard to believe, like I'd lied. I don't lie, Mr. Overman. I tell the truth."

"I'm sure you do," Maureen said. "It's just that one man's truth is another man's—"

"Nonsense." Luther walked to the door. "This is the way out."

Chapter Thirty-Nine

Driving away from Trust House, Gregory said, "You satisfied with the way that went?"

"Don't give me a hard time, Greg," Maureen said.

"Why didn't you tell me you'd recognized the photo in the *Post*?"

"I didn't know for sure."

"You could have shared your suspicion."

Maureen didn't know how to respond. She wasn't used to working with a partner. For years, she'd always kept some things to herself, not revealing the entire picture until she wrote the story or sent out a report. Since Grace's death, she'd told Go everything she'd done, just as she'd briefed editors or her partners. But in the past she'd never shared her hunches, the identity of confidential informants, or stuff she still had to check out. Did she want to change now?

Gregory said, "You know what's going to happened next?"

"I know you're going to tell me."

"Luther is going to tell Pettigrew that we think he drowned Sara."

Because she'd blurted out her suspicion. "Don't rub it in."

Gregory stopped at a traffic signal and turned to her. "So we shouldn't wait for Luther to talk to Pettigrew. We should confront Pettigrew first."

Maureen started to protest that she'd faced off with Pettigrew twice and gotten nothing. But she'd told Gregory that already.

Maybe a showdown with someone by her side might come out better. Maybe.

"You're still checked into to a room in Pettigrew's hotel," Gregory said. "We could go there and wait for him to get back."

"It's an idea," she said.

"Which means you don't want to do it. You don't want to confront him again. He still reminds you of your father."

Maureen exhaled, then counted to twelve slowly. It was time to get this out of the way. "Greg, find a place to pull over so we can talk." They were on Victoria Park Road, heading south. Gregory drove another two blocks, made an illegal U-turn and pulled off onto a paved area fronting a small park.

When the car stopped, Maureen said, "Look at me, Greg."

He turned around.

"Do you really think I dislike Pettigrew because he resembles my father?"

"I didn't mean what I said." Gregory looked toward a tree with yellow flowers. "Can we forget about it?"

"No. First you were a gung ho supporter of Pettigrew, now you're straining at the bit to confront him. Like you did my father."

"That was different."

It wasn't, Maureen thought. It was—and is—unfinished business.

Two weeks before Gregory's sixteenth birthday, the State Department assigned his father to London, a plum assignment. Maggie Thatcher had become prime minister, and everyone figured if Ronald Reagan was elected president, he and Thatcher would team up. The posting meant Gregory's parents would be going to two or three parties a night and wouldn't have much time for him. Gregory didn't want to leave Washington; he had less than two years left in high school. He protested, and his parents happily arranged for him to stay with Maureen's parents while they were abroad.

Gregory was delighted, and Maureen liked the setup, too. She'd started college and came home only for holidays, but it would be nice to have him around. They'd had their reconciliation and things were easy between them. Often Gregory would wait up for her when she went out with other friends. When she got home, late at night, she started telling him things she'd never revealed to anyone before. The secrets brought them closer together.

One night she saw the light on in Go's third-story bedroom. She started climbing the stairs, getting as far as her parent's bedroom on the second floor. Their door was ajar.

"Where've you been?" her father yelled.

"Out," Mo said.

"Don't get smart with me," he said.

"Come in here a minute," her mother said.

Maureen saw Gregory standing at the top of the stairs, shook her head at him, and went inside the bedroom. Her mother lay on her back on the bed, fully dressed, her eyes closed. Her father sat on the floor, still in formal attire but with his bow tie undone, two fingers of his left hand playing with his mustache. Another late party, Maureen figured, and too much booze.

She started to leave, but just then Gregory appeared at the bedroom door.

"You," her father shouted at Go. He tried to get up, but the effort was too much. "We'll talk tomorrow," he said to Maureen and slouched back against the wall.

"Another father-daughter talk?" Gregory said, his words so harsh and unexpected they startled Maureen. "Like those other chats you've been having with her?"

Her father's fingers went to his mustache again, covering his mouth.

"About how you really don't know why you married your wife?" Gregory shouted. "About how she's so cold, and how you really need a woman who's warmer and more understanding?"

"No!" Maureen yelled, thinking, He's going too far, I never should have.... Her mother turned on the bed so she could see Gregory.

"And how that justifies everything?" Go yelled.

Mo's father pushed himself forward enough to put a hand on the rug.

"Don't bother to get up," Gregory said. "I'm not going to let you sit on my bed like you sit on Maureen's."

"Greg, don't!" Maureen had never seen him this way, betraying a confidence, making more of it than it was.

From the bed, her mother said, "What are you saying, young man?"

"I'm not sure," Gregory said, "Mo won't talk about the details."

Her father found the strength to stand up. "Young man, I won't put up with this."

And her mother said, "Have you been drinking, young man?"

"He shouldn't be in Maureen's bedroom," Gregory said, almost yelling now.

"I can talk to my daughter whenever I want," said her father.

"Not when she's in bed, and not when you start touching her," Go said.

"He doesn't, he's never touched me," Mo said, wondering, Where did he get that idea?

Her father lunged toward Gregory, but he'd drunk so much he lost his balance after a few steps and fell to the floor.

"You're disgusting," Mo's mother said, staring at Gregory, and even later Maureen couldn't figure out whether she was talking about her father or Gregory or both. Go had said things her mother didn't want to face.

"All of you, stop it," Maureen yelled. "Go, you come with me."

She ran down the stairs. Gregory followed.

At an all-night diner on Wisconsin Avenue, Mo said her father hadn't really done anything.

"He must have," Go said. "The way he reacted. The way you look now."

"No," Maureen said, nothing happened and she could handle it.

"But you've never told your mother about it," Go countered.

"True," Maureen agreed, she hadn't told her mother about what he'd said. "How could I?" And that was all she'd said. But deep inside she'd felt more. She never told Gregory, then or later, that she'd begun thinking her father's visits were becoming too frequent and their talks too intimate. He'd never touched her, but he had seemed to move closer and closer.

Finally Gregory said he didn't know what had gotten into him, that the things Maureen told him had built up in his head all out of proportion, that he couldn't stand the thought of her father sitting on her bed whether he'd touched her or not.

"You're jealous," Maureen said. Gregory didn't say anything to that for a long time, then, grudgingly, admitted maybe he was, indeed, jealous. Only then did Maureen say she'd been thinking of moving out of her parent's house for good and maybe Gregory should, too.

The next day they packed and moved Gregory to a townhouse in Glover Park, down Wisconsin in the District of Columbia. He lived there with a couple of other students, and they rarely saw each other except when she visited on holidays.

A few years after she moved out her parents' house, Maureen's father died, leaving all his possessions to her mother except for a gold Rolex, which he willed to Maureen. She gave the watch to Gregory, who never wore it except when he was with her.

Now, in the Mustang in Lauderdale, Maureen held Gregory's hands in hers. "Confronting my father paid off for you then. You got me away from him, just like you wanted."

"That was different," he repeated.

"That's my point. My father's been dead for years, but you won't let loose of that night. You were jealous of my father. Now you're jealous of Pettigrew and want to confront him."

"No way," Go said. "I asked you to come to Florida because I wanted you to endorse him. Now that we think he murdered his sister—and probably Bridget and Grace, too—everything has changed."

A new thought came to her. "Maybe that's why you asked me to come down here. You want to play the scene with my father again, one way or the other."

Gregory was silent then, and Maureen knew he was really thinking about what she said. Finally, he grinned. "You know you could get busted for practicing the shrink business without a license."

Maureen laughed, but she wasn't going to let it go that easily. "I've spent more time with Pettigrew than you have. He's different than my father. Different than the public perception even."

"People usually are."

"So can we drop this business about my father?"

Gregory looked at the trees in the park again, seeming to examine every one at least twice, finally turning to her. "Yes."

"Forever?"

"Yes."

"Now hug me." They put their arms around each other, not much of a hug, but the best they or anyone could in the front seat of a Mustang. "OK. Now let's get Midas Man."

Chapter Forty

W walking into the hotel lobby from the parking garage, Maureen told Gregory she wanted to check for messages at the front desk.

"Hotels don't do that anymore," he said. "They flash a red light on the telephone."

"I know. But I want to announce to the world that I'm back in my room."

"Who would care?"

"We'll see."

When Maureen identified herself, the young woman behind the desk said, "Mr. Pettigrew said for you to come to his room when you got in."

"When did he leave the message?"

The clerk looked at the note. "A few hours ago." She told them a code to put into the elevator keypad to get to the top floor.

Riding up, Maureen said, "He may want to see me alone."

"Too risky," Gregory said. "Where you go, I go."

Maureen liked the sound of that.

They stepped out of the elevator into a small lobby with carved chairs and tables along the walls, the suite entrance a double door with a large lacquered frame, an ornate doorbell to one side. One panel stood open a few inches.

Gregory said, "Do you suppose he wants us to come right in?"

"We'll ring anyway." Maureen pressed the button. They could hear chimes inside. Seconds passed, then a minute.

"Try it again."

Maureen nodded. Again the chimes rang out. No one came.

"Now what?" Gregory asked.

"We go in."

They walked though a small entrance hall into a large living area. A floor-to-ceiling glass wall dominated the room, boats cruising down the Intracoastal in the foreground, the downtown Fort Lauderdale skyline in the distance, a long balcony to one side. On the left another window framed a view of Port Everglades and the channel to the Atlantic.

Maureen turned in a circle, examining the room. Simple, uncluttered furnishings so as to not detract from the views, everything neat and in its place, no sign that Pettigrew or anyone had been there recently. She walked through an open kitchen and dining area, each equally devoid of any sign of life and looked into a front room. An office, the desk tidy and uncluttered. another balcony behind it, this one with a view of the Atlantic. Maureen stopped at the open door, something keeping her from invading Pettigrew's work space, just as she didn't want anyone in hers.

She saw Gregory walking down a hallway and followed. They reached a door opening into a bedroom.

"We shouldn't," she said.

"If we're going to look around, we'll look around." Gregory stepped inside, and Maureen followed.

A large, round bed sat in the center of the room, chests made of blond woods standing around the sides. Flat television screens hung on three walls, the fourth opening to yet another balcony. A lone photograph, one of Sybarite at anchor, was mounted above a dresser.

"Poor guy," Maureen said.

"You were expecting mirrors on the ceiling?"

"There's not a single picture or portrait of a person in this entire apartment. Just the boat."

"So?"

"Most people have somebody," Maureen said. "Children, parents, grandparents, an aunt or uncle, even nephews and nieces.

There's not a single person in the whole world Pettigrew cares enough about to have a photograph of in his home."

"You're getting soft," Gregory said. "He doesn't deserve sympathy."

"I'm trying to understand the man."

Gregory walked toward the hall. "Maybe there's something in the room across from this."

Maureen followed, wondering about her reluctance. Were they breaking the law? The front door had been open, so technically maybe.... But how would she feel if someone walked in and discovered them?

She had expected a second bedroom, but the room across the hall was a small gymnasium, more exercise machines than she'd ever seen in a private residence, the mirrored walls making them seem even more numerous.

"Kennedy said he was Pettigrew's personal trainer. This is where they work out." Gregory walked among the machines, a connoisseur evaluating their worth. "Not bad."

Maureen sat down on a bench seat covered in black vinyl. "Everything is fitting into place. If Pettigrew works out regularly, he's stronger than he looks. He has the strength to hold his former wife under water until she drowned. Likewise, he could strangle Bridget if he used a garrote or something."

"He had alibis."

"Nobody saw where he was when Grace was drowned. And as for his telling the police that he was at his office when Bridget was killed, he could have left and returned by that helicopter on the roof of his office building."

"Unlikely." Gregory sat at an exercise machine, pushing against a metal bar. "The police could question the helicopter pilots. And they'd have to keep a log showing drop-off points for all passengers."

Maureen closed her eyes, blocking out the damn mirrors. It came to her then.

"Those little boats that ferry people all around town."

"Water taxis," Gregory said.

"Pettigrew could have changed into something casual, worn a big hat or something so no one would recognize him and caught a water taxi from his office to this hotel. He could pick up a car here, find and strangle Bridget, then dump her on the steps of your apartment."

Go thought about it. "Could be."

There were still questions in Maureen's mind. "Pettigrew left me a message to meet him here but he's nowhere in sight. Don't you find that strange?"

"We've checked everywhere...." Gregory stopped.

"Everywhere except the big balcony."

Maureen ran out of the room, down the hall, through the living room, and onto the balcony, Gregory close behind. "No one here," she said.

Gregory walked to the railing. "A beautiful view, wasted."

"We could check the other balconies."

"No."

Maureen had turned away from the railing, preparing to walk to another balcony, but the harshness in Gregory's voice made her stop.

"Look down there."

Maureen walked to the railing and looked down.

Roland Pettigrew lay on his back in the grass twelve stories below, eyes open, not moving, his body hidden from bathers around the swimming pool by a pump house, a rag doll out of place in his white dress shirt and maroon tie. Dead?

"Jesus," Maureen said.

"Mary and Joseph," came a voice behind them.

Fourquet walked onto the balcony and looked over the railing. "Again." He shook his head. "Don't you two ever stop?"

Chapter Forty-One

The medics put Pettigrew in the van, Fourquet standing about ten feet back, Maureen and Gregory farther away, police milling all around but ignoring them. One group strung yellow crime scene tape around the area where Pettigrew's body hit the ground while another kept curious tourists away. Other cops had gone upstairs with crime scene apparatus.

Fourquet walked to where they stood. "Fifty-fifty chance he'll live."

"Remarkable he's alive," Maureen said.

"He hit the ground on his butt or something," Fourquet said. "If he does live, he may never walk again."

"Is he conscious?"

"Or do much else," Fourquet said.

Maureen figured Fourquet would take them to the station next. But something was wrong. She could see it in Fourquet's face. His whole body, as a matter of fact.

"And no," he said. "He hasn't regained consciousness."

Yes, the lieutenant detective was suffering. His face seemed bloodless, his posture limp, his responses languid, disconnected. He looked at Maureen, then Gregory, then around the hotel pool as if seeing the scene for the first time. Pettigrew's body had fallen on grass four to five feet from the concrete floor that surrounded the pool. A few more feet and he would have been killed.

"I don't see any reason for us to go down to the station again," Fourquet said.

"Good," Gregory said.

"Let's sit down over there." Fourquet pointed to a group of aluminum chairs around a table with an umbrella. Maureen looked at Gregory He shrugged.

"So you think you were set up?" Fourquet asked. His questioning had gone on for an hour, but his heart didn't seem to be in it. He'd been thorough, though. He wanted to know what Maureen and Gregory had done almost every minute since they'd got back from the Palm Beach County Library.

The whole interview was just— Strange. Bizarre. Inexplicable. Maureen ran out of words. For one thing, this was the first time Fourquet had interviewed them together. Both other times Fourquet had followed what surely must be routine police procedure, separating witnesses or suspects. But now he didn't object when Maureen and Gregory exchanged glances, even interrupting the other occasionally to add something. Further, Fourquet's questions were haphazard, almost random, his tone flat. It was as if he'd given up. And now he was coming back to a throwaway line of Gregory's, that they must have been set up.

"It's a possibility," Gregory said. "Somebody could have known about the message Pettigrew left at the desk and figured we'd be going up to his penthouse. They were in the apartment until just before we got there and left the door ajar."

Fourquet lit a cigar. Another first, Maureen thought. No ceremony, no production, just pulled the thing out and lit it with the sort of lighter you could buy at a 7-Eleven, the cigar already unwrapped. He's definitely not himself today.

"A set-up," Fourquet said now. "I'm wondering the same thing. Too damn many coincidences here. And if you two are the killers, you're the biggest bunglers I've ever heard of."

Maureen let out her breath so loudly that Gregory jerked his head around to look. Fourquet noticed, too.

"Go back to what you told me before," he said. "What in the world does Luther having a picture of his sister hanging on his wall have to do with anything?"

Maureen had decided against telling Fourquet about the news stories they'd found in the *Palm Beach Post* but figured she should mention visiting Luther, since the detective might find out later. So now she said, "I was curious,"

"Just curious, huh?"

Yep. That's all I'm going to tell you, she said to herself. You might not remember what I told you at the police station, but I do. *Someday things are going to be different. You're going to want something from me.* You wanted to know if that was a threat, and I said, *No. A prediction.* One that's proved to be right on the money. Payback is so sweet.

Fourquet shook his head, looked away, then turned back quickly. "You plan to leave town soon?"

The movement startled her. "No."

"If you were, don't." he said.

Maureen moved her head just enough to let him know she'd heard him.

"I'm not going to hold you. But two things."

Maureen saw Gregory lean his body in her direction. Nice, she thought. Protective.

"One, I may call you down to the station later," Fourquet said. "Or someone else may."

This time Gregory nodded.

"Two, there's no way in hell I can keep this out of the papers. Your presence here at the scene of the...." Fourquet looked back and forth between them. "Accident, murder, we don't know yet."

Maureen and Gregory sat in the chairs, not moving, not saying anything, Maureen wondering when he was going to get to the point.

But Fourquet never did. He stood and looked around the pool, his face showing more life than before, almost its natural color. Most of the other cops had gone, a lone officer guarding the fall site, a couple of others on the balcony.

"I've got to get to the hospital." Fourquet walked away, his back straight, a military precision to his steps. Almost like his old self.

When he was out of sight, Maureen turned to Gregory. "What do you make of that?"

Gregory shook his head. "An overnight lobotomy?"

She smiled. "What's happened since the last time he questioned us that caused him to change?"

Gregory put a finger to his lips as if thinking, but Maureen knew he was faking. Finally he said, "Pettigrew was almost killed."

"My reading, too, Mr. Bones. Now the second question is, Why did that matter so much to Fourquet?"

Gregory said, "You think too much."

Maureen laughed. It was her line, but she didn't mind Go stealing it. Besides, she had more important things to think about.

Chapter Forty-Two

Gregory pulled the Mustang to a stop in front of his apartment and looked over. "Could Fourquet be the murderer?"

Maureen said, "I've been thinking about nothing else since we left the hotel."

"Fourquet was on the scene very quickly after each of the bodies was found, and he could have been there even earlier than anyone knew. He's strong enough to have overpowered any of them. He could have drowned Grace and strangled Bridget. And it would have been easy for him to throw Pettigrew off the balcony."

"Really?" she said. "Wouldn't he, or anybody, have to knock him out first?"

"Probably. I meant Fourquet was strong enough to lift and throw a body."

"But if he or anyone wanted to kill Pettigrew, wouldn't they throw the body far enough so it would hit on the concrete?"

"They'd try. But that would take more than just a push. Most likely, whoever did it didn't stop to think."

Maureen shook her head. "The whole idea is so far-fetched. A police officer murdering two people and trying to kill a third."

"You're assuming all cops are good cops," Gregory said. "Fourquet didn't impress me as a good cop from the very beginning."

"But...." Maureen didn't know how to finish it, so she asked about something else that had been circling inside her mind.

"Remember what Bridget said about Pettigrew saying he wanted to marry her."

"Yep."

"Do you believe it?"

"Yes."

"Why in the world?"

"Old men lust for young women." Gregory smiled. "The first old man Pettigrew sure did."

"Must be more to it than that. How about the idea that opposites attract?"

"Then they attack," Gregory said.

"Really?"

"Check it out."

Maureen thought for a couple of beats. "And us?"

"And us what?"

"Are we alike?"

"Not the last time I looked."

"You know what I mean," she said. "You're a shrink."

"I'm not a shrink," he said. "I'm a counselor, inactive for now, specializing in children."

"What do counselors say?"

"They'd tell you that common interests and common values are more important than anything else in predicting whether a relationship will work." Gregory was smiling again, so Maureen knew more was coming. "That, and not being able to keep your hands off each other for thirty years."

"But we didn't do anything for thirty years."

"I meant the next thirty years." Gregory leaned over and kissed her on the mouth.

She was surprised. It was the first time Gregory had ever started things. She kissed him back, letting their mouths linger together, then broke it off. "We'll finish this later," she said. "We've got work to do."

"We?"

"I've got a phone call to make. You can listen in."

"Right after I fix us bowls of ice cream," Gregory said. "This evening it's Chocolate Fudge Brownie."

Maureen set the bowl on a table beside the sofa and dialed a number. She heard Gregory pick up the phone in the bedroom. Eight-thirty in Lauderdale, five-thirty in Santa Fe. What would Melody be doing now? What was the best way to break the news?

Melody picked up and Maureen identified herself. "I have news. I'm not sure whether you'll think it's good news or bad."

"Try me."

"Roland Pettigrew fell twelve stories from a balcony and has been severely injured."

"That doesn't affect me."

"I thought maybe—"

"He's not a part of my life anymore."

Maureen said nothing. She'd wait as long as necessary. Finally Melody broke the silence. "Did he jump or was he pushed?"

"Nobody knows yet."

"But he'll live?"

"Probably. But he may never walk again."

"I guess that should make me happy. But it doesn't."

"Would you have benefited financially if he'd died?"

Melody laughed. "You are a snoop, aren't you?"

"There've been two murders and maybe this was an attempted one. Anything we learn might be helpful."

"Not a penny," Melody said. "I signed everything away for a good divorce settlement."

"One more thing. Did you deliberately hang up on me the last time we talked?"

"Yes."

"Why?"

"I panicked."

"Why?"

Melody paused, and Maureen knew she was making a decision.

"You can tell me," Maureen said. She'd never understood why this simple sentence worked so often. But it did.

"I was about to tell you something," Melody said, "and I didn't know if I should."

"What?"

"I guess it doesn't matter now."

Again Maureen waited.

"Remember I mentioned birth certificates?"

"Yes." Maureen started to tell her about phoning Jacksonville but stopped herself.

"I never really saw one," Melody said.

"But you suspect something?"

"I didn't say that."

Maureen felt something touch the back of her neck, and an idea hit her, one so strong and clear she decided to take another chance.

"You think Kennedy is Pettigrew's son."

The sound of Melody inhaling deeply came from the phone. "How did you know?"

The thought just came, Maureen almost said. Maybe the subconscious, maybe intuition, maybe even an angel. Didn't matter. It was the same power that told her Roland Pettigrew would be at the party even before they got there and that had warned her something was wrong in the market before she got Go's call in New York, the source of premonitions that had helped her so many times. It was the sum total of everything she knew, felt and experienced beforehand, little specks of ideas, thoughts, feelings, and facts that came together so marvelously every now and then—miraculously some people might say, the whole world changing in an instant. God? Who knows?

She'd let herself get sidetracked into thinking Luther was Kennedy's father because of their mannerisms. But it was equally logical that if Kennedy and Luther were close when Kennedy was a child—if Luther had helped raise Kennedy, for example—the younger man would mimic the older without realizing it. And if Pettigrew was Kennedy's father, the relationship would explain Kennedy's strange status at Pettigrew's party and in Pettigrew's life—mingling with the guests, carrying personal messages for the man, access to his penthouse, and Pettigrew putting Kennedy, his only child, through law school. Everything clicked.

"How do you know?" Maureen said, putting it back to Melody. Confirm everything, she'd been taught, and check every detail. If a man says his name is Smith, ask him how to spell it.

"Pettigrew told me one night."

"Why? How?"

"It's a long story. He was trying to explain.... I'll tell you about it some other time maybe."

"I have plenty of time now."

"I've said enough. It's all in the past. I've got to go."

"Before you hang up," Maureen said. "Who was Kennedy's mother?"

The phone went dead.

Gregory walked into the living room and sat on the sofa, an empty bowl in his hands. "I think we know who Kennedy's mother was."

Maureen nodded. "Now we have to figure out who killed Grace Pettigrew and Bridget."

"No we don't."

It surprised her.

"Fourquet's reaction to Pettigrew's fall made it clear that I'm no longer a suspect," Gregory said. "So you can't be an accomplice."

"But— " she started.

"You could go back to Wall Street tomorrow, and I could report for work at Providence Place."

Maureen knew more was coming.

"Better yet, you could kiss your job goodbye and we could go off together. Paris. Rome. Tahiti. Wherever."

It was tempting, but Maureen knew better. "My former partners have ruined my reputation and given my job to Rebecca. Eventually, I'll go back to New York and fight them, but I can't do that until the murders are solved."

"Why not?"

"My name has been smeared, and I'm totally without credibility until I clear it. That won't happen until this mess is resolved completely. Until then, I couldn't work effectively at any job." She looked to see if he understood.

Gregory took her hand. "We. We have to find out. We have to clear your name."

"I keep forgetting." Maureen smiled.

"I'm with you," Go said. "But do we have to solve everything tonight?"

She moved closer. "Tomorrow will do."

Chapter Forty-Three

They were at the Floridian again eating breakfast, rock blaring from loudspeakers, the overhead television sets muted, the crowd almost as large as Sunday's, but they were able to get a table. Maureen had decided to wear jeans, it being Saturday and all.

"Go, think back," she said. "Who first suggested you ask me to come to Florida?"

"No one actually. One of the nuns asked me if I knew anyone on Wall Street. Naturally I thought of you."

"When did Pettigrew start talking with the nuns about a donation?"

"Weeks or months before then, I think."

Maureen looked up from her bowl of fruit. "So sometime during those discussions, Pettigrew could have suggested they talk to someone on Wall Street about him."

"Maybe."

"And he could have assumed they would ask you for advice and you'd think of me."

Gregory held a stick of bacon in the air. "I see where you're going. But to make that work, Pettigrew would have had to know we were close."

"He'd done his research. Remember at the party, he knew you'd refuse the drink of champagne. And a little later Kennedy told me Pettigrew's information about our relationship was puzzling."

"Yes, but—"

"Pettigrew or somebody working with him knew there was a good chance I'd come to Florida if you asked."

Gregory said, "Why go to all that trouble?"

Maureen said, "If my partners wanted to get rid of me, a good first step would be to get me out of town where there was a possibility of a confrontation with Pettigrew."

"But your firm doesn't do business with him."

"Everybody is always soliciting business. The partners could have approached Pettigrew, and he could've told them they had to get rid of me before he'd even consider it. He knows I'd never say anything good about his companies."

Gregory stared at her. "Surely you're not saying somebody killed Pettigrew's wife just to get you in trouble."

"Of course not. She was killed for some other reason." Maureen picked up a second piece of toast. "The point I'm making is that if Pettigrew knew there was going to be trouble, he and my partners would find it to their mutual benefit to get me down here."

Gregory sipped from his cup of coffee. Maureen decided this was an opportunity to again bring up the subject she'd been trying to get Go to talk about since she arrived in Lauderdale.

"Of course you had a choice," she said. "You didn't have to invite me."

Gregory pushed his plate aside.

"But you did," she persisted.

"Yes."

"Why?"

Gregory looked up at a television monitor. *The Today Show* broke for a commercial. Finally he looked back at her. "For a smart woman you can be very dense."

"Tell me."

"I would have grabbed any excuse to get you down here."

"Did you really think you needed a reason?"

Gregory shrugged.

"You didn't," Maureen said.

Gregory reached over and took her hand. "And you didn't have to wait for an invitation."

They sat there like that, oblivious of the din around them, until a waitress came and picked up their empty plates. There were many more things to say and more feelings to get out, but Maureen felt better. The first step was the hardest. The others could wait.

"Now," she said. "Who killed Grace? And why?"

Gregory smiled. "Good. I like these easy questions."

"Well?"

"We might make more progress if we backed into this. Start with motives. Think of motives and possibilities we haven't thought of."

"OK." Maureen said. "What are motives for murder?"

"Money, sex, power..."

"Revenge, greed, fear, maybe others," she finished.

"Which one applies here?"

"Let's go though the list one at a time." Maureen took a pen from Gregory's shirt pocket and lay a napkin on the table. "Who benefited from Grace Pettigrew's death?"

"Pettigrew. He got rid of a thorn in his side."

Maureen wrote his name on the napkin. "Who benefited from Bridget's death?"

"Unclear. She was allied with Grace, but surely not a big threat to Pettigrew."

"If Pettigrew had been killed, who would have benefited?"

Gregory clapped his hands together. "His son. Kennedy. When Pettigrew dies, he'll inherit everything."

"Not necessarily," Mo said. "It would depend on Pettigrew's will. And, Kennedy wouldn't necessarily gain control of the Trust."

"Who would determine that?"

"The remaining individual trustee and the bank," Mo said. "The bank would probably go along with any qualified person nominated by the individual."

"And who's that? The other individual trustee."

Maureen searched her memory, finally bringing up an image of the Trust reports she'd seen on microfilm, a signature page. There it was, the name. "Luther."

"You didn't tell me that."

Again she reached back, trying to remember everything she'd told Go after coming back from West Palm the first time. He was probably right.

"I guess not," she said. "Pettigrew appointing an employee he could control as a trustee was so predictable, it didn't seem worth mentioning."

"So Luther could recommend Kennedy as the second trustee," Gregory said, "and the two of them would run the show."

"Exactly."

"Is that motive enough for murder?"

"What do you think?" Maureen let it lay there, the answer obvious to her. People would do much worse to control a billion dollars.

"Did Kennedy have an opportunity to murder Grace and Bridget and toss Pettigrew off the balcony?"

"He showed up at the lagoon soon after you jumped in to retrieve Grace's body," she said. "He could have killed Grace just minutes before we got there and hid somewhere nearby until we came along."

"Were his clothes wet when you first saw him? "

Maureen tried to remember. "Don't know. I was watching you." Gregory didn't say anything to that, but Maureen didn't care. She was rolling. "Kennedy could have killed Bridget almost anywhere and dropped her on your apartment stairs when he saw us coming."

"Maybe," Gregory said.

"And Kennedy must have been who pushed or threw Pettigrew from the hotel balcony. He probably had a key to get into Pettigrew's apartment to set up the exercise room. The message the hotel clerk said was from Pettigrew could easily have come from Kennedy. She'd think the chauffeur was speaking for his boss."

She watched Gregory process what'd she'd said, admittedly bold theories with no proof. Finally he said, "If Kennedy is the murderer, who could prove it?"

"There's only one person who has all the answers." Maureen pushed her chair back. "Let's go talk to him."

Chapter Forty-Four

Gregory drove up the ramp of the parking garage behind Broward General Medical Center and pulled into the first available space, one on the top floor. "You sure he's going to talk to us."

"Nothing's sure," Maureen said. "But it's worth a try."

After showing some ID at the hospital entrance, they picked up admission badges and got Pettigrew's room number. "Security," Gregory said. "That's what this century will be remembered for."

"And the impossibility of being completely safe," Maureen said.

"Even if you're Midas Man."

They found Pettigrew in a private room on the fifth floor—the furniture, drapes and wallpaper more like a motel than a hospital unit—no guard or anyone at the door, so they walked in. He was sitting up, IV tubes in his left arm, clear plastic pouches of liquid hanging above them upside down (like bats, Maureen thought), a telephone on the table by his right, the bulge of a body cast visible under the blanket.

A chalk board with Pettigrew's name, a doctor's name, and a phone number hung from the wall opposite the bed. Maureen recognized it as a number for Pettigrew Enterprises. His next of kin.

"Check into a hospital, and you find out who your real friends are." Pettigrew smiled as he said it, and Maureen wondered if he knew how close he'd come to death. "Lt. Fourquet was by here earlier."

Maureen said what she'd say to anyone in a hospital bed. "How do you feel?"

"I won't be able to dance for a while." Pettigrew smiled again, the expression different than any she'd seen before he fell, almost sincere. Or he was faking it better? Gregory walked to the window and looked out, Maureen knowing he was turning the interview over to her but he'd be there if she needed him. She sat on a straight chair beside the bed.

"Make yourself at home," Pettigrew said.

Pretending to be a tough old bird to the very end. Maureen figured she could sit there making small talk forever before she got to the big questions, but didn't see any reason to wait. Pettigrew would either tell her or he wouldn't. "Who did it?"

"Did what?" he said.

"Pushed you off the balcony."

"Who said I was pushed?"

"OK. Were you pushed or did you jump?"

"Funny." Pettigrew was clearly in a good mood. "That's word for word what Fourquet asked, too."

"And you told him?"

"I don't remember."

"Hard to believe," Maureen said, thinking too late that Luther had cut off the conversation when she'd said that to him.

"But irrefutable," Pettigrew said. "No one can ever prove you can remember something you say you don't. If you're ever in court, remember that." He laughed.

"But you can remember what happened before then?"

"I might. I might not."

"Who was on the balcony with you?"

"I don't remember." Pettigrew caught himself. "If there was anyone, that is."

"Why won't you tell?"

Pettigrew laughed. "Don't remember that either."

"Was anyone in your apartment before you went to the balcony?"

"You know the answer to that. I don't—"

Gregory turned around. "Were you in pain?"

The question took Pettigrew by surprise, and what came out next seemed spontaneous. "Oh God, yes."

Finally, Maureen thought, a normal human response from the man.

"Until I blacked out," Pettigrew added quickly. "Since then I've been so drugged up, they could cut me in two and I wouldn't notice."

Gregory said, "Have they told you your prognosis?"

"They say I'll never walk again or do much of anything below the waist." Pettigrew tried to smile. "But doctors have been wrong before. I may fool them."

Now Gregory nodded toward Maureen, messaging that he'd done his job. He'd started Pettigrew talking.

Maureen stood and moved closer to Pettigrew, standing above him, looking down. "We know a lot about you that you wouldn't want to get out. Things you've been keeping secret for years."

"Not that old stuff about changing my name."

"No." Maureen paused for a count of ten. "We know that you killed your sister by drowning her in the Atlantic."

If the accusation surprised Pettigrew, he didn't show it. "There was an official investigation. The Coast Guard said it was accidental."

"And we know other things," Gregory said, surprising Maureen.

Pettigrew swiveled his head. "I doubt it."

"We know that Kennedy is your son. And we're pretty sure who his mother is."

"You can't prove that," Pettigrew said, then seemed to reconsider his answer. "That's ridiculous."

"But someone could prove it," Maureen said. "Somebody with authority to collect DNA samples."

Pettigrew stared at the wall across the room. "No one has that authority."

"The police or FBI could get it. Once they believe Kennedy's parentage has some significance in a murder case."

"Get out!"

Neither Maureen nor Gregory moved.

"Get out." Pettigrew pushed a button that called nurses.

Maureen knew she didn't have much time left. She leaned over the bed, her face close to Pettigrew's. "What I really want to know is which of my partners you've been dealing with."

Most of Pettigrew's face stayed stoic, but a tic at the side of his left eye betrayed him. She was right. One or more of her partners had been working with Midas Man behind her back.

"Yes," said a voice on the intercom.

"We're leaving," Maureen said. And then, almost under her breath, "But we'll be back."

In the elevator going down to the main floor, she said to Gregory, "He was surely cheerful during most of that."

"Morphine derivatives. They do the job, but sometimes patients leave the hospital addicted."

Of course. Go knew that from his training as a nurse. Or staying in a rehab center. But the drugs weren't sufficient to keep Pettigrew's face from betraying the secret about working with her partners. Did that have anything to do with the murders?

They'd left the top of the rental car up, and the inside was hot already. In February. Imagine.

"So?" Gregory said. "What do you think of Pettigrew now?"

"His story about not remembering what happened on the balcony is preposterous."

"But he may be able to get by with it."

Maureen fastened her seat belt. "Agreed."

"So he's protecting someone. Who?"

"Who else but Kennedy?" Gregory held the car key in his hand. "If Kennedy is his son, Pettigrew wouldn't want the world to know he'd been pushed or thrown off the balcony by his offspring."

"A son trying to kill his father?"

"Sons have been trying to kill their fathers for thousands of years. Think of Oedipus."

"He didn't know."

"And sleep with their mothers." Go grinned. "Or surrogates for them."

"Beside the point, I'm sure you know."

"What I'm saying is some sons have been so badly abused, they eventually revolt." Gregory started the engine. "Who knows how Kennedy feels about his father? If, that is, he knows Pettigrew is his father."

"Surely he knows by now."

"Maybe. But we haven't established that yet."

"I prefer economic motivations for murder." Maureen closed her eyes. "Money. Power. Survival."

"Kennedy again. If Pettigrew dies, Kennedy is his sole heir."

"Depends on Pettigrew's will."

"And we already know Luther could help Kennedy get control of the Pettigrew Trust. Control of a couple of billion dollars. That economic motivation enough for you?"

Maureen closed her eyes and thought about it. When she was ready, she said, "Maybe we should confront him. Kennedy. "

"Our record on confrontations isn't good so far."

"But what have we got to lose?"

Kennedy sat behind Luther's desk playing with the black-ball cigarette lighter, a boy messing around with his uncle's stuff, the big desk not fitting him nearly as well as it did Luther, but when Maureen and Gregory finally tracked Kennedy down, this was where he said to meet. He wore the same outfit as when Maureen first saw him at the party, a blue blazer with a white handkerchief barely sticking out of the pocket and tan slacks.

"You use Luther's desk now?" Maureen said.

"He recommended I try it out."

Gregory walked to the window and looked out, Maureen knowing he couldn't possibly be interested in the view again. He was getting out of the way. She liked this sort of partnership.

"The photographs," she said, sitting down. "They're gone."

"What photographs?" Kennedy's voice was flat.

"The ones of the attractive black woman. And a child."

"Maybe I took them down. Or maybe Luther did."

Now! Maureen told herself. "The child was you."

There. She'd said it.

Kennedy lay the black ball on the desk. "Luther told me you might say that."

No denial. No confirmation. No information spilled. Not a bad strategy, Maureen thought.

"In fact Luther's been telling me a lot lately," he said. "Sometime when you're with him, ask him to tell you the story about the Black Knight."

Interesting, but she wasn't going to be diverted. "Settle a bet for us. I say a son wouldn't try to kill his father. Gregory says it happens all the time."

"What I've heard is that that part of Freud's theories has been discredited," Kennedy said. "Like so much of the rest of it."

Maureen stood up and walked to where Gregory was standing, silently asking for help. The sound of a lawn mower came from the garden below.

Go turned toward Kennedy. "Your clothes were already wet when you jumped into the lagoon to help me retrieve Grace's body."

"Not the way I remember it," Kennedy said.

"And Bridget was in the garden down below shortly before she was killed and dumped on my doorstep," Gregory said. "Someone saw her there and feared she'd heard something."

Maureen realized he was making this up.

"Wasn't that at night?" Kennedy said. "How could anyone have seen her in the dark?"

"Easy enough if someone turned the flood lights on."

"Or maybe just the smaller overhead lights," Kennedy said. "The ones we use for parties."

Now Maureen was sure. Kennedy was playing with them and would continue the game forever. Like Pettigrew. Still, it would be interesting to see how he worded his non-denial denials.

She said, "How did Pettigrew meet your mother?"

Kennedy said, "Who said he did?"

"She was a pretty young woman."

"That's past tense," Kennedy said. "Who said she's not alive?"

"Is she?"

Kennedy started to say something, then stopped, and looked around the room. Was that moisture in his eyes? Tears?

Finally he said, "Is yours? Your mother. Alive."

"No," Maureen said.

"You say that with such certainty."

"I was at the funeral," Maureen said. "We had an open casket service."

"I wish...." Kennedy dropped his head to his hands.

Yes, she thought now, those are tears.

Kennedy swung his chair around to the wall. More silence. Finally he dug a handkerchief from his pocket, put it to his face, and turned around. "You're not going to learn anything more today. Not here anyway."

"One more question—" Maureen started.

"No!" Kennedy hurled the cigarette lighter across the room. It slammed into the paneled wall opposite the desk and burst into pieces, ceramic bits flying in all directions, the impact sounding like a gunshot.

Maureen and Gregory stood in silence, an unspoken message passing between them: It was time to leave. "We can find our way out," she said.

Kennedy watched them walk to the door. His tone softened.

"I heard you walking up the stairs to get here. Why not take the elevator? Down the hall on your right."

"They fixed it?" Maureen said.

"I didn't know it was broken," Kennedy said.

Chapter Forty-Five

Now Maureen and Gregory sat on the wrought iron bench at the back of the garden, the spot shaded from the afternoon sun by the bamboo and pine hedge that separated Providence Place from the Trust headquarters. Gregory hadn't objected when she said she wanted to catch her breath.

"This is where it all began—where Bridget used to meet Grace," Maureen said. "They would sit here and talk."

"And where they dreamed up their plot to distract everybody while Grace went to look for some documents. The so-called secret papers."

"Which nobody has ever found."

"Who's looked?"

Boats passed on the Intracoastal in the distance, the boathouse off to the left, the mower somewhere on the other side of the house falling silent.

"Maybe...." Maureen said.

"Maybe what?"

"Bridget said she and Grace used to leave notes for each other underneath slats of this bench." Maureen pushed herself off the seat, bent down in front of the bench, and reached underneath. "Move."

Gregory stood up. Maureen felt along the bottom of each of the slats, working left to right, front to back, the texture of the wood on the bottom rougher than on the seat. Finally, she touched something taped to one spot near the back and tried to work it loose with her fingers. It wouldn't budge. "Help me."

Gregory walked around the bench, lay down on his back, and slid underneath. It took him a moment or so, but eventually he pushed himself out and held up what looked like black electrical tape wound around something. He handed it to her.

A key, Maureen realized as she unraveled the tape. A key to what? She sat back on the bench and handed it to Gregory. "Any ideas what this might fit?"

"Not a very big key." Gregory said. "Bigger than a mail box key, a little smaller than a key to a house door."

"A boat key." The thought came to Maureen from nowhere. No time to think whether the message came from angels, her intuition, or subconscious.

"Maybe."

Maureen looked up at the second floor of Trust House, trying to see if Kennedy or Luther was peering down at them. If so, they were too far back from the window to see.

"We need leverage," she said. "Something that will get Pettigrew or Kennedy to tell us what happened on the penthouse balcony. If we knew that, maybe we could understand everything else."

"No shit, Sherlock."

Maureen hit Gregory on the arm harder than she'd intended. "So how do we pressure them into opening up?"

He rubbed his biceps, pretending to be hurt. "I'm too wounded to think."

"What is it that Pettigrew fears most? And what would Kennedy, in his newly discovered role as heir, be equally fearful of?"

"You're going to tell me."

"Exposure," Maureen said. "Something that would bust up the Trust and bring everything crashing down."

"And how do we accomplish that?"

"Weren't you just talking about secret papers? If they show illegal activity by either Pettigrew or the Trust, he'd lose control of both. And maybe Kennedy wouldn't inherit anything."

"But we don't know where they are—the documents, whatever they are."

Maureen held up the key.

Gregory stared, the light bulb in a bubble over his head almost visible. "They're on Pettigrew's boat."

"That's what Grace and Bridget thought," she said.

"And now they're dead."

"We'll be more careful."

Chapter Forty-Six

A dopt an attitude," Maureen said as they walked toward the parking attendants outside the Radisson Bahia Mar, the hotel next to the new one where Pettigrew lived and Maureen rented a room. "Look like you belong here, and no one will stop us." She'd been there before, visiting Pettigrew's yacht.

Gregory, beside her, said, "Why didn't we go through the lobby of your hotel?"

"Too many people know us there."

When they were almost at the hotel entrance, Maureen turned right into the marina. "Still amazes me. No gates, no screening, no security, not even when you get near the multi-million dollar yachts"

"It's a minor tourist attraction," Gregory said. "Somewhere around here there's a plaque proclaiming Slip 18 as a Literary Landmark. Travis McGee was supposed to have lived there on *The Busted Flush*."

"Too bad he's not around to help us."

Maureen led as they went down an aluminum ramp to the floating docks, their shoes causing the metal to reverberate like dozens of marching feet, but when they reached Pettigrew's yacht, Gregory boarded first and helped her on.

"Bridget's home away from home," Maureen said.

"When she was alive."

"Don't go there," she said. "You know what *Sybarite* means?"

"Sybaris was the most magnificent city in ancient Greece. A place of luxury, splendor, and wealth." Gregory walked to the cockpit door. "Until it was sacked and burned to the ground."

"Proving once again that nothing lasts. I wonder if Midas Man knew that when he adopted the name." She handed Gregory the key they'd found taped under the garden bench at Trust House.

Gregory put it the lock and slid the glass door aside. "Why would he leave important documents here?"

"It's the way Pettigrew thinks." Maureen stepped inside. "He wouldn't leave anything important in his office, his apartment, or Trust House. Too many employees and cleaning staff coming and going all the time there."

"But people work on the yacht, too."

"Pettigrew told me he had the stateroom doors reinforced. He could restrict maintenance to the exterior and the main cabin."

"The salon," Gregory said.

"Salon?"

"That's what they call the living, dining, and kitchen area."

She laughed. "And I thought you were wasting time down here." Like old times, kidding with Go even when things were serious. "You've been learning really important stuff."

"I even know the difference between a sportfisher, a cruiser, and a sports convertible. Also that a cruiser is sometimes called a sedan."

"Forget it."

Nothing seemed to have changed since Maureen had been in the cabin with Pettigrew. The brass still gleamed, the teak smelled newly oiled, the sofa and a reading chair sat near the door, the dining area and the galley straight ahead, scrubbed and uncluttered. So peaceful then. But now every motion of the boat, each creak from inside or out, signaled danger. They could be caught. They could....

Stop thinking like that, Maureen told herself. She and Go would do what they had to do and leave. That was all there was to it.

"Do we search this area first?" Gregory asked.

"Don't think so." Maureen walked through the cabin toward the front of the boat. "Grace told Bridget she thought the documents were hidden in the bow, and Bridget said she tried to break into a safe she found up there."

She tossed her purse on a counter in the galley, ducked her head, and slipped into the passageway leading to the staterooms. Gregory followed. A small door stood ajar to her left revealing the head—a tiny room with a shower, toilet and wash basin. She opened the door on the right. Two bunk beds side by side, less than a foot between them, no room for anything else. She moved on.

Then, straight ahead, she saw what Pettigrew had told her about. Brass bands crisscrossed the stateroom door at the end of the corridor, a curved metal frame encased its sides, and a stainless steel plate extended eight to ten inches around its brass handle and keyhole.

Maureen pushed down on the lever and pressed against the door. It held fast.

"The key," she said.

Gregory put the shiny metal in her hand. "It'll never fit."

She knew he was right but tried it anyway. The key wouldn't go in. She turned it over and tried again. Same result.

"OK, now what?" she said.

"Stay here. I'll be right back."

Gregory walked down the passageway and through the salon, disappearing when he got to the sliding door that separated cabin from cockpit. Maureen wondered what the heck he was doing, leaving without explanation when she needed him. She didn't have to put up with things like this when she worked alone. Maybe pursuing information with a partner wasn't such a good idea.

She heard a scraping noise on the deck above her. Was that Gregory or someone else? More sounds came from somewhere above the bow, then from inside the stateroom. Or was she imagining things? Then there were two knocks on the other side of the stateroom door. She hadn't imagined those.

"Can you hear me?" Gregory's voice sounded as if it came from the bottom of a cave, but Maureen could make out the words.

"How did you get in there?"

"The forward hatch. It's big enough to get through, and it wasn't latched. Now I'll try to open this door from the inside."

The forward hatch, Maureen thought. What had Pettigrew said about it?

Gregory banged against the door. "I need tools."

"How could I get them to you?"

"Drop them though the hatch."

"I'll look."

Maureen turned and made her way back to the salon. Had to be a screwdrivers and wrenches around somewhere, maybe a hammer even. She was so absorbed in those thoughts that it took a while to notice the sliding glass door. It was closed. Hadn't Gregory left it open? No matter. Find the tools. Where would Pettigrew or his crew put them? The galley. That was a possibility.

Something growled under the floor. A turning noise. A motor starting. She could feel vibrations. Then a second motor turning over. The clank of diesels. Maureen remembered Pettigrew telling her about them, the horsepower and all, but she didn't have anything to compare the information with so she hadn't retained it. Not important. The important thing was, Who'd started the engines? Nobody on board except her and Gregory. To her knowledge, anyway. Then she thought of the superstructure above the cabin—the flybridge they called it, the place where the wheel and all the controls were located. Somebody could have climbed up there while she and Gregory were talking. Could have? They did. Got to stop him. Or them.

Maureen hurried to the sliding glass door, put her fingers on an indentation in the metal at one end and pulled. It didn't move. Stuck maybe. Try again. Again it stayed put. Was it jammed? No. Must be locked from the outside. She looked around for something to break the glass. What? Nothing heavy in sight. Then she remembered what Pettigrew had said. *While I was at it, I had unbreakable glass installed throughout the cabin... Now nobody can get in unless I want them to.* Or out, Maureen had said, not thinking twice about it then. Now she understood. We can't get out until he's ready to release us.

Unbreakable glass. Was there such a thing? Must be. Jewelry stores. Windows in cars they use to carry the President in. What else? What did it matter? She kicked the door. Solid. Like it must feel to kick the hull.

She should tell Gregory what was going on.

Maureen ran though the cabin and down the passageway. At the stateroom door, she yelled. "Someone locked the door."

Gregory didn't respond at first. Then he said, "Hold on."

Hold on? Where did he think she would go? Imprisoned in the cabin, the back of her neck hurting…. Then she knew. The hatch would be locked, too. Pettigrew said he'd fixed the forward hatch so it could be locked from either inside or out. Only now did she realize that didn't make sense if security was his only goal. The only reason to secure an opening from the outside was to keep people in.

"The hatch is locked or stuck," Gregory yelled from the other side of the stateroom door.

It was so obvious now. Someone had deliberately left the hatch open, then locked it after Gregory entered the stateroom.

The boat moved. Had she imagined it? Maybe a wave had caused the hull to rock? No, *Sybarite* was definitely moving backward, pulling out of the slip. Somebody cast off the lines. The boat had left the dock.

"Did you feel that?" Gregory asked.

"Yep. We're moving."

The stern of the yacht turned, and Maureen visualized it backing into a channel between docks. Slowly the vessel stopped. Maybe this is as far as it's going, she thought. Or she hoped. Maybe someone was testing the engines or something. Maybe it will go back into the slip now.

No luck. *Sybarite* began moving forward, slowly at first, then faster.

"Be right back," Maureen yelled to Gregory.

She eased her way along the passageway, the boat's forward motion forcing her to take long steps, and looked out the cabin window. The Bahia Mar docks passed by, the few people on them not seeming to notice the boat. Probably wouldn't even if she yelled. So many strange things went on around docks that nobody paid attention to anything. Locked in. Definitely a first for her. Usually corporate executives tried to lock her out.

When they reached the Intracoastal, the boat turned left. South. Toward Port Everglades. And if it reached the port and turned left again into the main channel, toward the Atlantic Ocean. And then where?

She knew. They were going out to sea.

Chapter Forty-Seven

Of all the places Maureen could sit in the yacht, she felt the most comfortable sitting on the floor next to the main stateroom, legs stretched out in front of her, back to the door, knowing even when she and Gregory weren't talking that he was on the other side ready to listen. She couldn't see out the small ports in the passageway from there, but she wasn't interested in watching the water anymore. It was clear where the yacht was going. Farther east into the ocean, beyond the sight of land.

She'd watched from the salon as *Sybarite* turned into the Everglades Ship Channel, passed the tall condominium buildings on the left and a barren beach dotted with Australian pines on the right, then glided through jetties on either side until they reached white water. The tiny waves splashed harmlessly off the Bertram's hull.

Farther and farther out they went, the row of hotels and condos along the beach growing smaller, fewer and fewer boats around them this far out, even the freighters and cruise ships waiting at anchor receding in the distance. She wondered if they'd reached the Gulf Stream. She knew it was deeper and choppier than water closer to the shore, but how did you tell where it began? They couldn't draw a line in the ocean.

Maureen knocked on the door. "Talk to me."

Gregory's muffled voice came back. "Want me to read you the comics?"

"Tell me who you think's up there on the flybridge."

"Pettigrew, maybe," Gregory said, no conviction in his voice.

"He's supposed to be in the hospital."

"A miraculous recovery?"

"Even Pettigrew couldn't pull that off."

"OK," he said. "*You* tell me who's taking us out on this ride?"

Maureen had been thinking of little else since they past the channel buoy. "My money's on Kennedy."

Gregory didn't answer.

"You still there?"

"No, I'm walking around the block."

Maureen smiled. "So you agree?"

"Kennedy seemed genuinely sorrowful."

"About his mother. Not about Pettigrew."

Maureen waited, knowing Gregory was thinking about it.

Finally he said, "Well Kennedy is strong enough to strangle Grace and Bridget and throw Pettigrew off the balcony. But somehow he doesn't seem...."

"Think about it," she said. "Kennedy could have learned Grace's plans from Bridget. He was friendly with her. And later, after Bridget talked to us at the swimming pool, she could have told him what she told us. Kennedy might have realized then that she knew too much."

Gregory said, "She was supposed to have gone back to Providence Place."

"There was nothing to keep her from going through the opening in the bamboo hedge behind it and into the garden at Trust House. She could have met Kennedy there."

"And he killed her?"

"There or someplace else. Then he took her to the stairway in front of your apartment."

Gregory said, "And why did Kennedy throw Pettigrew off the balcony?"

"To kill him."

"Why?"

"You said sons always kill their fathers." That should rile him.

"I didn't say always."

"OK. Maybe it had more to do with the billion dollars Kennedy might inherit if Pettigrew died."

"Why rush things?' Go said. "Eventually, he'd get the money anyway."

"A million reasons," Maureen said. "Maybe Kennedy thought Pettigrew was losing his grip. Maybe his empire is closer to crumbling than anybody knows."

Again no sound from the stateroom.

"So you agree with me?"

"I don't know," Gregory said. "I'm too busy looking through these books."

"What books?"

"The ones I got out of the safe in the bow."

The books in the safe, the ones they had been looking for. Gregory hadn't told her he'd found them. "You crumb bum. You radish. You lousy—"

Gregory said, "Do you want to know what's in them, or not?"

The diesels were quieter now, or perhaps Maureen was straining so hard to hear Gregory's voice that her mind shut out everything else.

"There were two accounting books in the safe," Gregory said. "Nothing else."

"How'd you get it open?"

"Used the same key that unlocked the sliding door to the cabin."

So Pettigrew had a new cabin lock made to match that of the safe, or vice versa, Maureen thought. Made sense in a twisted sort of way. Fewer keys to carry. But why didn't it fit the stateroom door, too? Maybe two keys made him feel more secure than one. "Describe the books."

"Both the same. The hard covers are light green. The pages inside have ruled blue lines and a few red ones. Nothing fancy."

"Go on."

"Each page has a series of dates written down the left hand column. Next to them are names of companies, followed by two columns of four and six-digit figures."

Maureen could see them. "The third column is probably the number of shares purchased or sold, the fourth the amount of money involved. Read me the first pages of each book."

Gregory read them. The dates started in the late seventies when Pettigrew took control of the old man's fortune. The share numbers and dollar amounts in one book were much smaller than in the other, but the pattern of purchases and sales was consistent. Transactions in the book with the smaller numbers always took place before those in the second, sometimes two or three weeks in advance, often just a few days.

Maureen understood at once. One book, the one with smaller figures, listed Pettigrew's personal purchases and sales. The other listed the Pettigrew Trust transactions. Her suspicions were right on target. Pettigrew had used his knowledge of what the Trust would buy or sell to make money for himself. He knew major purchases or sales by the Trust could cause stock prices to rise or fall. It was a clear-cut case of systematic illegality, especially if the trades involved companies Pettigrew controlled.

"Flip to the back of the books and read me the last pages."

Gregory did so.

The same patterns prevailed but the number of shares grew larger and the dollar amounts were much bigger. And—this made Maureen's heart sing—they involved stock in companies Pettigrew controlled.

"We've got him," she yelled. "If Martha Stewart deserved five months, Pettigrew should get fifty years."

There wasn't any reply.

"Did you hear me?"

"That's backward, Mo," Gregory said. "He has us. We're locked in separate compartments of the boat, and he or somebody is taking us out to sea."

Yes. But....

"And there's another detail," he said.

"What?"

"The books aren't titled. There's nothing to indicate on the covers or anywhere else that Pettigrew is connected with either one. And I doubt this is his handwriting. It's too neat."

"Doesn't matter," Maureen said, her spirits bouncing back. "The Securities and Exchange Commission can reconstruct the trades from brokerage records." It was an interesting bit of subterfuge, though. And why in the world would Pettigrew keep the detailed records of transactions that would incriminate him?

"Now I've got a question," Gregory said.

"Shoot."

"Why are we being held in separate compartments?"

The question had occurred to Maureen, too, but until now everything else seemed more important. The answer came to her.

"So whoever is up there can deal with us one at a time."

Chapter Forty-Eight

Maureen heard a noise behind her. Something rolling. A sliding glass door being opened. She stood up, and ran down the passageway. When she got to the cabin she saw the door to the cockpit had pulled to one side.

"Time to come out," a voice said. It came from outside. Who? Male, but with her hearing dulled by the throb of engines, Maureen couldn't identify him. No matter. She could escape now. She rushed through the cabin, and ran into the cockpit. As she reached daylight, someone jumped from the side and pushed past her.

She heard the cabin door sliding behind her and swung around. It was closed. Reflections of the sun and sea prevented her from seeing inside. She cupped her hands to the sides of her face and pressed against the glass. A man crouched in shadows at the back of the salon. He wore a blue blazer and tan or gray pants. That was all she could see. No help. At separate times, she'd seen both Pettigrew and Kennedy in outfits like that. Even Gregory had one. It was a male uniform.

Now whoever it was bent low, his back still to Maureen, pulled up a hatch in the cabin floor, crawled down into the opening, and disappeared. Maureen pushed sideways against the glass, attempting to slide the door. It held tight. Locked from the inside this time. First she'd been locked in, now she was locked out. Whoever had rushed past her had a plan, but she had no clue what it included. All she knew for sure was that their captor had sunk beneath the floor to where the engine was. To below the water line.

Maureen stood in the cockpit torn between two strong impulses. She wanted to break the glass somehow, rush into the cabin, and confront whoever had pushed past her. At the same time, she felt she had to rescue Gregory. He'd been locked in the bow stateroom since before Sybarite left the Bahia Mar marina, no way to look outside, no idea where the yacht was now. Forget about whoever crawled into the engine compartment, she decided. He's not going anywhere. Help Gregory.

That issue settled, Maureen's next thought was to edge herself around the side of the yacht and try to open the hatch above the stateroom where Gregory was imprisoned. She looked over the side—the left side, the port side, she remembered, both words having four letters. She didn't like what she saw. The chromed metal railings that started at the bow didn't come all the way back to the cockpit, leaving a three or four foot gap. There was no way she could to edge along the narrow walkway without something to hold on to. It was barely wide enough for a shoe, and with the boat rocking she'd fall into the sea. She'd drown. Like Grace Pettigrew. Like Sara Pettigrew before her. Like Roland Pettigrew claimed almost happened when he was a boy.

Why didn't the boat's designers think of this problem? The answer came almost as quickly as she posed the question. To get to the front of the boat in rough weather—to toss an anchor overboard or something—a person would go to the front stateroom and crawl out the bow hatch, the opening she was trying to reach. The one that was locked.

Maybe there was another way. Maureen climbed up a chromed ladder from the cockpit to the flybridge. The higher she went, the more the boat rocked. She didn't like being at the mercy of uncontrollable elements. How had she gotten herself into this mess? Answering a phone in New York. Maybe sitting at a desk there wasn't so bad.

At the top of the ladder she found two chairs sitting side by side, each padded and covered in white vinyl, a wheel in front of one. She wondered who occupied the second seat when Pettigrew was at sea. An L-shaped cushioned area, a place for guests to sit, stretched out in front of the two seats. Who would Pettigrew put there? Business prospects, probably, but Jesus, what did that matter now?

Maureen rested her knees on one of the cushions and looked down. The front of the yacht slanted down to the deck—like a windshield but opaque—the hatch not many feet away. Metal tubing ran down each side of the incline, but there was none in front of where she knelt. She could slide down.

Glad she'd worn jeans, Maureen began climbing over the edge, one leg on the seat, the other on the slanted front. A piece of cake if she stayed in the middle.

The hatch popped open. Gregory's head rose above the deck.

"How?" Maureen said, the only word that came to mind.

"I heard a door slide shut about five minutes ago," he said. "Then there was no noise at all. I decided to check the hatch again. Someone had unlocked it."

"Whoever let me out must have unfastened it, too," Maureen said. "Now he's down in the engine room."

"Not anymore," said a soft Southern voice behind her.

Maureen turned around.

Luther Benjamin Washington stood at the top of the metal ladder, grease on his face, no shirt, his shoulders and arms more muscular than she could have guessed. "Why don't you two take seats so we can have a good talk?"

Chapter Forty-Nine

Even sitting on the flybridge in front of the wheel, an unbuttoned sport shirt on now but his arms still showing grease, Luther managed to look dignified. Maureen sat in the chair beside him, Gregory on the bench seat in front.

After Luther appeared, they'd looked at each other just long enough for Maureen to signal Gregory and for him to nod back, an unspoken agreement passing between them: They'd listen to what Luther had to say, all the while on guard for whatever trickery he might have in mind. Together, they could overpower him and take *Sybarite* back to shore whenever they wanted.

"We'll troll while we talk." Luther inched the throttle forward. The engines, idle while he was below, turned faster. "Just speak a little louder than usual."

Maureen said, "What were you doing down in the engine room?"

"I needed to get something."

"Why did you lock us up?"

"I wanted to talk to you, and I knew you wouldn't listen to the whole story back on shore."

"A God-damned drastic way of getting our attention," Gregory said.

"Do you want to know what's been going on?" Luther turned to Maureen. "Do you want to know the cause of two murders, an attempted murder, and you being fired?"

Her mind jumped ahead. "The elevator, it wasn't broken."

Luther smiled. "We have much to discuss before we get to the elevator."

So she was right. The elevator was the last detail of a complex thought—a probable chain of events—that had come to her. Angels, intuition, her subconscious? Again she didn't care.

Gregory, a puzzled look on his face, was staring at her. Maureen gave him a half nod, silently sending the same message as before. They'd listen now, act later. She turned to Luther. "It's your show."

"That being the case, I'll propose some ground rules. Mainly, I ask you not to interrupt me with questions." He looked at her first, then Gregory. "If there's anything you don't understand when I'm finished, I'll answer then. Agreed?"

"Agreed," Gregory said.

Maureen took longer. "I'll try to restrain myself."

Luther took his time getting started—squinting at the compass, aligning Sybarite with the shoreline, adjusting the throttle. When he began talking, his voice and manner were the same as in his office, unhurried and polite, his eyes scanning between them for bounce-back.

"First, my congratulations. You've discovered a great deal of information since you arrived in town. More than anyone else."

"Get on with it," Maureen said.

"To really understand the story I'm going to tell you, you need to know about me and the event that influenced everything I did for the rest of my life. It happened during the Korean Conflict, a little war that came soon after World War II long before either of you were born. Officially it wasn't even a war."

"We've read about it."

"Please. You promised to keep quiet."

Maureen put a hand to her mouth and turned it, pantomiming the turning of a key. She'd keep quiet if at all possible.

Luther resumed his story. "I was in the Army in Korea. I signed up when I was fifteen, no birth certificate, nothing else to show my age, but they didn't care. They needed bodies. After boot camp, they sent me overseas and then straight to the front lines. I saw death and terrible injuries there, injuries I thought were worse than death, men crippled for life without legs or manhood. I saw what we call bravery and what we call cowardice. I learned those words don't mean a thing. Men do what they have to do when they're afraid."

Luther looked eastward toward the horizon, talking as much to himself now as to them. Like Pettigrew had done, Maureen thought, like we're not even here.

"I was afraid for days. I felt completely alone. Then God came to me." Luther stopped, and Maureen knew her face must have betrayed something.

He learned forward. "Hard for you understand, but try. I didn't see a burning bush or a flash of light. But one night after days of despair, when combat had quieted down, He came to me. One minute I felt one way about myself and the world, the next minute—maybe it took longer than that, I don't know—I felt completely different. I knew then I'd never be alone again. I understood God had plans for me, even if I didn't know what they were. I knew that as long as I was true to myself and to God, no harm would come to me. And none ever has."

Luther paused again, and this time Maureen showed nothing. He turned his gaze back to the sea.

"Soon after my Enlightenment, they took me out of combat and sent me back to the States for retraining. While on the way there, en route to camp, my father died, and I was the only male left in the family. They gave me a hardship discharge. The series of events was so fortuitous that I knew God had intervened in my life. And I knew what His purpose was for me. I was to protect my family, every member of it, no matter what. This was the mission God assigned me.

"Ironic, wasn't it? I found God and old man Pettigrew— Reginald Pettigrew—started making big money about the same time. That's part of the reason I made such a production of telling you all about his history. Maybe even then I wanted you to understand how everything fit together.

"Anyway, soon after I got back home, I went off to Florida A&M, the only public college in Florida that was open to me. After I earned a degree I went back to Jacksonville, where the family was, and went through the motions of getting a job. None of the white firms would hire me, and black accountants said they didn't have enough business to pay a decent salary. So I set up my own practice.

"I attracted nickel-and-dime stuff, keeping books for a few small businesses and doing income taxes for them and anybody who walked in the door. I eked out a living and had enough to help the family. Equally important, I was my own man, and proud of it. Family was my whole life, and I was particularly fond of Evelyn. I watched her go through school and grow into a young woman."

He turned toward Maureen. "You've said you read about things that happened before you were born, but reading is not the same as being there. The country was undergoing enormous change. The Supreme Court handed down Brown vs. Board of Education outlawing 'separate-but-equal' schools. Rosa Parks refused to give up her bus seat to a white man. Eisenhower sent the troops to Little Rock. You can't possibly understand how important all this was to us. The decisions and the actions changed everything." He looked to see if Maureen understood, but she didn't move. "When you came to my office, the last time you were there, I told you I was disappointed when Evelyn chose to go to Bethune Cookman, and I told you about her getting a job in Palm Beach to gather material for her magazine exposé. What I didn't tell you is that when Evelyn came home after her second visit, she was pregnant."

He stopped there—for dramatic effect, Maureen figured—but again she didn't react.

"We all wanted to know who the father was, but Evelyn wouldn't tell us. I begged her and begged her. She was adamant, so there was no father listed on the baby's birth certificate."

And so even if Melody had seen Kennedy's birth certificate, Maureen thought, she wouldn't have known anything. But Maureen knew. She'd made a mistake in thinking Luther was Kennedy's father, but she was right this time. There must be more to it, though. Give him enough rope. "Why are you telling us all this?"

"Because if you understand it, you'll understand that what I did was right."

"And what you did was?"

"No." Luther's voice was harsh. "I will not tell you anything unless you let me tell this my way."

"Let him talk," Gregory said.

His intervention startled Maureen, coming from the side like that, but maybe Go was right. She'd wait. But she wouldn't shut up forever.

"The baby was a boy," Luther went on, "and Evelyn debated a lot about whether to name him for Martin Luther King or Bobby Kennedy. Finally, she decided having one Luther in the family was enough and she picked Kennedy. I was glad."

I doubt that, Maureen said to herself.

"Kennedy's skin was pale, just as it is now. He could pass for white, but that wasn't an option in Evelyn's mind. She said he'd be raised black, at least as long as he stayed in Jacksonville. And she didn't want anything to do with the father. She would raise him by herself.

"But soon after the baby's first birthday, Evelyn had a change of heart. She said she wanted the best for Kennedy and knew she couldn't get it by herself alone. She told us the father's name, and asked me to see if he would help financially. She saw it as her right. She'd been taken in by young Fritz."

So Roland Fitzgerald Pettigrew was Kennedy's father, exactly what Maureen had figured. One detail to clear up, though. "Fritz? Why not Fitz as in Fitzgerald?"

"Fritz was what Sara called Roland when they were children, and later everybody else called him that, too. Why Fritz instead of Fitz?" Luther shrugged. "Who knows how children's nicknames get started?"

"The name sounded strange from the beginning," Maureen said.

"Evelyn told me the whole story then," Luther said. "Their affair started when Roland Fitzgerald was at Harvard working on his MBA. They met when he came home for the summer. He flattered her, told her he wanted to hear her opinions. Gradually she started telling him what she thought of Palm Beach and Palm Beach society. To her surprise—and his I suppose—his views were similar to hers. They were both outsiders.

"Remember too, Fritz was just a couple of years older than Evelyn. She was an attractive young woman, and Fritz was a healthy young man—physically anyway. He told her how lonely he was, how he felt unwanted. He even told her the story about almost falling off the yacht. You may have heard a version of that—with or without phony tears."

"On his boat," Maureen said. "With the tears."

Luther leaned over the wheel, looking down at the instruments, obviously nervous for the first time since he'd started talking. "But an exchange of philosophical views wasn't all young Fritz wanted. He wanted in her pants, and he would have said anything to get there. He'd had his first sexual experience while at college—not with another student, it came out later, but with a prostitute. With Evelyn he wanted to see what it was like without having to pay."

He looked out to sea. "I don't know what her sexual history had been up until then, but whatever it was, I'm sure she was more loving than anything young Fritz had ever experienced."

Maureen felt a tinge of sorrow for the old man. He had to push through a big mental barrier to talk about his sister's sex life, the difference in generational attitudes still big.

"Who knows what might have come of the affair if it had gone on?" he continued. "But one evening Sara—Roland's sister—came back to the mansion unexpectedly, heard noises in his bedroom, and walked in. Caught them in bed, like a scene in the movies. Evelyn told me later she'd never seen a grown man so scared. He acted like a little boy, she said, a frightened little boy."

A trace of a grin moved across Luther's face. "Sara was angry for days. She didn't care so much about what happened but where it happened. In her house. In a community where she'd been ostracized because of her husband's coarseness. Where she was just getting into society. She thought Palm Beach socialites would do something terrible—something like banning her from all parties again—if they found out."

But no one in Palm Beach Society would care, Maureen was thinking. They'd forgiven themselves and others for much worse things. She remembered the stories in the *Post* about how popular Sara had become. Roland's affair with a maid would be an amusing piece of gossip, nothing else. They'd never even mention it in front of Sara.

Luther said, "Sara's belief was naïve, but that's what she thought. She was, after all, just poor white trash from the Eastern Shore, and she was alone. She offered Evelyn money to leave, but I'm proud to say Evelyn wouldn't take it. Then, before Sara could do anything else, summer ended and it was time for Fritz and Evelyn to go back to their schools."

Maureen had heard enough to make up her mind. Luther's story was an accurate account of what happened. Every word rang true. But she still didn't understand why he was telling them this. He'd said if they heard the story they'd understand why he did what he did. No way, she thought, not if he'd done what she suspected.

"Unknown to Sara and everyone else, Fritz and Evelyn kept getting together," Luther said. "They met in Daytona Beach on school holidays. Evelyn was already there, at Bethune-Cookman, and Fritz could fly in. Thanksgiving, Christmas, Spring Break. It was a forbidden affair, which probably made it even more exciting for both of them. Until June, a year after old man Pettigrew died. That was the month my sister went to the Palm Beach mansion for the second time. And this time she was pregnant.

"Sara was really furious then. She'd just finished what she considered a very successful season in Palm Beach society, and she planned to buy a northern residence to follow the society circuit. And now, Evelyn's pregnancy was going to ruin it all.

"She offered Evelyn a much larger sum of money and told her to get an abortion. It wasn't legal then, but Sara said my sister would know where to go. She was wrong. My sister not only didn't know where to go for an abortion, she wasn't going to get one. No matter how much Fritz begged her to do it."

"That was the motive!" Gregory almost yelled. "Roland was afraid his sister would replace him as a trustee of her husband's trust in retaliation for embarrassing her."

Maureen had figured that out already. "Roland knew it would be easy for Sara to persuade the bank trustee to vote with her. And he must have figured any of the men who took her to parties—the banker, the lawyer, the financier—would love to have his job. Were probably lobbying for it, in fact."

"So he killed Sara." Go looked at Luther for confirmation.

"I wasn't there," he said.

"But you learned about the drowning and have had years to think about it," Maureen said. "How could you not know?"

Luther looked out into the water as if trying to figure how to phrase his next sentence. Finally, he turned and faced them. "What you've guessed seems to be a reasonable conclusion from all the available facts."

"It was the first murder," Maureen said. "The murder that paved the way for little Fritz to become a billionaire, and set the stage for Grace and Bridget's murder more than thirty years later."

"Nobody could prove anything now," Luther said,

Gregory said, "And now you're going to tell us that Pettigrew killed Grace and Sara, too."

Luther looked to his left, then his right, then slowly back to Maureen.

"Not exactly," he said. "Not exactly."

Chapter Fifty

Not exactly. Some part of Maureen knew what that meant, but the pictures in her head were out of focus, the pieces jumbled, refusing to stay still.

"You OK?" Gregory asked.

"Yes," she said.

"You're holding the back of your neck again."

Mo smiled. "I'm OK. Now Luther's going to tell us the rest of his story."

"But I've got to tell it in my own way." Frustration showed on Luther's face. "And I've got to tell you everything that's significant. To me."

"Go ahead," Maureen said, and Gregory nodded agreement.

Luther took a deep breath. "After Sara drowned, my sister thought her problems were over. Evelyn was in love, and she was sure she'd be with Fritz for the rest of her life. But the day after Sara's funeral, Fritz told Evelyn he'd never see her again. He said he had big plans, plans he needed to be alone to accomplish. You know what that meant?"

"I can guess," Maureen said.

"Until Sara's death, Evelyn's race hadn't mattered," Luther said. "But afterward, Fritz knew he'd be dealing with bankers, brokerage houses, judges, and lawyers. They wouldn't like him having a black girl friend. Not thirty or forty years ago. It was the nineteen seventies. Florida was barely a generation out of segregation and still very much a part of the South."

"My sister was hurt and disgusted," he said. "Here was a man she'd loved and respected offering her money and telling her he'd never see her again. She told him to go to hell and came home to Jacksonville."

Luther grinned broadly, as if about to share a dirty joke "You know Pettigrew's impotent?"

Maureen, remembering what Melody told her, nodded.

"Well, before Evelyn came back to Jacksonville she told Pettigrew she'd put a voodoo hex on him. She made up a story about going to West Palm Beach and finding a voodoo priest who performed a two-hour ceremony with dead chickens and chants and anything else she could think of," Luther said. "She said he'd never be able to get it up again. Pettigrew scoffed, of course, but you know what? From what I hear, he hasn't been able to since."

It was Maureen's turn to grin.

Luther became serious again. "A year after she came back to Jacksonville, Evelyn had a change of heart and asked me to approach Pettigrew about support. I agreed, but I knew I couldn't just go down to Palm Beach and accuse a rich man of fathering my sister's child. I might never come back."

Luther put his hand inside his shirt pocket, as if fishing for cigarettes. "You look skeptical, but I had solid reasons to be fearful. A few years before three national leaders—King and the Kennedys—had been gunned down in public places. If the country wasn't safe for them with all their security, Palm Beach sure wasn't safe for me."

"The truth of it doesn't matter," Gregory said. "If you believed that, it was true for you."

Luther pulled his hand away from the shirt, nothing in it. "So I decided to make sure the story would come out even if something happened to me. I tape recorded a statement from Evelyn, got it transcribed and had her sign the document in front of two witnesses and a notary. Then I put the whole bundle—the tape recording, her statement and a letter outlining my plans—in a safe-deposit box. I kept one key, gave the other to a close friend and put his signature on the card at the bank. After that I drove to Palm Beach to confront Roland Fitzgerald. A black knight off on a mission."

"A black knight off on a mission," Maureen repeated, remembering Kennedy had suggested they ask Luther to tell them about the black knight. OK. Now he had.

"But I got a surprise," Luther said. "The Palm Beach mansion where Evelyn worked was vacant and up for sale. The phone books and city directories didn't have a listing for a Roland Fitzgerald or anything close to it. Neither did information. Fritz had vanished.

"I admit my search wasn't as thorough as others might have made, but I couldn't go from door to door, mansion to mansion, asking if they knew what had happened to Roland Fitzgerald So my first trip didn't produce anything. I went back to Jacksonville, and phoned some friends.

"One of them had a friend who had access to the *Post's* files, but they were no help. After Sara's drowning Fritz had dropped out of the news. Another friend said he'd check records at the courthouse as soon as he had time. And one told me—I'll always remember it word for word--'Fitzgerald coulda died. Or changed his name'."

"You found out that Roland changed his name," Maureen said.

Luther looked up. "You found it, too?"

Maureen nodded, but Luther was intent of telling all the details.

"It was a long shot, but by that time I'd reached the point I'd try anything," he said. "I stayed in West Palm over the weekend. Monday morning I went to the Palm Beach County Courthouse and searched public records. There it was, bold as brass. Petition to Change Name. Petition Granted. Roland Fitzgerald had changed his name to Roland Pettigrew."

Luther smiled now, his first happy expression since he started his story, proud of himself after all these years. Maureen let him enjoy it.

"I still hadn't found Fritz, though. Neither the phone book nor any of the city directories had a Roland Pettigrew, and there wasn't any Internet to search back then. I got discouraged and went back to Jacksonville."

"Adventures of the black knight delayed," Maureen said.

Luther smiled again but didn't stop. "Eventually I started making a little money and wanted to invest it, so I began reading the financial magazines. One of them, I think it was *Forbes*, carried a little article in the back about 'a young man to watch' in Fort Lauderdale. And there he was. Roland Pettigrew—the man Evelyn knew as Roland Fitzgerald—picture and all. I knew once again that God was in my life. He'd just told me to wait."

"Or you got a lucky break."

Luther ignored her. "It wasn't hard to get to Fritz once I knew what city to look in. He wasn't famous yet, and he didn't have security guards."

Again he grinned, and Maureen knew the old man was relishing what he was about to say.

"I found the man who called himself Pettigrew living with his first wife in a waterfront mansion, the place we now call Trust House. I went right up to the front door, introduced myself to the woman who answered the bell, and said I was there on behalf of the mother of Roland Pettigrew's child. She thought I was joking or something but agreed to relay the message. When she did, ol' Fritz set some kind of speed record getting to the door."

No wonder Melody said to check birth certificates, Maureen thought. She knew all about Pettigrew fathering Kennedy, even if she'd never seen a piece of paper with his name on it.

Luther said, "I don't know what Pettigrew told his wife, but he took me for a tour of the garden. We walked around the lagoon where they found Grace's body last Friday, and then we went down to the boathouse."

Maureen could see it—Roland, a small white man in his mid-twenties about to take over the world of business but scared to death someone would learn what he'd done to get there, and Luther, a tall black man in his forties, a combat veteran, not caring about Roland's sister being drowned but caring very much about own sister and her child, walking around the garden, getting acquainted. Must have been quite a sight. Better yet, something to hear.

"I told Roland about the material in the safe-deposit box in Jacksonville," Luther said. "I said it would be appropriate for him to send Evelyn a check every month. He said 'How much?' and I gave him a figure. He said it was acceptable.

"Then I decided to see how afraid he was. I told him it would be appropriate to hire a bookkeeper to come in every so often to check his books and see that he had written the check. I wasn't really serious, but wonder of wonders, he said he might need a CPA to do some auditing. I didn't take him seriously. Not at first.

"Evelyn's checks started coming to Jacksonville regularly, every month the first week of the month. Then I decided to see what Pettigrew meant by needing a CPA to do some work, so I went down to Lauderdale again. It turned out his idea of an audit was to sign a piece of paper saying certain books had been audited without going to all the trouble of looking at them. I told Pettigrew I wouldn't do it.

"That didn't faze him. He came up with a new offer. I could keep books for the Pettigrew Trust. It would be a part-time job with a decent salary, nothing underhanded." Luther looked at Maureen. "So, you see, being true to myself paid off again."

"You blackmailed him," she said.

"I didn't look at it that way," Luther said. "What I was doing was just a reverse form of a common business transaction. In business, they say, 'I'll do this for you, if you do that for me.' What I was saying to Pettigrew—by implication, never directly—is I won't do that to you, if you do this for me. I won't raise a stink and my sister won't go to court if you keep supporting Kennedy."

"Where is she?" Maureen said. "Evelyn."

"I'm coming to that."

Maureen could see that Luther was losing patience. But so was she. "Go on."

"And maybe you won't think what I did was so bad when hear what happened next. I began coming down here regularly, mostly on weekends, and Roland and I started spending a lot of time together. We developed a strange bond. I had something on him, but somehow he got the idea that meant he could trust me—that he had some power over me, too."

Gregory had been staring at the ocean while Maureen and Luther talked. Now he said, "It happens. A person being blackmailed has to trust the blackmailer to carry out his part of the bargain—that he won't tell what he knows as long as person being blackmailed keeps up his end. That trust established, why not trust him more?"

"Sounds dangerous," Maureen said.

Luther extended both arms in front of his body and pushed his hands outward, as if clearing the air of the subject. "Eventually, Pettigrew offered me a full-time job. I would be in charge of the accounts, but I'd have other duties—some administrative work, but more important I'd be the public spokesman for the Trust. I knew I was being given the job, at least partly, to be his token black, but I didn't care. Even then, I had plans to get Kennedy involved.

"Later Roland made me a trustee of his own Pettigrew Foundation, one he set up to handle his personal charitable contributions. I saw those books, too, but didn't work on them. Would have been a conflict of interest."

Maureen said, "You have an interesting set of ethics."

"All the time I've worked for Pettigrew, I've always been my own man. I've been true to myself and my principles," Luther said. "I've never lied to anybody."

"But you're not above blackmail."

"Neither were you and Mr. Overman." Luther adjusted the wheel. "Back when you were threatening to tell Mr. Pettigrew that Kennedy was preaching at a local church."

In Maureen's mind, the two incidents were different, but she didn't argue. She wanted to learn.

"A few months after I started working for Pettigrew, I was able to get him to double the monthly checks he wrote for Kennedy's care. Evelyn appreciated that. But then, everything changed again."

Luther paused, and Maureen could see him pushing himself to talk about something unpleasant.

"Evelyn vanished. Disappeared without a trace."

Maureen didn't let anything show on her face, but she was thinking, No wonder. No wonder Luther blew up when she asked him earlier about Evelyn's whereabouts.

Luther looked away but kept talking. "Maybe we should have seen it coming. We knew she'd become radicalized by the experience with Pettigrew. His betrayal became a symbol of white oppression. She wanted to hurt Pettigrew, but by then she couldn't harm him without damaging her son's welfare, too.

"She started talking about ways to hurt all white people. The Black Panthers became her heroes, and as time passed she became more and more agitated. Then one day she asked her older sister to take care of Kennedy while she went shopping. We never saw her again."

Until this moment, Maureen had been immune to Luther's attempts to engage her sympathy, just as she'd been with Pettigrew. Now she weakened. "Surely there was some way to trace her."

"At first the family thought she was coming down here to be with me, to confront Pettigrew, so we didn't do anything for a while. Then when she didn't show up in a month, we put out word to all of our relatives and friends. They hadn't heard from her, either. We checked the few records that were available to us. Eventually we found out she had no up-to-date driver's license, no car registration and no credit cards. She'd vanished from the face of the earth.

"Maybe she got mixed up in some crime— Maybe she— Who knows?" Luther turned back to Maureen. "I never told Pettigrew that Evelyn was missing, of course, but I did start going back to Jacksonville every weekend to spend time with Kennedy. I didn't want him raised by nothing but women. And I kept sending Pettigrew's checks to Jacksonville, depositing them in a joint account Evelyn had with her sister.

"I kept looking for her everywhere I could think of. I researched techniques of finding missing persons, and I paid a private detective. The answer was always the same. This is a free country. It's possible to disappear if you want to."

Luther looked out to sea. Maureen waited until he was ready to speak again.

"I put Evelyn's photograph on the wall behind my desk and later added the second photo of her with Kennedy. You know something?" he said. "Pettigrew saw those pictures a thousand times but never asked about them. But when it was time to send Kennedy off to college, I didn't have any problem getting him pay the bills. We pretended he was just helping an employee.

"Kennedy went to Florida State, where I wanted to go but couldn't. When he graduated I wanted him to get a graduate degree in theology somewhere, but he wouldn't. He wanted to play and party. So I arranged a job for him with the Pettigrew Trust. Officially he was a security guard, living on the grounds and patrolling at night. In fact, he was Pettigrew's chauffeur and trainer with hours so flexible he could go to law school on the side. Nova Southeastern was close enough to make that possible."

Every one of these details is important to Luther, Maureen was thinking, but she needed to push him ahead. "You were Kennedy's surrogate father, but his biological father down the road paid the bills."

"You might say that."

"Because you were blackmailing him. Don't you see an inconsistency in bragging about how truthful you were when your job and your status and Kennedy's welfare rested on a lie—that Evelyn was alive?"

"I assume she is," Luther said. "She's just missing."

Enough, Maureen thought. Get down to it. "When did you conclude Pettigrew probably drowned his sister?"

"Not long after I started coming to Lauderdale to 'audit' his books."

"And when did you first go out on a boat with him?"

"Quite a while after that."

"Who was the third person on board?"

Luther pursed his lips. "At first there was a captain. Then just the two of us."

Maureen waited a beat, then. "And who was at the wheel?"

Luther put a hand to his mouth and stared at the floor.

"A truthful answer, now," Maureen said. "Who piloted the boat?"

"You're a smart woman," Luther said. "You've guessed I did."

"In fact, in spite of all his bragging, Pettigrew never took this or any other boat out single-handed after his sister died. Either you or Kennedy was aboard with him. He's afraid to go out by himself."

"True enough. But not important."

"It's a symbol," Maureen said. "A symbol of your relationship with Pettigrew."

Luther looked at Maureen as if he didn't know what she was talking about, but she was sure he did.

She locked her eyes on his. "You've been running things since soon after you arrived in Lauderdale. You've made all the decisions: What stocks to buy or sell, what companies to acquire or divest, maybe even what contributions to make or withhold."

Luther opened his mouth, but no words came out.

"You're the mastermind of the whole deal. The Trust. The businesses. The billion-dollar personal fortune. It was probably even your idea to contribute to Providence Place so you could expand the Trust House property."

"You can't know that."

"I know that Pettigrew is a frightened little man who couldn't run a corner drug store," Maureen said. "And I know you're the only man at Trust House who knows what he's doing. You controlled everything."

Luther looked first between Maureen and Gregory, at the horizon, back to them, then back to sea again. Finally he said, "I'm not going to deny it."

"So you get the credit for everything," Maureen said.

Luther nodded.

"And the blame."

Chapter Fifty-One

They sat in silence for minutes, Maureen looking toward the shore wishing she knew more about how the South Florida coastline appeared from the ocean. Was that Pompano Beach in the distance? Boca Raton? Lake Worth, maybe? They were all so damn flat, not one with enough tall buildings to make a decent skyline, not a single landmark she recognized.

"We should head back in," she said.

Luther nodded. "In fact, it's time for you to take the wheel. I've got to go below and do something."

"I've never...."

"Or Gregory can sit here." Luther looked at Go. "You'll find it steers pretty much like a car."

Gregory stood and went to the wheel. "Turn it around. Then I'll take over."

The boat circled, Luther pointing it away from land at first, then just as Maureen was about to protest, toward shore. He showed Go how to work the throttle and gearing system, the chromed handles topped with red and black balls. "Be back soon," he said as he crawled down the ladder.

When he was out of sight, Maureen turned to Gregory. "What do you think?"

He rubbed stubble on his cheeks. "Why is he telling us all this?"

"That bothers me, too."

"Another reaction. You're both very quick to indict Pettigrew for murdering his sister. But nobody alive except Pettigrew knows what happened out in the ocean that day. It could have been an accident, one he's been blaming himself for ever since."

"A possibility."

"And you notice that in all of his explaining Luther hasn't said who killed Grace or Bridget, or who pushed Pettigrew off the balcony."

"True." Maureen brushed hair off her forehead. "You're making the boat go faster than Luther did."

"I'm more anxious to get back to shore. I'm using more power and angling directly toward the Port Everglades channel."

Maureen appreciated this, but there was something about Gregory's attitude she didn't like. He was putting down everything they'd learned. Hadn't he heard Luther confirm her guess that he ran everything? Didn't he remember finding the account books that documented Pettigrew's insider trading? Couldn't he see that if Pettigrew had been exposed....

"Promise me one thing," Gregory said. "When the showdown comes, leave the physical stuff to me."

Maureen could feel her anger rising then, her heart beating faster, adrenalin spreading through her body, as if Go had reached out and hit her. Damn him. They'd solved the problem and now he was looking for a fight. Didn't he see....

"Here comes Luther," Gregory said.

She'd settle with him later.

Gregory offered the wheel to Luther, but he waved Go off and sat on the bench seat at the front. From there, he had to look up to see Maureen and Gregory as they sat side by side on the raised helm seats. Maureen's mind formed an image of a King and Queen with a Jester at their feet. Now it was up to Luther to amuse them.

"Think back to the party the night I arrived," she told him. "Pettigrew tried to scare me away. 'Don't mess with me,' he said. Then Kennedy found me and apologized."

Luther just sat there.

"You had a part in that," she said.

He nodded. "Pettigrew came upstairs and told me what he'd told you. I told Kennedy to go back and apologize for Pettigrew. I wanted Kennedy to find out more about you."

"He asked if Go and I were an item."

"Unfortunately," Luther said, "you kept asking so many questions he couldn't get much out of you."

"My partners. Have you dealt with them?"

Luther barely hesitated. "Someone from your firm came down and solicited Pettigrew's business. Roland referred her to me, and I told her I wouldn't deal with them as long as you worked there."

"Rebecca?"

"That was her name."

Everything fit together. Rebecca. Pettigrew. The nuns. Luther. Two murders and a murder attempt. Their solution was pretty obvious now. But first they had to get off this boat.

She turned to Gregory. "Now what?"

"We're going in the Port Everglades Channel."

"I don't think so." Luther grinned.

"We are," Go said, his voice louder.

Luther leaned back against the vinyl-covered seat cushion. "You know what a thru hull is? Or a seacock?"

Gregory nodded, but Maureen shook her head.

"A thru hull is an opening, a hole if you will, in the bottom of a boat, usually below the waterline. Thru hulls bring in sea water to cool engines, clean heads, or perform similar chores."

So? Maureen wondered.

"A seacock," Luther continued, "is a valve that shuts off a hose attached to the thru hull."

"I didn't fly from New York to get a lesson in marine hardware," she said.

"It's relevant to your present situation. Listen and you may learn something."

Luther was stealing her line. You can learn a lot by listening.

"Remember when you saw me pull up the hatch in the floor of cabin?" He stopped long enough for Maureen to recall it. "I went down to the engine room."

Maureen nodded, a flicker of understanding running through her mind, the idea leaving as quickly as it came.

"What?" Gregory said, concern in his voice. "When?"

"You couldn't see me, because you were locked up." Luther turned back to Maureen. "There're two big diesel engines down there. Pettigrew probably told you the horsepower and all."

"You opened the seacocks!" Gregory rose from his seat.

"Go down there and look if you wish." Luther seemed amused. "But you'd be wise to listen to me."

Gregory looked to Maureen. She lowered her head a fraction of an inch, leaving the decision to him. He stayed where he was, standing with one hand on the wheel.

"The seacocks were already open," Luther said, his tone that of a professor lecturing students. "They had to be to cool the engines. What I did earlier was disable the shutoffs."

"How?"

"I unbolted the handles. Now the seacocks are stuck open and can't be closed."

"Where are they? The handles."

"The bottom of the ocean. I threw them overboard on the way up here."

Gregory sat back down. "And now?"

"You know about the cylinders around the strainers?" Luther leaned forward.

Maureen shook her head, and Gregory looked blank.

"No? Then I'll explain. Marine engines are cooled with water from rubber hoses attached to the seacocks, but there's all kinds of junk in the ocean. The water has to be strained. People who maintain the engines need to know when the strainers are about to clog up, so each filter is surrounded by a transparent cylinder."

"So?" Maureen said.

"I broke them."

"You broke the cylinders?" Gregory said, louder than before.

"They're made of a hard plastic. All it took was a couple of whacks with the back of a wrench."

Gregory inhaled loudly. "So now water is coming in through the seacocks and spilling out into the hull?"

Luther nodded. "Naturally I disabled the bilge pumps, too."

Maureen looked between the two men, wondering why neither was saying the obvious. They weren't going to say it, so she would.

"We'll sink."

Luther smiled. "And there's nothing either of you can do about it."

"Take the wheel," Gregory said to Maureen. "I'll go below and check."

She stared at Luther. "You want us to drown."

"Precisely."

"That means you'll die, too."

Luther nodded. "The difference between us is I don't care. I've finished everything I was put on earth to do. I don't mind leaving it."

Chapter Fifty-Two

Luther was right about one thing. The boat did steer pretty much like a car. Maureen was at the wheel now while Gregory searched below deck seeing what could be done. She had a million questions, but one seemed more important than all the others.

"How long will it take for the boat to sink?"

"I don't know," Luther said. "I've never sunk a boat before."

The bastard is enjoying this, she realized. Don't give in. Act as if everything is under control. "We have enough time to get back to shore."

"I doubt it. It's farther away than it looks."

Maureen saw the microphone next to the wheel and stared at it, realizing too late that Luther would see her looking.

"Naturally I made sure the radio couldn't be used," he said. "Lift the microphone up. High. Over your head."

Maureen picked it up and pulled. The end of the cord dangled in the air.

"I cut it earlier. It can't be mended."

She said, "There must be a life raft or something."

"There used to be an inflatable boat attached to the back of this one. When you boarded, you didn't notice it was gone."

"We'll put on life vests."

"I think you'll find they've been taken off the boat, too."

"But why?" she demanded. "Why tell us everything you've told us and then decide to sink the boat?"

"I thought that if you knew my whole story, you'd understand. But it's clear you don't. And never will."

Of course not, Maureen thought. Nothing justifies murder. And then she understood another piece of the puzzle. "You taped the key to the bottom of the bench in the garden."

Luther smiled. "I couldn't be sure you'd find it, but it was worth a try. You put things together so well I could often predict what you'd do next."

"It was the key Bridget used to get into the boat when she stayed here overnight. The one Grace gave her. The one you..."

Before she could finish Gregory appeared on the flybridge ladder, his shoulders bare. "Water is spilling into the hull from holes in the filters. Not a gusher, but steady. There's several inches in the bottom already."

Maureen said, "Could you tape the breaks in the cylinders?"

"You won't find any tape on the boat," Luther said.

"Could you wrap them with something else? Or maybe stuff cloth in the holes?"

"I donated my shirt to the cause," Gregory said. "Fabric slows the flow but doesn't stop it."

Luther laughed.

Maureen and Gregory ignored Luther and talked about options as if he weren't there. He'd done his worst already.

The most obvious option, they agreed, was to increase the boat's speed and head it directly toward shore, but Gregory said revving up the engines might make water come in faster. He agreed to angle it more directly toward land, though.

Maureen examined the radio cord, trying to figure some way to re-attach it, but the cut was clean and the rubber-like wrapping would require more than an ordinary knife to penetrate. It occurred to her then that a radio wasn't the only way to communicate with shore, but she'd have to wait to try the idea.

"We could fire an emergency flare," Gregory said.

Luther smiled. "They're gone, too."

"Or honk the signal horn."

"Disabled also," he said.

Maureen opened compartments in front of and to the side of the helm, looking for something that might help. Nothing in any of them but some maps and a key tied to a miniature red buoy. No life vests, nothing that would float in the water except the key. And then she realized what the key fit, what it might unlock...

"The cushions," Gregory said. "We can use them to float on."

"I threw away all cushions with any buoyancy." Luther pointed to the vinyl-covered padding he sat on. "These thin things wouldn't hold up anybody."

Maureen said they could always hope another boat would come close enough to signal for help, but Gregory told her that was unlikely. By custom, boats stayed far apart while fishing; and the ones that got too close were warned away.

"I've read of fishermen shooting at each other for intruding," Luther said.

"Shut up." Gregory's voice came out like a bark.

"No, Greg." Maureen held up her hand, her palm toward Gregory. "I think Luther has more to tell us."

"I do, indeed," Luther said. "In the time you have left, you want to hear the rest of the story? Or would you rather run around the boat chasing rainbows?"

No doubt in Maureen's mind. She had a plan now, but it was too early to try it. Meanwhile she'd come too far not to confirm her suspicions.

She looked at Luther. "You and Pettigrew became partners."

Luther leaned back. "You might say that, although we may have had different ideas about who was in charge. After I let him know that Evelyn told me about his sister's drowning, I got very little back-talk. We divided the work along traditional lines. He was Mr. Outside, I was Mr. Inside—a common arrangement in corporations and government. He made the public appearances, talked to the bankers, and made the speeches. I ran things."

"The perception is always that Mr. Outside has the power," Maureen said. "Like the President."

Luther shook his head. "Not with us. I knew three secrets— the drowning, Pettigrew's name change, and that he had engaged in insider trading. Taken separately his sister's drowning and him changing his name weren't much, but put them together and they looked mighty suspicious. Add the insider trading, and.... Well, it was enough to keep him in line."

"Insider trading even back then?"

"Early on, I discovered Pettigrew was buying the same equities for himself as for the trust. I took that idea and ran with it. I was the one who built a billionaire-dollar empire."

"Illegally," Maureen said.

"For Kennedy," Luther said. "A memorial to my sister."

"Good God, Mo," Gregory said. "The boat is sinking and you're talking about securities laws."

"What the hell do you want me to do?"

Gregory opened his mouth and shut it, slipped from the seat, and began crawling down the chromed ladder.

"Let me know if you want help," Maureen yelled after him.

She turned back to Luther. "All the while, you and Pettigrew were buying and selling companies with no regard to all those people you hurt when you closed plants and sent the jobs overseas. Or destroyed pension funds. And you're supposed to be a man of principle."

"We had a clear duty," Luther said. "We were to invest old man Pettigrew's money to produce maximum income for the blind, the deaf, and the elderly, and for crippled children. That was all. Nothing about workers or pension plans or plant closings."

"But you had a separate agenda. You wanted to make Kennedy rich and powerful."

"Happily my agenda and our legal responsibilities coincided."

So there it was. Noble ends justify any means. The pursuit of stock market wealth for a good cause, or even a selfish one, can be completely divorced from the actions of the companies invested in.

Maureen remembered what she'd told Rebecca: *We don't whip the horses, we just bet on them.* She'd been wrong. Absolutely wrong. People are responsible for actions of the company's they own. If they aren't, who is? Officers and directors? Not a chance. They're in it for themselves. Just look at the big salaries and bonuses they pay each other.

The was one more thing to ask Luther about. "You named those buildings for Pettigrew."

"A sop to boost his tiny little ego." Luther paused, looked around, and smiled broadly. "Nothing wrong with that. Or anything else we did."

Nothing illegal, nothing most investors would consider immoral, just a good man doing his duty as he saw it. And now he was going to kill them.

Chapter Fifty-Three

What was Gregory doing down there? What in the cabin was so interesting? Should she leave Luther and join him? Maureen considered the questions only briefly. If Gregory wanted help, he'd ask. She had a plan, but if it didn't work she didn't want to die without knowing all the answers. This was her last chance.

Were there any more easy questions to get out of the way before she asked the hard ones—before she made the accusations? None Maureen could think of, so she decided to go for the jackpot. She fixed her eyes on Luther.

"You said you'd tell us the cause of two murders and an attempted murder. The fact is you killed Grace and Bridget and tried to do the same to Pettigrew."

Luther looked away, scanned the horizon, breathed deeply, and turned back.

"Everything was going wonderfully until that bitch.... Until Grace began digging into things that weren't any of her business."

There it was, the breakthrough. Maureen knew Luther would spill it all now. Just like in business. Time after time when she questioned executives at corporations about to fail, they got to a point where they had to talk to someone to try to justify what they'd done. Or failed to do.

"Grace was out of control," Luther said. "You heard her at the party. She'd learned or guessed there were incriminating papers in my safe. She told Bridget she had the combination."

"How do you know that?"

"They were out in the garden one day planning for Bridget to disrupt the party so Grace could sneak upstairs. My window was open, and I overheard them."

"What was she going to do with them?" she said. "The papers."

"Give them to you."

Maureen heard herself gasp for breath. If she hadn't been on the scene, hadn't flown from New York to Lauderdale, Grace and Bridget might still be alive. The accusation, poisonous and unwanted, jumped into her consciousness. No, she thought. Don't blame yourself. You didn't invite any of this. You didn't hurt anyone.

"So the night of the party when Grace came inside Trust House, you strangled her and dumped her body in the lagoon. You were able to get back and forth quickly because the elevator was operating. The guard lied to us when he said it was broken."

Luther nodded. "He said what I told him to say."

"Why in the world did you keep records of the illegal trading in the first place? You must have known they could harm you."

"For protection," Luther said. "For leverage with Pettigrew. I convinced him he'd go to jail if anyone ever found out, but I could say I was just a bookkeeper doing what I was told."

"Plausible."

"I made three copies. All by hand, no photocopies. If anyone found one, I wanted them to think they had the original. One set of copies I kept in the safe in my office. Another I put in the safe deposit box I still share with a friend in Jacksonville. The third I kept in the boat, a reminder to Pettigrew. That was the one Mr. Overman found. I heard you talking."

"Costa Rica," Maureen said. "When were you planning to go to Costa Rica?"

"Never."

"Bridget found a pamphlet from a Costa Rican bank in the boat."

"A decoy to throw you off track." Luther grinned, proud of himself. "You probably thought Pettigrew was about to sail away."

"It occurred to me."

"And Bridget?" Gregory stood at the top of the ladder. "Why the fuck did you have to kill Bridget?"

Luther leaned to his side, looking around Maureen to see Go. "She knew all about Grace's scheme. If she ever told the police about it, they'd conclude that I murdered Grace."

"You wanted to throw suspicion on me," Gregory said "You killed her in the garden but put her body on the stairs leading to my apartment."

"It worked. The police held you overnight."

Maureen said, "Then you called one of Pettigrew's attorneys and arranged for his release."

Luther nodded.

"You tried to kill Pettigrew," she said. "When we came to your office the last time and I asked about the photograph on the wall, I told you too much. You knew you weren't the only one who'd guessed Pettigrew drowned his sister. You figured that when we confronted Pettigrew with what we knew, he might sell you out."

Luther lowered his head a fraction of an inch.

"So Pettigrew had to go," she continued. "You had his confidence, so you probably had a key to his suite. You may have trained with Kennedy in his exercise room."

Luther straightened to face Maureen. "It was going to be so simple. With Pettigrew dead, the police would have concluded he was the killer and for some reason committed suicide. Then I and the bank trustee could appoint Kennedy as the third trustee."

"You overpowered Pettigrew and threw him over the balcony. But he didn't die."

"A few more feet and he would have landed on the concrete."

"When he didn't, your whole enterprise failed," Maureen said. "From that point on, Pettigrew knew you'd killed Grace and Bridget. He could start blackmailing you."

Gregory said, "I'm surprised you didn't try again. Try to kill Pettigrew."

Luther shrugged. "There are police guards at Pettigrew's hospital door now. He must have phoned Fourquet and asked for protection right after you two left."

"But why?" Maureen said. "Why does Fourquet always side with Pettigrew?"

"Haven't you heard? Fourquet is planning to run for sheriff. Pettigrew will finance the campaign."

So that's it. Now all the offbeat, unprofessional things Fourquet had done made sense. From the very beginning—starting when Grace Pettigrew's body was found in the lagoon—he never treated Pettigrew as a suspect. He's twisted every development in Pettigrew's favor. He wanted Midas Man's money. Maureen remembered what Fourquet told her in the police station parking lot. *I'm not going to be a cop all my life.* He had bigger plans.

Maureen became aware that something had changed on the boat. It was quieter. The engines. She could still hear the clank, clank, clank of an engine but.... The sound came from only one engine. That was it. The other engine wasn't running. She looked at Gregory.

"The water has reached one engine," he said. "It's just a matter of minutes before the other one stops, too."

"And then?"

"It'll come up through the engine hatch and begin filling the cabin."

"And then...."

"I don't know how high it has to get before the boat sinks."

So it's now or never, Maureen thought. Gregory volunteered to handle what he'd called the physical stuff. Well, she'd let him do the heavy lifting, but she'd help. Could she signal him without Luther intercepting her message? She could only try.

"Let's go below," Maureen said, looking at Gregory. "I want to see this for myself." She stood and faced Luther. "Take the wheel."

Gregory started down the ladder, and Luther moved toward the wheel. Maureen turned her back to Luther, using her body as a shield to keep him from seeing what she was doing. She opened the compartment at the side of the wheel, the side opposite from Luther's approach, and reached for the key and miniature buoy she'd seen there earlier. She felt Luther watching. Could he see what she was doing? She closed her fingers around the key, pulled her hand up, and closed the top.

From behind her, Luther said, "I'll adjust the throttle so we can all go below together."

Maureen eased past him, keeping her hand that held the key out of his sight. She looked down at Gregory, already in the cockpit, heading toward the cabin door. "Wait."

He stopped. She scrambled down the ladder and whispered, "Do you remember what you did to the bodyguard at the party?"

"Sure."

"When Luther gets in front of the stateroom door...."

Gregory's expression told Maureen he understood. She looked up and saw Luther starting down the ladder. "Come on see what you've done," she shouted at him.

Suddenly the boat was quiet. The second engine had died.

Luther followed Maureen and Gregory down the ladder and into the cabin, just as she expected. They knew too much to leave alone, even when Luther thought he'd blocked every way of getting information off the boat.

Maureen looked down the passageway and was relieved to see the stateroom door already open. Luther must have unlocked it when he came below before. Gregory pulled the engine hatch open, the flimsy fiberglass below the tan carpeting less than an inch thick, certainly no match for the water roiling six inches below the cabin floor.

She saw Luther looking at the water, too, and asked, "You sure you're ready to die?"

"I've done everything I needed to do in life," he said. "Kennedy is all there's left of the family, and I've assured his future. The mission God gave me has been accomplished."

"You can't be sure about that."

"The bank trustee has already signed papers appointing Kennedy to replace me. I've sent a copy of the account books to the Securities and Exchange Commission, and my friend in Jacksonville will find other copies in our safety deposit box. With that evidence, the bank and Kennedy can have a court remove Pettigrew as a trustee."

"Those account books," Maureen said, moving toward the passageway leading to the front stateroom. "Gregory saw them, but I haven't."

"I'll get them," Gregory said.

"No, I will." Luther pushed himself past Gregory. "Pride of authorship and all that."

"He'll destroy them," Gregory yelled.

"Let him go." Maureen pulled the key and miniature buoy from a pocket in her jeans. "Luther seems to think the account books need a bodyguard."

Gregory stopped, and Maureen was sure he'd received her message. *Bodyguard.* The key word. The only word that was necessary.

Luther walked down the passageway, his back seeming much broader than when he sat behind a desk. He stopped at the door to the stateroom.

"Now," Maureen said, realizing as she said the word that it wasn't necessary. Gregory was more than halfway down the passageway, his body hurtling toward the stateroom. Luther started to turn around. Gregory's shoulder rammed into Luther's side, his forward momentum so great that Luther's body seemed to leave the ground as it crashed backward and fell onto the stateroom's double bed. Gregory fell to the passageway floor.

Maureen stepped over him, closed the stateroom door, and locked it with the key.

"Good job, Go," she said, putting her hand down to help him up. "We've won."

He got up slowly. "Now all we've got to do is swim a million miles back to shore."

"Nope." She smiled. "My fussing with the radio microphone was a diversion. I knew all along that I'd left my purse in the cabin."

Gregory didn't understand what she was talking about. She walked to the galley and picked up her purse. "I knew my cell phone was in here. You told me there are cellular base stations on the roofs of condos near the beach."

"Are we close enough?"

"Cell phones have a range of three to five miles on land, but it's much farther offshore." She began walking toward the cockpit. "When I researched telecommunication companies, I read of fishermen using their cells almost twenty miles out. Halfway to Bimini, they said. And a range of ten to twelve miles is common."

Gregory said, "Luther didn't think of that."

"He's part of the generation that dislikes and distrusts cells. We needed to lock him up because he'd have tried to grab the phone when he saw what I was doing."

Maureen could tell Go was pleased, but she knew he wouldn't congratulate her until much later. He hadn't thought of the idea, so he'd be gruff.

"Well don't just stand there, Mo," he said. "Get out there and make your call."

No time to gloat, even if Maureen had wanted to, every minute counting now. From the cockpit she could see water sloshing inside the cabin, four or five inches above the floor already, rising another inch every few minutes. How much time did she have? No way of knowing.

She reached 9-1-1. The woman who answered asked if she'd radioed the Coast Guard. She started explaining the situation but before she was halfway through the phone went dead. Damn. She remembered more about what she'd learned. The farther out at sea a cell phone called from, the worse the reception and more chance of a disconnect.

Maureen called the emergency number again and got a different person. She described their plight quicker this time, and the woman asked where the boat was. Maureen said she didn't know, but she guessed it was off Pompano Beach or near it. The woman said to hold on while she got through to the Coast Guard. But while Maureen was waiting, the phone clicked off.

Try something different, she told herself. She dialed 4-1-1, ignored the prompts and got a real person. He gave her the Coast Guard number and offered to dial it for her, no extra charge, but the phone went dead again. She punched in the number as she remembered it. A recording said, "Your call cannot be completed as dialed." Damn. She tried again, changing the last digit. Another bum number. This wasn't like her. She usually remembered numbers and figures, getting them right the first time. Calm down.

Gregory's voice came from inside the cabin. "Mo, we've got to let Luther out soon."

Maureen understood. Leaving Luther locked inside the stateroom while the boat filled with water would be murder. But first she had to get the call through. "Not yet," she yelled.

She tried 9-1-1 again and this time told the woman who answered to give her the Coast Guard number before she tried to get through to them. She did. Again the connection broke. No matter. She had the number right this time.

"Hurry, Mo."

"I am."

Finally she got through to someone at the Coast Guard, but a couple of questions revealed he was somewhere south of Miami. They'd never reach Sybarite on time, she thought. The guy said he'd try to get one of the Lauderdale auxiliaries out to them; meanwhile he'd call one of the private towing services. Also, he'd see if there were any copters already in the air near her.

Until that moment Maureen had thought there were fleets of helicopters and boats standing by at Coast Guard stations on every shoreline in the country. Impossible, she realized now, but.... Finally Miami Coast Guard said a helicopter was on its way. Exhausted, she clicked off.

Now she could see the water had risen higher by five or six inches. Gregory should get out of there, but he couldn't leave until Luther was safely out of the locked stateroom. He would be a problem, but they had no other choice.

"Let him go," she yelled.

"OK."

Now all they had to do was wait and hope the boat didn't sink before help arrived. Luther could still give them trouble, but he didn't have a chance against the two of them. They'd shown him that. Maybe he'd learned his lesson.

"Mo," Gregory yelled, something close to panic in his voice.

"What?"

"He's gone."

"What?"

"Luther's not there. The stateroom is empty."

Maureen remembered then, only then, something she'd forgotten. Earlier Luther had unlocked the deck hatch above the stateroom so Gregory could get out. After they'd locked Luther in the stateroom, he could crawl out just as easily.

More than a foot of water covered the cabin floor now. Maureen sloshed through it to the stateroom and found the account books on top of one of the teak shelves next to the bed exactly where Gregory must have left them. Thank God Luther hadn't touched them. They'd be valuable back on shore. If they got there.

She searched the boat's interior, using one hand to open doors, the other to hold the records. The heads. A second stateroom. A closet. Luther wasn't in any of them. That left only the engine room, and it was filled with water. Luther couldn't have hidden inside there. She went back to the cockpit.

"Nothing and no one up here," Gregory said from the flybridge.

"But then where did he go?"

They stared at each other, then in almost the same instant turned and looked down into the dark green waters of the ocean. Did Luther slip and fall overboard? Maybe the boat took an unexpected bounce when he stood up. Or did he jump? Was he so convinced that they'd all drown that he opted to speed the process for himself? Or did he think he could swim to safety?

A flapping sound caused Maureen to look up. She saw a helicopter coming straight toward them. Hard to believe it had gotten there so quickly. But there it was, the slanted red slash that anywhere in the country announced that the Coast Guard was coming. She turned to Gregory. He'd seen it, too.

"Maybe Luther saw it coming and decided he didn't want anything to do with the Coast Guard or anybody else."

"Anything could have happened."

"One question we have to decide quickly. Do we tell them?"

"That Luther was aboard?" The thought had floated through Maureen's mind, too. If they didn't tell anyone, who would know that Luther had been on the yacht? They could say they'd taken the boat from the dock by themselves, got in trouble, and phoned for help. It would save an awful lot of explaining.

The copter flew closer. Soon its blades would make too much noise to talk over.

"We do the right thing," she said.

Gregory nodded. "We tell them everything and take our chances on their believing us. We'll never know what happened to Luther."

"And neither will they," Maureen said.

They couldn't talk without shouting until they got back to shore, but when they landed and the blades stopped Maureen asked the pilot, "How did you get to us so soon?"

"We were almost there when you phoned."

"Why?"

"The Lauderdale cops phoned us. A lieutenant named Fourquet convinced an officer to begin a search. Some V.I.P. named Kennedy was worried about his uncle." He turned to Gregory. "Is that you?"

Chapter Fifty-Four

Hope it's still true, Maureen mused, the back of the plane getting there the same time as the front. Already she felt the rush of air pressurizing the cabin, the high she always felt at take-off. No difference there. And so much cheaper back here in coach, the cost of her ticket and Gregory's combined less than the first class ticket that brought her to Lauderdale. Alone. A nice tradeoff. Having Gregory sitting beside her was considerably more important than anything the front cabin offered.

Three weeks and three days now since she'd left New York. Might as well have been three years. Her life had been transformed in so many ways she could barely remember what it'd been like before. For her, every change had been for the better. She couldn't say that about everyone she met in Florida.

Pettigrew was out of the hospital, recuperating in a nursing home. A nice place, she'd been told, but not at all what Midas Man wanted. He'd asked for round-the-clock nurses at his penthouse, but a judge had frozen his assets and a temporary receiver had decided private nurses weren't necessary.

Maureen felt a little sorry for him now. Imagine, living like a frightened little boy for more than forty years, all the while having to feign an aura of power. And now his life would get worse and worse—the court appearances, the news stories, the probable personal bankruptcy.

Fourquet came out of the experience only slightly better. He'd been put on traffic patrol pending conclusion of an internal police investigation. The department's preliminary assessment was he hadn't broken any law, but his investigative work was so sloppy he'd given the impression he had a personal interest in the outcome of the case. Yeah, Maureen thought. That's about the way they'd phrase their findings. One step short of a whitewash. It wouldn't matter to them, for example, that Fourquet had lied to her, saying Gregory was being held at the police station for arraignment via closed-circuit video. Televised hearings were only held in the County Jail, she'd learned. Fourquet had been blowing smoke.

No matter. Fourquet's career in law enforcement had reached a dead-end. Any idea of him running for sheriff was downright ludicrous now. And Fourquet's back-up plan, the one police discovered when going through Pettigrew's files—that Fourquet would become director of security for Pettigrew Enterprises if he lost the election—was just as dead.

Luther had never been found. A Coast Guard helicopter searched for him for hours but eventually gave up. The pilot said his body had probably been swept north by the Gulf Stream until sharks.... Maureen didn't like to think about it.

She'd miss Luther, an honest man with a strange mix of ethics. Always tell the truth, but it was OK to mislead, blackmail, break securities law, and even murder for a good cause. He wasn't the first person—and wouldn't be the last—to believe a higher calling justified any means. And Maureen knew she couldn't throw stones. She'd attempted to blackmail Luther and Kennedy, if only for information.

Kennedy grieved the disappearance and presumed death of his uncle, but he hadn't blamed Maureen and Gregory. He always knew Luther had a fatalistic streak, and he wasn't surprised that the proud old man would prefer death to discovery.

And now that all the secrets were out, Kennedy revealed he'd suspected for years that Pettigrew's interest in him was more than that of an employer for an employee. He didn't want anything to do with the old man or his money, though; Luther had left him enough money for law school. He'd become a full-time student, but his future plans were unknown or unknowable.

He'll be all right, Maureen knew. Anybody who could spellbind an audience of young people as he had at the church was sure to have a bright future in law or half-dozen other fields.

Some things Maureen would never know. Would Grace have attempted to steal the account books if she hadn't heard a Wall Street analyst was coming to town? Would Luther have killed her? Bridget too? Would Pettigrew be up and walking now? Her feeling was those events would have come to pass anyway; something or somebody else would have triggered them. Impossible to calculate, of course. What she did know was that her life had been forever changed.

"Can you live on it?" Gregory said.

"What?"

"A dollar a year."

Almost as if he'd been reading her mind. A dollar a year was the salary Maureen had agreed on to manage investments of the Pettigrew Trust. She'd replace Luther, temporarily at least, and there'd been talk of her becoming both chief operating and chief finance officer of the Trust, with someone else being a figurehead president. She hadn't made up her mind about that.

"I guess I'll have to be like you," she said. "Live on my savings."

"Not for long. I'll have to go to work soon."

"Well, not for Providence Place. Or any organization the Pettigrew Trust supports."

"You don't want to be accused of any conflict of interest. Me neither."

"You don't sound unhappy about it."

"I can always get a job." Gregory reached over and took her hand. "But if you want to consult with me, it'll cost you."

"Really?"

"All the Cherry Garcia I can eat."

"I'll pay you half that."

"Deal."

They were silent for a while, but Go wasn't finished with the subject. "Why did you take it?"

"What?"

"The no-pay job advising the trust."

Maureen searched for right words. "Because nobody else cares."

"That's broad."

"There are thousands of pension funds and charitable trusts in the country that retain investment advisers to do one thing: Grow the money. Make it a bigger pile. The trustees figure that's their only job. They never stop to think that what they're doing may hurt the same people they're supposed to help."

"Trustees like Luther," Gregory said.

"Luther's an excellent symbol for what's wrong. He thought he had one purpose in life. Help Kennedy. He didn't care who he hurt to do it. Almost all of Wall Street is like Luther. Pension fund managers, for example, never consider whether the companies they invest in outsource jobs overseas without considering domestic options, or.... You know the list."

She could hear the passion in her voice. Good. She hadn't felt this strongly about something in years. "Except for a very few socially-conscious mutual funds, nobody on Wall Street cares about the things companies do without regard to their consequences. Pollute the environment. Provide miserly medical care. Discriminate against women or minorities. All the while lavishing huge salaries and bonuses on a few people at the top."

"You think you can do better?"

"You're damned right."

"Will you miss the money? The money you made on Wall Street?"

"I never wanted to be Midas. Imagine, everything you touched turning to gold. You couldn't eat, or read, or even wash your face."

"Or make love to a woman," Go said.

Mo squeezed his hand.

Chapter Fifty-Five

The trading room looked exactly as before. The same men and women peered into computer monitors, typing commands and talking into phone sets. Just as noisy, too, the same expletives mixing with the clicks and chatter, the buzz occasionally punctuated by a victory whoop. A few traders looked up as Maureen passed, but none of them said anything. Just as well. She didn't want to talk until she'd finished what she'd come to do.

She found Rebecca sitting at her desk—Maureen's desk—in her office—Maureen's office—eyes fastened on a monitor, phone to her ear. Maureen walked across the office and stood on the other side of the screen. Almost a minute went by before Rebecca noticed her.

"You," she said.

"Yes." Maureen narrowed her eyes. "Me."

"What do you want?"

"Did you enjoy talking with Luther?"

Rebecca's expression, her movements, and her body froze in place, one hand suspended above the keyboard.

"I know all about it," Maureen said. "Also that the partners didn't know you had talked with either Luther or Pettigrew."

"I kept them informed."

"No you didn't." Maureen was bluffing now, but sure of herself. "Neither were you speaking for them when you told me I'd been suspended."

"You've talked to them."

"Not yet. But I will."

Rebecca seemed to shrink. "They won't believe you."

"They will. There's a federal investigation going on in Florida. If necessary, prosecutors can get phone records, e-mails, memos, anything they need. All someone would have to do is tell them about you. They'd do the rest."

Rebecca said, "The partners saw the article in the *Times*. If it had been wrong, they would have corrected it."

"Odds are, they didn't see it. One just had a heart attack. One is staying home to help with a new baby. A third has been out of town. But even if they saw the article, they'd figure whoever was in charge would take care of it. And with me gone, no one was in charge."

Rebecca opened her mouth but no sound came out.

"And my account," Maureen said. "I logged into it and discovered you didn't do what I asked. You didn't sell me out."

"I couldn't get around to it. I'll—"

"No you won't. You won't do anything except what I tell you." Maureen put her hands on the desk and leaned over. "What you're going to do now is type out a letter of resignation."

"I won't."

"Or you'll get a subpoena telling you to come talk to prosecutors. I can't even count how many crimes you've committed. Fraud. Malfeasance. Misrepresentation. Who knows what else? You'll never work in the securities business again. You'll probably go to jail. And for a lot more time than Martha Stewart."

Rebecca stared, then stood, and walked to a window behind the desk.

It was a lousy view, Maureen knew. Nothing outside but an unremarkable building across the street and a glimpse of gray sky. She wouldn't miss it, but she had to finish this business, had to pretend she wanted her office back. Everything depended on the next few seconds. She didn't really know if Rebecca could be convicted of a crime, but she knew she didn't want to tie herself up giving depositions and testifying against the young woman for months, possibly years. She wanted to get on with her life.

The time had come to hammer in the last nail. "The afternoon I got the telephone call from Gregory, you asked me to look at a stock that had come alive," Maureen said. "I told you it looked like Pettigrew was planning to grab control of the company and gut it."

Rebecca turned and faced her.

"You knew all along that the Pettigrew Trust was buying it," Maureen said. "Luther told you."

Rebecca put a hand to her mouth.

"And you were probably trading it for your personal account. They'll put you under the jail for that."

Rebecca's lips pressed together. Silent seconds built into minutes. Finally she said, "If I resign, will you let it go? No prosecution, no civil suit."

"As long as you stay out of the securities business."

Rebecca wet her lips with her tongue. She stared into a corner of the office. She moved her shoulders, almost shrugging. Then she sat in front of the monitor, typed on the keyboard, and pressed a button. The printer across the office started.

Maureen knew she'd won, but she didn't say a word.

Rebecca walked across the office, picked up her letter, and signed it. She handed it to Maureen. "You've taught me a lot."

"Get out," Maureen said. "Get out of my sight. Don't talk to the traders outside. Never come back."

Rebecca walked from the office, not saying another word.

Maureen logged onto the computer, and was surprised to see her password still worked. She pulled up her personal account. The stocks, bonds and money market cash totaled more than seven digits.

Rebecca's failure to sell everything in the account gave Maureen a second chance. She could hold onto what she had and let it grow. Or she could sell it all with a few clicks.

In Florida she'd decided she wanted out. She wanted a new life. She hadn't owned those stocks and bonds. They'd owned her. All those times she'd woken in the middle of the night wondering if she'd made a mistake, all those days she'd checked stock prices every hour, even every ten minutes, the market was never far from her mind no matter what else she was doing. It had become an addiction.

Now Kennedy and the bank trustee wanted her to work fulltime on the Pettigrew Trust. She was willing. That meant she'd still be thinking and studying and talking about the market every day. Why not keep her holdings?

She looked up. The Gandhi poster was still on the wall. *Do the right thing.* That was it. She couldn't in good conscience trade for the Trust account at the same time as hers. That was what Pettigrew and Luther had done.

If she sold now, though, the tax consequences would be horrendous. Maybe she could put her holdings in a blind trust. Just leave things as they were, with vague general instructions to the trustees. She wouldn't know what they did with her money.

Who was she kidding? The names of the stocks and bonds she owned now would remain lodged in the recesses of her mind, and any prudent trustee would hold on to most of them. She looked at the Gandhi poster. There was really no choice. Let her trustees start with a clean slate, even if she'd take a beating on taxes.

Maureen's fingers hesitated over the keyboard. Did she really want to do this? *Do the right thing.* The words came to her mind again as if from a loudspeaker. She pushed the keys. The smaller holdings would be gone in seconds. Traders would take a little longer getting rid of the big blocks, but they'd be gone before she left the building.

She was out of the market. Free! From now on stocks and bonds would be abstractions, little puzzles to figure out for the Pettigrew Trust. She'd have no personal involvement.

She wrote a resignation letter, left it on the desk next to Rebecca's, and walked out of office. She waved at the traders as she passed through the trading room floor but didn't talk with them. They'd learn about her resignation soon enough. Rebecca's, too.

Gregory was waiting in the lobby.

"One great meal and a show before we go back to Lauderdale," Mo said.

Go nodded, put his arm around her, and they walked down the street together, away from the deals, away from the short-term mentality, away from the idea that all that counted was the bottom line this month, this quarter, this year—day and night, forever, consequences and tomorrow be damned. Maureen knew better. There were more important things in life than making a big pile of money.

Author's Note

This is a work of fiction. I made it up, every bit. None of the characters in this novel should be confused with any of the many fine billionaires—fifteen at last estimate—who live in South Florida or with any of the marvelous police officers who protect the area.

Also, readers are cautioned against drawing any conclusions from this story about the real Fort Lauderdale or the real Palm Beach and their diverse inhabitants. Astute residents will realize, for example, that I've taken liberties with geography to make room for the fictitious Providence Place and the equally ethereal Trust House, neither of which is really anything else. The same goes for the hotel where Pettigrew lived and the building that housed Pettigrew Enterprises.

Similarly, readers with knowledge of the stock market will realize there are no listed companies named Qualflex or First National Travel USA; they are just as fictitious as the people who trade them. And the news stories supposedly found in the *Palm Beach Post* are equally imaginary and, if true, more likely would have been found in the *Palm Beach Daily News,* which, alas, is not available on microfilm. The Federico García Lorca and John Maynard Keynes quotations are from The Columbia Dictionary of Quotations, Columbia University Press.

Finally, I happily acknowledge that Chunky Monkey is a registered trademark and delicious product of Ben & Jerry's Homemade, Inc., now a subsidiary of Unilever, that Phish Food and Cherry Garcia are proprietary flavors licensed to the company, and Cherry Garcia is a trademark of The Estate of Jerry Garcia. Yes, another estate.

I am grateful for the help of many people along the way. Big thanks, in particular, to John Dufresne, Les Standiford, and Lynne Barrett, who taught me all I know about lining up words left to right to create flesh, facts, and feelings; to good friends Andrew Kingston and Natasha Grinberg, who listened and reacted with intelligence, insight, and tenderness to every chapter of this novel; to Joyce Sweeney and her Thursday Group, for comments, critiques, and support over the years; to Albert Pacer, Antonella Novi, Caren Neile, Carol Berry, Ed Johnson, Felix Mitchell, Henry Grinberg, Hobbit Forest, Jackie Reece, Jo Bailey, John Bond, Kate Godar, Mary Anne Robertson, Mary Free, Shelley Lieber, Steven Greenleaf, and others who read this or previous versions of the manuscript; to Jim Rich, Dan Moogan, and Randy Kires for information and advice about motor yachts; and to Dr. Henry D. Holland and others I met on the Internet who provided excellent, often firsthand, information about polio.

Any errors are mine, and I'm open to corrections, comments and even mild criticism. Enjoy!

About the Author

Jack Nease was a reporter, editor, and columnist for four Florida newspapers before earning an MFA at Florida International University. He has since taught creative writing and journalism at Florida Atlantic University and divides his time between South Florida and the Pacific Northwest.